BENDING DESTINY

By

Anne Barclay Morgan

Cover Illustration Copyright © 2013 by Angela Deane
Cover design by Angela Deane
Author photograph by Brent Mashburn

"Bending Destiny" Copyright © 2013
by Anne Barclay Morgan
ISBN: 978-0-9898660-1-9

Preface

After listening to one of my short stories, Melanie Almeder, the poet and Associate Professor of English, insisted that I expand the story into a novel. Without Melanie's encouragement and editorial skills, *Bending Destiny* would not have been born.

Each page wrote itself as the characters introduced themselves to me. I did not know any of them before I began. Their likes and dislikes, their dilemmas are all their own.

While writing down their stories, my husband and I eloped. To Brent Mashburn, I am profoundly indebted for being the inspiration for the transformative effects of such intense sharing between two people. He sprinkled smiley faces in the manuscript, and offered to help create the recipe for the Tea for Dreary Colds. To my intense amusement, he announced, "You have a *very* active mind!"

I am deeply grateful for the insights and assistance of these marvelous and talented friends, who live on two continents.

Sylvie Blum-Reid, author and Associate Professor of French and Film, made very helpful suggestions.

Kim Rose, writer/poet and strategic communications/public relations director, gave her enthusiastic support.

Gael Morgan, my beloved sister, made excellent comments rooted in a shared appreciation for character and for language.

Lisa Chan, acupuncture physician, reflexologist and shamanic healer gave the book her special blessing.

Elisabeth McCarty, spiritual channeller and writer, shared her great insights.

Joana Morris, Reiki Master, shamanic healer and psychic, gave the ultimate accolade: many passages made her feel good.

Sarah Bewley, talented writer of plays and mysteries, did a wonderful job of editing the final draft and sharing her discerning perceptions about the story.

Angela Deane, gifted artist and creator of banterbanner.com, took the vision I had for the cover and made it better.

Why write a novel? I was searching for one to read and I began writing to entertain myself. My curiosity pushed me toward considering answers to questions that popped up during the writing process. One of the most important ones being, what creates community?

Bending Destiny found its title by addressing the fundamental question: To what extent are we, the quirky, complex members of the human race, ruled by destiny? In other words, is freewill an illusion?

So, welcome to *Bending Destiny*, and enjoy!

Anne Barclay Morgan
November 2013

I. The Keeper of Practical Order

Behind my back, friends call me Bossy Barbs. With rolling eyes, they whisper, "She's at it again!" But after all, *someone* has to organize things. In order for things to be right, you have to tell people what to do. It's a simple process: you explain, they do. Some of us, I'm not going to mention any names, are just not skilled at organization.

With our annual Summer Full Moon Party scheduled to take place on our village green the following Saturday afternoon, I had to take charge of building the platform for the welcoming ceremony and the band. Tom Bates, a skilled carpenter under other circumstances, eyed me with considerable skepticism when I explained, in my most patient voice, that this year's platform had to be larger than previous ones.

I tried a winning smile. "You must have forgotten, Tom, that animals will take part in this year's opening ceremonies."

Tom's stormy grey eyes narrowed. "People take up a lot more room than those animals ever will," he retorted.

I huffed, and started drawing diagrams in the dirt, pointing out possible placements for both two-legged and four-legged species on stage. The long and short of it was that arguing about the rudiments of platform design did not suffice. I decided then and there to help out with its construction. Tom didn't bother to hide his dismay. His crop of unruly black curls shuddered, but I was not deterred.

My father taught me at a very early age how to wield a hammer and drive in nails. "Never know when this might be useful, Barbara," he would say whenever he wanted to teach me a skill, one that he had learned as a boy. Fueled by a desire to focus on what he loved best, he was a good instructor. He inspired me to learn all the skills that he chose not to implement.

As a child, I trailed after my father just long enough to become the Repairer of Our House or better yet, the Keeper of Practical Order. I began to oversee all those details that he preferred to delegate, while he buried himself in a history book. His eyes would shine when he spoke about the latest read. All too soon, his eyes would glaze over as he relived history in his mind.

I often wondered which side he picked to be on. To me, people are on one of two sides in every history, those who win out after tremendous difficulties and many battles, or those who lose after a final and bitter struggle. He was hard to pinpoint and he never seemed to mind losing. He rather liked both points of view. I ground my teeth. "But only one side can be right!" I argued, never hearing a reply, since my father was once again lost in his book.

Like most of the dwellings in our village, our house has undergone almost continual renovation and a few expansions. A great-great-great-grandmother added the second story onto the ground floor. So I had had plenty of scope for plying my new skill. The garden still boasts the nail-studded plank displaying my first forays into the practical arts. My father wanted it on permanent display.

Tom Bates pouted as only a man of his bulk could. But I did not have to remind him that the platform for our village party could only benefit from my proficiency.

To his considerable relief, new developments pulled me off track. My hammer remained in its place of honor by my back right pocket. Heavy, sturdy, reliable and patient, it was ready, but I was not.

"What? She's coming? Now?" I was hooked all right, and Tom gloated.

Instead of hammering next to him, I began a round of speculations and attempts to find out more about Anne Beauchamps, who was due to arrive at her new home the afternoon before our party.

Everyone in the village knew that Anne was the granddaughter of our beloved Mrs. Goodheart, the wise woman, a natural healer and counselor, and the baker of very crisp Choco-Cheery-Charm Cookies with tiny bits of chocolate. I spent many an hour after school sitting at her kitchen table sampling the latest batch and asking ticklish questions, ones that I was reluctant to ask my parents. She never spoke to me about her family, but then again, I never asked, being much more interested in my own life.

All I knew was that Mrs. Goodheart left the village to stay with her daughter and grandchildren in France on a regular basis. They never visited her. Before her passing, Mrs. Goodheart requested we welcome her youngest grandchild Anne Beauchamps, who would be coming to live in the house.

After fruitless searching for more information about Anne, I returned my attention to the all-important platform. I pulled out my hammer and joined Tom on the green. He gave me a sour look, knowing he would now have to compromise. While my presence made him less than cheery, I was grateful to be active. It took my mind off of unresolved, and therefore fruitless, speculations about our soon-to-be-newest inhabitant.

By Friday morning, visitors began streaming into our village, which guidebooks describe as "quaint," being devoid of any glass-paneled bank buildings. Since I grew up surrounded by wood and stone, the cottage style seems commonplace. Only the impressive sighs and appreciative comments of visitors about the wood, "gleaming with care and age," and the odd-shaped stones, "bursting with unique character," made me look at the jumbled buildings, not for their familiarity or for what needed to be repaired, but for a certain harmony of line.

What I do notice and value, is that our inns and shops cater to my tastes, and those of other villagers. I like things that are made by hand; after all, my hands are rough with calluses, my nails blunt. With considerable pride, I expound to visitors that villagers create quite an array of handiwork, from jellies and condiments, woven baskets, whimsical lamps embellished with pressed flowers and leaves, soaps and creams from home-grown herbs and flowers, to garden ornaments made of iron and stone.

Charmed Necessities, at the far end of the village green offers all of these items and more. I still can't quite grasp that this shop, which has been handed down through my mother's family for generations, is now fully my own.

Other village shops provide us with all sorts of things, from fruit wines and cider to fresh produce grown in our fields and greenhouses. And, I remind visitors, in spite of our traditional appearance, we are *not* locked into a historical time warp. Wood and stone are all very fine, but without the most efficient heating and insulation, they can be unbearable in the depths of winter. Villagers understood long ago the importance of adapting to the times. The latest technologies are considered for their potential to improve the quality of our lives. However, the making of *wise* choices, versus a whole-hearted and indiscriminate embracing of all the latest trends, has always been a top priority. I admit that Bossy Barbs has never assisted in that decision-making process, or even attended any of the relevant village meetings, focusing her attention instead on the two all-important "V's:" Visitors and Villagers.

Tom called me back from my reverie about our village with a curt request to finish hammering my section. I eyed him with my frostiest glare. "I'm just about to complete *my* portion of the platform. What about *yours*?" All he had to do was gloat with arms crossed over his thick chest. My mental meanderings had cost me. His portion was done.

To my intense disappointment, the vehicle that brought Anne Beauchamps to the village that Friday afternoon sped by. Torn between wanting to go have a closer look and the needs of platform construction and visitors, I muttered under my breath and tried to glean at least some information from a distance. It was too sunny, the windows of the vehicle reflected our antics back to us and Anne remained a mystery.

By late Friday afternoon, Tom Bates and I parted on more cordial terms. While forced to modify the platform according to my design, he was appeased by my absences and inattentiveness. He could now boast about having done most of the work himself.

On Saturday morning, Colleen, my childhood mentor and also the assistant manager of *Charmed Necessities*, arrived a full hour before opening time in order to help me prepare for the inevitable deluge of visitors. Colleen, who is one of the most vivacious members of the Shaw family, shook her profusion of red tresses when she noticed that I was restocking shelves without any of my habitual enthusiasm.

"What's bothering you, Barbara?"

"Well," I began and then stopped. "It's just that..." stopping again. I sucked in a deep breath and lunged into full sentences. "Anne Beauchamps must have spent her first night in her grandmother's house. I'm just wondering whether she liked it."

Colleen's locks shook again, but she grinned. "Pay attention to what you're doing!" she admonished.

She was right, of course. But Mrs. Goodheart had played such a central role in our lives that I couldn't help being curious about her granddaughter.

Moments after we opened, *Charmed Necessities* filled with visitors. The wooden floors creaked under all the shuffling feet. Both rooms reverberated with chatter and exclamations. The colorful items clashed with the rose-patterned linens on the tables and chairs and with the festive clothing of visitors. The colors and heady scents all began to blend together like an overgrown flowerbed.

Colleen, with her lovely voice and gracious manner took good care of the visitors. In lilting tones, she answered all the redundant queries about the purity of the ingredients in the body care products. So, I stole a few precious moments and slipped over to see my neighboring shopkeeper, Megan Sullivan.

Megan managed *Chalice Lore* as best she could in place of her absent parents and brother. Her shop, almost double the size of *Charmed Necessities*, was even more cluttered than my own, with products as diverse as garments, gauntlets and games. Oblivious to the many visitors filling the aisles, Megan sat behind the counter staring into the distance, dreaming. When I stood between her and the light, she smiled and wafted down from her perch, her wispy attire and her long blonde hair flowing behind her as she moved toward me and hugged me.

"Barbie, you caught me off-guard!"

I grimaced. The nickname bestowed on me by Megan's father, the erratic Papa Sullivan, was a source of ongoing amusement for others. I should have been born blond with abundant curves and slender, long legs. Instead, my hair is thick and black and I am built to wield a heavy hammer.

"Megan, do you know anything about Anne Beauchamps?" I blurted out before she could utter another word.

Two years my senior, Megan has known me for all of my twenty-five years. She was no doubt expecting my question.

"Not any more than you do." Her answer was ready, pat and most dissatisfying.

On very rare occasions, Megan could be persuaded to use her innate gift for "second sight"–I don't know what else to call it. Already at the age of six, she "saw" her beloved older brother scoring three goals in a row in a very well matched soccer game months before it happened.

I always disapproved of this strange aptitude, even if I wanted her to use it for me, just this once. However, Megan was just as ambivalent about her inexplicable ability, and rarely bothered to use it.

But I knew her just as well as she knew me. Having loaned her Kissing Bough for use during the

Summer Full Moon Party, I knew she would be rather curious about its effect, even though she didn't want to try it out herself.

As a student of myths and storytelling, Megan's father first visited our village almost thirty-five years ago. Discovering that the shopkeeper of *Chalice Lore,* a middle-aged woman with a kind smile, had a strong interest in all things Irish, he lingered. He was standing under a Kissing Bough when Megan's mother, the shopkeeper's daughter, then a breathless 23 year-old, barged into the shop with a rush of wind, and ran smack into him. She glowed and seemed so right that he kissed her then and there, and that was the end of that. They were married a few months later. He only returned to Ireland to finish his degree, and hastened back to his new life in our village. He encouraged his daughter Megan to make her own Kissing Bough, not because he felt trapped by her mother's, but because he felt that it brought him such good luck.

"So Megan," I began in casual tones, "What will happen under your Kissing Bough?"

Megan's eyes gazed into the far distance. I was tempted to look over my shoulder, but I knew that I would only see some overstuffed shelves.

Megan's words jerked me back to the present. "Several people will fall for each other under the Kissing Bough."

"What about Anne Beauchamps? Will she attend? What does she look like?" I slipped my questions in, hoping she would take the bait.

Megan frowned as if my questions were too mundane. "Of course she will, Barbie, and she's blond, unlike you." This was not much to go on, but better than nothing.

For the rest of that frantic morning, I hovered between wanting to check up on the platform and tending to visitors intent on browsing and acquiring items or information, or both. But on this particular Saturday, the day of our Summer Full Moon Party, visitors were certain to be crowding my path down our main street to the green. Besides, the wind chimes by

the front door kept tinkling with all the comings and
goings. I was forced to stay put until closing time at 3
PM, just half an hour before the opening ceremonies. I
ground my teeth and patted my hammer in my back
pocket. Soon, soon enough.

A stout man with short, grey hair scattered
around the fringes of his shiny head entered the shop
wiping his forehead. His white shirt was already limp
from exertion. Opening the glazed windows in the
storefront and in the back had brought in a much-
needed breeze on that sunny summer morning. But he
needed more than that: my loveseat would hold him
until he caught his breath.

"Welcome to *Charmed Necessities*. May I
suggest that you rest for a moment in my special
alcove?" As I gestured to the loveseat, I looked
straight into very vivid blue eyes.

Few people remember eye color. "They are sort
of brown," friends might say with a puzzled look as
they try to recall their hero or heroine's eyes. I, on the
other hand, am able to describe a pair of eyes in great
detail, the various shades and striations in the color,
the size of the pupil in relationship to the iris, the
translucence. This time, however, my mind registered
vivid blue and nothing more. While I had never met
him before, this man's eyes resembled those of my
mother, or better yet of Great Aunt Hopie, a long
deceased relative, who chose to become enmeshed in
village affairs rather than marry, much to the secret
dismay of those villagers whose lives she rearranged.

After he lumbered over to the proffered seat, he
sat down with such firmness that the loveseat
squeaked. Only two other people have ever been able
to make that happen. There was Mary Lisa MaGuire,
who has the habit of throwing herself onto anything
horizontal when she starts to scream with laughter.
The loveseat protested then with such a resonant
screech that all the glass in the shop tinkled.

The all-time champion of squeaking is my old
schoolmate. His grandfather, who raised him, was
such a lover of Ancient Rome that he renamed his
grandson Horatio Caesar. My schoolmate's chagrin

was so great that he began to stuff himself with all manner of food. Desserts coated in sugar became his favored antidote to his name. He sat next to me in many a tedious class, so I know just how shy he is. His thick glasses make him look like an earnest owl with tufts of light brown hair sticking out around the ears. The rectangular, brown plastic frames are always coming loose from being smashed on his face once too often.

The day that Horatio Caesar leaned forward as he sat down on the loveseat, his glasses crashed to the floor and a lens popped out and rolled under him. As he groped for his glasses and the missing lens, the whole loveseat fell forward and landed on top of his sprawling body. We heard the crackling of squashed glass.

Mr. Blue Eyes, my would-be relative, sat and took deep breaths. I pretended to re-arrange some dried flowers in a copper urn on the adjacent table. I waited: still no word from him. I flicked specks of invisible dust off the chintz tablecloth. He was still speechless. I grew impatient and began to walk away.

"Wait!" he ordered. His voice was not that of any relative; his elocution was too brusque. "I want something special for my wife!" he barked, sounding like a big and polluted city.

"What is your wife's favorite color and scent?" My patient smile was pinned in place.

"Blue and gardenia."

I scurried off to select a variety of products and returned with an armful. Only glancing at them, he bellowed from the loveseat, "I want them all gift-wrapped."

My selections, though tasteful, were quite eclectic, so his extravagant choices took me aback. Our village boasts an impressive number of greenhouses, so fresh gardenia sprays are always available. Wreaths and bouquets of fresh and dried flowers are as popular with our customers as with us, but few get three of them at once for the same person, along with soaps, perfume-essences, massage oils, candles, a pillow, and even a blue garden angel. These small statues possess secret ingredients that help plants grow, even when placed in big city window boxes.

Colleen shook her red mane and took over. She has that enviable knack of making gift-wrapping seem effortless and fun.   Colleen presented a running commentary, as she twirled the paper and ribbons in cadence with her voice.

"She's a swirling gardenia girl, with blue, blue eyes and a touch of sunshine in her smile," Colleen began. Our visitor relaxed as the banter continued.

When I presented Mr. Blue Eyes with the bill, he smiled for the first time. After he handed me the exact sum from an overstocked wallet, he commented in flat vowels from his seat, "It's my wife's birthday. She wanted to visit your village. She's talking to the people down the street."

I warmed to him. He was not only my long-lost relative and did not know it, but he thought of his wife's happiness.

"She has no idea where I am, this is a surprise." He gestured to the overstuffed gift baskets as my evaluation of him went up another notch.

With a groan from the loveseat, Mr. Blue Eyes rose, and grabbing the two bulky baskets, limped out the door that I held open for him. As he passed, he looked hard at me and rumbled out a reluctant thank-you. I glanced at my watch, only thirty minutes until closing.

Fifteen people lined up in front of us both, and Colleen never once lost her expression of unqualified joy. My heart filled with renewed gratitude. Colleen had had the dubious honor of watching over me from time to time as I grew, so she understood the depths of my dilemma six years ago better than I had. When I had been forced to become the sole owner of *Charmed Necessities*, Colleen left her own occupation to help me out and has remained ever since.

As another visitor burst in, grey-haired and imposing, I called out, "Sorry, we are closing for the Summer Full Moon Party." Undeterred, the robust woman went straight to the rack of straw hats, picked out one with an abundant spray of fuchsia flowers and came straight to me. Sixteen customers now, I sighed.

As Colleen and I were closing up *Charmed Necessities* well after three, I thought about Anne Beauchamps for the first time in hours. A hint of apprehension ruffled my eagerness to attend our festivities. Would she enjoy our village life? Would she like her new home? Would she want to stay? I was determined to meet her and find out.

II.   Bumping Practice

Just as he had in our school days, Horatio
Caesar, that Master of Loveseat Squeaking, saved the
seat next to his for me. I slipped into the folding chair
at the edge of the fourth row just as the opening
speeches began on the platform of my design. I had
already heard Bessy Macintosh practice her poem of
welcome, so her melodic phrases flew straight past me,
as I scanned the crowds for unfamiliar blond heads.
When Bessy uttered her last line, the listeners yelled
out their appreciation. Their delight was so infectious
that I forgot about my search for an unfamiliar Anne
and became caught up in the ceremonies.

Jimmy Delane got up on stage and began to
warble. Since the tender age of ten, he could mimic the
voices of so many birds and wild animals that at least
one creature always tagged along somewhere in his
vicinity. Beginning with hoots, Jimmy shifted into
high-pitched trills, whistles and then onto cooing. The
crowd watched as owls and geese, followed by doves,
flew toward the platform and perched in the
overhanging oak tree and on the wood around him.
They all answered back, so the airwaves were filled
with chaotic vibrations. With only a slight mental
twist, you could imagine St. Francis of Assisi
communing with the birds. Jimmy ended this
conversation between species with a sudden flap of his
arms. All the birds rose up and flew off. In awe, the
crowd applauded.

The ribbon that was to be "cut" marking the official beginning of the festivities was one of our special creations made of edibles for four-legged creatures. Laced with fresh carrot slivers, tender green shoots, and an occasional lump of sugar, the ribbon looked delectable.

Little Joanie MacLever climbed onto the platform with her two white goats. Their heads were festooned with ribbons and fresh flowers that flopped down over their foreheads. They looked just as two favored pets should–docile. Appearances can be ever so deceptive. Why should two pet goats become unnerved at the sight of at least eight hundred people sitting in rows, surrounded by an even greater number of people standing, all staring up at them? We were docile, but they began to prance a bit and hold up their tails. They could not butt heads with all of us, but they were getting ready to try.

Joanie looked so worried that Jimmy Delane stepped forward. The goats turned and charged. Adept at this sort of thing, Jimmy swerved at the last moment. The darling goats butted each other's heads. Jimmy was then able to lead them, somewhat chastened, back to Joanie. Recovered from their stage fright, they followed her around in a circle as the ribbon was lowered to well within their reach. In less than two minutes the ribbon was cut by hungry goat nibbles, and the crowd shot up clapping in fervent appreciation and began hugging itself. Mary Lisa MaGuire laughed with such complete abandon that she ended up on the stage floor.

Horatio Caesar did not hug me, of course, but he bounced up and down in his sneakers. He beamed, and his cheeks puffed out even as his glasses bopped up and down on his nose. I behaved in a rather undignified manner myself; I raised my hands over my head and waved them back and forth as I began some energetic steps of the Whirly Girly Dance. I became so exhilarated that I slammed into the chair in front of me, bumping its former occupant. He looked around, startled. Whoops, a stranger, a Mr. Green Eyes with tawny flecks and brown streaks. Let's call him Mr. Mostly Green Eyes.

I was elated and proud of it. We had passed the first party hurdle with flying colors. The platform held fast. I beamed at Mr. Mostly Green Eyes, "Sorry about that. Enthusiasm can be so infectious." His eyes sharpened and he was about to speak, when his pretty friend nudged him into leaving his row. So that was the end of that.

Next on my agenda was the Hapless Hatless Potato Race. I never missed the sight of the eight to twelve year-olds hopping toward the finish line encased in potato sacks and wearing floppy hats. Made of light green felt lined with silk, the identical hats are so tall that their tops flop over to one side. Keeping them on requires a firm hand and concentration. No pins, elastic bands, or adhesives are allowed. No potatoes participate. Furthermore, the race has nothing to do with carrying or moving any. That's part of another long story that my father would have been best at unraveling.

We formed quite an eclectic audience. Children, who were too young to participate, looked on with envy. No doubt, those floppy green hats seemed like an emblem of maturity. Those above the twelve-year limit tried to look bored. But those who had raced down the green before could not hide their interest.

I pretended to be impartial but Horatio Caesar, who knows almost all my secrets, whispered into my ear, "She will do very well, don't worry." I turned to him and glared. It is bad enough to be accused of worrying, even worse is having one's innermost thoughts exposed. Somehow, Horatio Caesar had surmised that the slender and graceful Melissa Crane would be my very first choice for a younger sister. He continued to gaze at me with those big, limpid hazel (with a haphazard splash of green) eyes. I clenched my teeth to keep from retorting. Persons with a knowing attitude are just so persistent.

This year's Master of the Race, Patrick Doweran, by occupation a renowned master chef, boomed out the rules for all to hear. In order to be a winner, you had to finish the race in your sack with your hat on your head. If at any time your hat fell off or you bumped another contestant, you were disqualified. Bumped contestants would be picked up and placed two yards ahead. There would be one winner in each of the three height categories, with a yellow, red or blue chest ribbon denoting the appropriate category.

After Patrick yelled out "GO," a few contestants fell down and lost their hats. I stopped breathing and crossed every finger as I stared at my favorite, Melissa with her long black hair waving as she leapt forward. When she hopped across the finish line, a winner in the red or tallest category, I squealed and, to his dismay, hugged Horatio Caesar hard. He patted my back in an avuncular manner.

From where we stood, I observed three unfamiliar blond heads on female bodies. One of them looked promising. Her hair was sleek and well cut, her clothing chic. She stood a little bit by herself. As I walked toward her, she turned and headed away from me. I put on some speed. To my consternation, her clothing was in subtle shades of tan and cream, the colors worn by at least 67% of the female and male partygoers.

I began a light loping pace, braking for a moment as I espied Mr. Blue Eyes with a comfortable looking woman hanging on his arm. That moment of curiosity cost me. Gathering speed, I whizzed past more people, including the winning Melissa, surrounded by friends. I shouted out "Congratulations!" She looked up and beamed. I waved at her sideways, and ran smack into a hard body.

This was no fun. My limbs tangled with a pair of strong legs and down I went, clutching a pale blue shirt, thinking, 'nice soft material, nice shade,' before I hit the grass. A heavy weight came down on top of me. I groaned. All my bones were broken; I just knew it.

Pause. I looked up and saw a shaved cheek and jaw, and oh no, dangling down over us, the Kissing Bough, a limb covered with special herbs and flowers, dried with care, and bows in shades of blue and green, so like Megan. There was no mistaking it. Miserable is too nice a word to describe the way I felt. This was one spot, I had vowed, I would never be under, ever, unless with the man of my dreams.

The male body picked himself up off of me. A voice penetrated my misery. "Are you all right? Are you hurt? Answer me!"

Shaking my head, I looked toward the voice. I gulped; it was the man whose chair I bumped during my euphoric Whirly Girly Dance. His eyes became as acute as a falcon on an involuntary fasting regime.

"We meet again," he said without smiling.

I groaned again, and lifted my hand to point. The doomed man followed my gesture upwards.

"What is that?" he asked.

"Just help me up, please," I muttered.

He pulled me to my feet with a huff. My hair was all over the place. I was crumpled and aggrieved, but in all fairness, none of my bones were broken. Looking at Mr. Mostly Green Eyes, I managed to say "Thank you" and even "I apologize for running into you again, I was trying to find someone."

He grinned, oh my, and said, "You found *me*."

I stiffened. "I was seeking out our latest inhabitant. I want to welcome her to our village. You were in the way."

He stopped smiling, and asked again, "What were you pointing at?"

"That is the Kissing Bough made by Megan Sullivan."

I said the truth, just not all of it. With an amused gleam in his eye, he stepped toward me. I stepped back. No legend was going to influence *my* life! Regaining some of my agility, I turned and threw a generic phrase over my shoulder, "Have a happy party!" 'Speed, Barbara, Speed,' I whispered to myself as I ran away from the scene.

I stalked by Master Chef Patrick who was enjoying some moments of flirtation with Ms. Horizontal, otherwise known as Mary Lisa MaGuire. She was not sideways so she was not laughing, and nor was I.

That Kissing Bough had become an undeniable menace to my peace of mind. Papa Sullivan had a lot to answer for. Even when I was small, he would laugh at my determined practicality. "Barbie, wake up and see the dew drops and the sparkles and dance a bit, before you get on with your day. You can have Magic in your life and be merry!"

I shook myself, not that "M" word. I did not like it, not one bit. That was one word I never, ever wanted to hear. I did not want to hear it as a child. And I did *not* want to hear it as an adult. It reminded me of that other dreadful word, the one that begins like 'telephone,' but ends with 'pathy.' I didn't like words like 'Omen,' either. 'Enchantment' was another appalling term. And that all encompassing word 'Mysticism,' made me shudder outright. I like my hammer and nails, thank you very much.

The sight of Mr. Blue Eyes, that afternoon's Love Seat Squeaker, proved to be the perfect diversion. Sitting next to him on a curved bench in front of the ash grove at the far end of the green was the plump and pleasant-looking Mrs. Blue Eyes. Observing them surrounded by the contents of two large gift baskets, I forgot about my mishap and regained a sense of well-being.

When I approached for a better look, Mr. Blue Eyes gestured for me to come meet his wife. Introductions went straight over my head. As I held out my hand, my father's warm hazel-verging-on-blue-eyes gazed up at me. Mrs. Blue Eyes managed to speak first.

"Your shop has such lovely things." She gestured to the multitude of objects scattered on the bench around her comfortable form. "What is your name, my dear?"

"My name is Barbara Mahoney."

Mrs. Blue Eyes quivered. "What a lovely name. Are you, are you by any chance..." She paused, too long for my taste, and then began again. "Are you by any chance related to James Mahoney?"

"That was my father's name." My heart began to pound. His eyes in her face and then his name–that was just too much for a mere coincidence.

"Oh my, oh my, so *that* is why you look so familiar. You have," she paused and squinted up at me, "You have his features, his chin."

I did not add that I had his somewhat sallow skin tone and almost black hair. The chin was enough. But how could this stranger have his eyes, which even I do not?

"But what a delightful surprise! James is my much older half-brother! We lost touch after he left home for university. How is he?" Simple delight radiated from the roundness of her face.

I plopped down on the bench between her and the blue garden angel that her husband had given her from *Charmed Necessities*. A long lost relative, whom I had never even heard about, and she had not grasped my use of the past tense when I spoke of her older half-brother. Village party and disastrous events were two phrases that I had never put together, until now.

"My father died six years ago in a freak accident," I replied in flat and even tones, and then added to make this conversation as brief as possible. "My mother died with him."

Mrs. Blue Eyes, who must be my half-aunt, was aghast. "Oh my dear, I had no idea!" Ready tears formed in her eyes, and I stiffened, tears were not my forte. A torrent of words followed, which helped to squelch the rising flood.

"I only thought that James might have some connection to your village because of his passion for history. He always had his head in a book. When he left for university, he *immersed* himself in studying history. He just stopped communicating with us. Silence all these years." She sniffled. "So, I had no idea where he lived, or what he was doing." She looked at me with my father's eyes filled with

teardrops. "I didn't even know he had a daughter."
She wailed and the tears began bubbling over. "I am
so sorry, so very, very sorry."

She looked so very upset that I felt the need to
comfort her, rather than run away. "My father never
spoke about his relatives, except to say that he grew up
in the big city and didn't like it. He never talked about
his life or his family before he moved here." This
didn't sound very comforting even to my ears. "He
lived and breathed history. Always." That was better,
and it was true, too. He just didn't breathe and live his
own history.

My new half-aunt regained some of her
composure and color. "How very like him! Since I
am–was––sixteen years younger than James, I only
remember how eager he was to leave home. You must
know, my dear, that he was *so very* kind to me before
he left, even though my mother was his stepmother
and was very strict with him." She patted my knee to
reassure me. "He would entertain me for hours with
tales of ancient kingdoms, in particular about King
Arthur."

What my half-aunt described was all too
familiar. When I was little and my father told me
tales, I often felt King Arthur was alive , even though
his historical existence is much debated. My father
made me feel that The King could ride up into our
village at any moment.

All the same, it was a bit disconcerting to think
of my father having had a life, and even some of the
same interests, before I was born. In some strange
way, I thought that his existence had begun and ended
with me. As Mrs. Blue Eyes poured out more
reminiscences, I tried to accept the sudden appearance
of this new relative.

Mr. Blue Eyes listened to our conversation
without much surprise. Maybe his business inured
him to shocks. Yet, none of these revelations explained
to me why he looked so familiar as well.

When my new half-aunt finished her stories
and regained her composure, I turned to him and

asked in an off-hand manner. "By any chance, do you have any relatives living in our village as well?"

Mr. Blue Eyes was succinct and to the point. "I did not know that I did, until I met you."

My next question was phrased with some care. "Your eyes remind me of my mother's, and yes, while I have my father's features, I inherited her eyes." My vivid blue eyes have always been a source of consternation to me. They looked just right in my mother's pale face framed by her long reddish hair, or better yet, with Great Aunt Hopie's fluffy white head. My sallow skin and dark hair made those vivid blue orbs look unreal. My mother's appearance was authentic, mine is fake.

Mr. Blue Eyes didn't flinch. "My father's family raised me in the city. My father died when I was two. I have no memories of my mother. She had to hand me over. My father's family made her promise not to stay in touch with me. I never knew much about her, except that she had blue eyes."

It was my turn to quiver. I had vague memories of my Grandmother Boyle, a quiet woman with those same vivid blue eyes and a straight back, who died when I was small. "My mother was my Grandmother Boyle's only child, I mean," I cleared my throat, "her only daughter. Before she met Mathew Boyle, she lived in the big city." I paused to observe that Mr. Blue Eyes remained as calm as a flat lake. "I was told that her sister, my Great Aunt Hopie, was most upset that she left our village to live the big city." Great Aunt Hopie expounded to one and all about it. It fell under her favorite topic, "The Evils of Moving away from Our Village."

Mr. Blue Eyes raised an eyebrow. Ah, a reaction.

"I was commanded never to ask Grandmother Boyle about her move to the big city and why she came back. My mother was adamant, now I understand why. She was forced to leave behind her son."

Mr. Blue Eyes blinked a few times, but his stoic facade gave no other indication of hearing for the first time about his long lost mother. He asked no further questions. His mother, or lack of her, was all part of the unchangeable past. Instead, he focused on the present. After some mental calculations, he stated, "You are my half-niece."

I nodded, lost in my own private irony. The joke that I made to myself earlier that day, turned out to be on me. This portly man, who was supposed to be my long-lost relative and did not know it, was indeed my half-uncle.

During the Summer Full Moon Party, I had acquired two new relations, Aunt Phoebe and Uncle Christopher, as they invited me to call them. They seemed pleased enough with me, but my life had been clear-cut without them.

With an innate sensitivity that I managed to appreciate, they gave me their contact information saying how busy I must be with the village party. A perfect way to bow out, I wished them a lovely evening and walked off.

I, the Practical Barbara, Keeper of *Charmed Necessities*, felt very unlike myself. I headed toward a clearing under the ancient oak tree at the far edge of the village green and tried to think. Two unsettling events in one afternoon seemed just about as much as I could handle. I was wrong.

Hands grabbed me from behind, whirled me around, and a very male pair of lips kissed me hard. Catching my breath, I looked up in consternation at a face I had not seen for way too many years, a face that I had adored in secret all through school, a face that I never thought to have so close to my own. It was now thinner, with more laugh lines around the agile mouth and flashing eyes. A face filled with zest for living, a face as fickle and changeable as the moon.

"Barbie!" he exclaimed with delight. "How is my Barbie?"

I was speechless, but Sean Sullivan didn't care. He spun me around again, picked me up and threw me in the air, so that my head touched the Kissing Bough. He was delighted. I should have been, too. I could not have dreamt of a better outcome for my youthful yearnings. My one and only hero, my secret love, was kissing and hugging me under the Kissing Bough made by his sister Megan.

I voiced my first coherent thought. "The Kissing Bough is supposed to be under the group of trees at the center of the green."

At first taken aback, Sean began to twinkle. "That's my Barbie. After I return to her from my travels of six long years, and not having seen her serious blue eyes in forever, she greets the prodigal boyfriend with details of organization!"

I sputtered. This was not a dream. Only a Sullivan could tease me like this. "Sean, what are you doing here? When did you get back?"

He laughed. "First, it is the organization that gets to her, then she remembers to ask about me," he crowed.

And then some answers, at last. "I got here an hour ago, too late to see our Hapless Hatless Potato Race, but just in time to find you, Barbara Blue, just where I wanted you, too."

His family charm always had the same effect on me, I felt myself being wrapped around his little finger. I was never fully convinced that I liked it. But my secret yearnings had come true. Sean Sullivan had named himself as my boyfriend, he had kissed me, and under the Kissing Bough at that. The six years of distance melted away, forgotten.

Sean put his arm around me and walked me toward Megan and a group of friends. What we talked about, I could never recall in detail. The whole group moved as one toward the platform. The band was setting up. The fuchsia and aqua lights glowed in a long string above the platform as dusk grew across the sky. We stood watching, and chatting. My village, my party.

III.   If My Thigh were not Blue

Our Summer Full Moon Party came to a
graceful end when the moon was high in the night sky.
The lights dimmed, visitors returned to their vehicles,
some villagers walked home singing off-key. Oblivion
hit me like an over-sized brick the minute I crawled
under my comforter.

My first thought the next morning was relief;
the platform had not collapsed under the band's abuse,
not even when Chicken Charlie and his Gang stomped
out their music. Well-being flooded my entire body.
Surrounded by the old walls of this room where I had
slept since infancy, I felt like a vessel in a safe harbor.
The wooden beams above my head were dark, the
room was small and comforting, and the bed was just
wide enough for me.

And Sean was back home, and everything he
said and did made me glow. So much promise, so
much to look forward to.

I stretched like a happy kitten, and then pulled
back in pain. I must have done something to my right
leg. Peering under the comforter, I stared at a nasty
bruise that ran down the length of my right thigh.
Disbelief invaded my mind. In my well-ordered life,
that disfigurement just could not exist. Then the
memory hit me of my hands clutching a blue shirt
followed by the conviction that all my bones had been
broken. Gritting my teeth, I remembered the stranger
who made this ugly bruise.

My socialization slipped away from me like the thinnest silk in opened palms. Mr. Mostly Green Eyes escaped our village just in time, because I entertained the most unpleasant desires, not at all in keeping with village etiquette. Malevolent thoughts were my only companions, as I lay there unwilling to move.

Then I remembered where we had fallen. The village green felt soft against my back, as I lay covered by a hard body with a direct view of what hung above me. The Kissing Bough was no laughing matter, and at that particular moment, I was close to crying.

However, this visitor didn't know of about the Kissing Bough's significance. Maybe that meant it would not work. He had not kissed me either, because I backed away from him. Maybe that meant it would not work. He had attended our party with a pretty woman. Maybe he was already taken. I did not see him after that incident. Maybe he would not come back into my life. All my maybes seemed reasonable and logical, but I knew the stories of the Kissing Bough all too well to dismiss every disquieting thought.

I forced myself to focus on why I was so very happy. My secret love had returned to our village, when I never thought he would. To my surprised delight, Sean, who'd haunted my dreams ever since I can remember, had hugged and kissed me under that very same Kissing Bough.

But I would have felt much more ecstatic if the Kissing Bough events had happened in reverse order. Sean should have kissed me first, before I acquired this nasty bruise. Then I would not be lying in bed the morning after feeling uneasy and looking, at least on one thigh, quite blue.

Some officious person, having witnessed my downfall with a stranger under the Kissing Bough on its chosen tree, must have moved it to that other tree where Sean kissed me with such gusto. Gratitude for that unknown person welled up. I counted on a golden lining to the Bough-Encounters.

Three unnerving events at a single village party, and only one warmed my heart; Sean's kisses felt as good as I had always imagined they would. In school, I envied the girls four years ahead of me who were the recipients of his first kisses. I knew who they were, but for Sean, I was always the young girl next door with a hammer in her back pocket. At an age when he began to yearn for feminine curves, all I had to offer was a prosaic whack on a piece of wood. How could I ever tell Sean that his Little Barbie shifted into passionate daydreaming about him behind his back?

Besides, he left for the big city just as I was beginning to look a bit less immature. His visits during his university years were brief, though he did come back for the memorial service six years ago. Now, I knew first-hand just what I had been missing all those years.

In spite of these conflicting events, my primary mission during our village party was successful. When Megan introduced Anne Beauchamps to me, I was panting after dancing a jig with Sean, who covered a lot of territory in too few minutes. Anne did not seem to mind. She was not the woman I was pursuing before my crash under the Kissing Bough; her hair was longer and her face rounder than chic could ever be. Where I had expected sophistication, Anne displayed a quiet manner. Poised might be the big city word, but in our bucolic surroundings, she exuded serenity. Getting to know her better became a priority well ahead of other projects such as learning more Gaelic, or laying the foundations for a new barn, or raising a new breed of chickens with lavender eggs. (I made that last one up.)

After plunging into work clothes, I picked up my hammer from the table by my bed and slipped it into my back pocket. Standing in front of the long mirror in the hallway, I talked myself into a good mood. I felt strong and competent, as I admired the sturdiness of my limbs. My apprehension faded in the morning sunshine. I would see Sean, and we would continue where we left off, and that was all that mattered.

Ignoring the twinge from my right thigh, I descended the narrow wooden stairs to the kitchen. A quick breakfast, and I was ready to face my self-imposed task.

For a summer day, the air was refreshing, cooled by the breezes from the lake. Rolling hills surround us, forming a crown. The jewel of the crown is a lake, large, wide and wise. Yes, a wise lake. Rather odd, isn't it? According to my father, that lake has protected us many times from invasions, from prying eyes, from governments, from bureaucrats, from stray persons. What to most, including my father's undutiful daughter, is a haphazard dense fog, is in reality, he assured all listeners, a deliberate strategy to keep all invaders out and hopelessly lost on the steep slopes below us.

I listened to these tales and yawned. My father, living in his mind and in the times he loved most, never noticed. I had perfected the art of dozing with my eyes half-open.

Taking energetic strides towards the village green, I remembered sneaking after Sean when I overheard him making an assignation with one of his adolescent charmers. Leaving my hammer behind, I hid behind a series of trees on the green and near the creek, all the way down to the lake. This vast body of water glistened, so I crept after them taking care to remain low to the ground. He never guessed that he was being followed; his manner was too assured, and his attention remained fixed on his companion. Thanks to Sean, I learned about many a nook and cranny in those woods by the lake.

I stumbled. Pull yourself together, Barbara! Time to focus on your goal of dismantling the platform in sections for storage until our next event.

Arriving at the scene of the opening ceremonies, I took out my hammer from my back pocket and began plying sections apart. Tom Bates arrived a bit later. One look at him, and I knew. His stubble was thick and dark, his voice deep, his eyes shadowed. Even when he barked out orders, I decided not to argue with him, the day was just too fine, and he looked so hung-over.

Half of the platform was ready to cart away, when hands grabbed me from behind and whirled me around. I was more prepared this time.

"Sean, I didn't hear you!"

Sean grinned, delighted with himself. "Barbie, Barbie, you need to play. Let Tom Bates finish up, and come off with me!"

Time alone with Sean would be like the main present at the very best of birthday parties. However, his timing was lousy. I had a reputation to keep up. Organization just had to come first.

"Sean, you tempt me, but there is a lot for me to do. Why not meet up later?"

With a bemused expression, Sean looked as if his beloved puppy had burst into doggie adulthood and developed a mind of its own. "Barbie, you win out. But I won't be kept waiting for long."

That night at the Sullivan House, Sean, my hero, welcomed me with a smiling Megan by his side. The evening became a merry event in the company of brother and sister, with aching cheeks and lungs.

Sean teased me about my first attempt to nail two boards together. I hit the board instead of the nail with such force that everything went flying, including me. He joked about our teachers, who found it hard to maintain their dignity in the presence of such a light-hearted Sullivan. Megan teased him about his youthful pride when his upper lip sprouted miniscule hair growth. I was a good audience. My sides and face throbbed. Laughing non-stop can be such hard work.

Sean's farewell hug and light goodnight kisses made me float all the way back to my bed and comforter with promise of so much more to come. Just before slipping into deep sleep, I became aware of just how delightful the evening's shimmering moments were after years of adjusting to my changed circumstances. Like a bubble, the feeling of joy rose in my throat. I could not quite believe that all this happiness was real.

By the time *Charmed Necessities* opened on Monday morning, peace and cleanliness had descended onto the village. Even Colleen let out her red locks that resembled a glorious halo. Yes, that was just the way I felt, radiant, with the glimmer of so much more joy waiting for me just ahead.

That morning provided a welcome surprise. Anne Beauchamps entered the shop carrying a full basket. Walking past the bins and tables, she paused in front of the garden angels and reached out to touch one with a fingertip. She looked up and smiled.

In the daylight of the shop, Anne was neither slender, nor sturdy. Her shape matched her rounded cheeks. Her shoulder-length blond hair was smoothed back, framing the pale tan of her face and arms–a working tan, as fellow gardeners would call it. With clothes the same color as her skin, she would have looked almost bland, but for the pale pink glow of her lips and cheeks, and the blue-gold shining through the hazel in her deep-set eyes. Her demeanor was unobtrusive, but I could feel her presence all the way from the counter. I drew near.

"Let me introduce Colleen Shaw to you, Anne. She manages *Charmed Necessities* to perfection." Greetings were amiable.

Anne lifted her basket onto the counter. "I hope this food is to your liking, Barbara. Thank you for making my introduction to the village such a warm one." How I deserved such praise or food, I did not know. But I persuaded Anne to stay and enjoy her own feast with us. Anne smiled, Colleen beamed, and I was ravenous.

In between bites of thick slices of homemade bread coated with spicy mustard, fresh greens and hearty slices of cheddar, we answered Anne's questions and asked a few as well. It was only practical.

During her visits to France, Mrs. Goodheart had regaled her granddaughter with stories about village inhabitants.

"Is it true that Patrick Doweran began his cooking career by working as a sheep herder?"

Indeed, Patrick the Cook, or as he preferred to be called, Master Chef Patrick, had discovered goat cheese at a young age and began tending the goats of

Old Giles Hughie. He went to the farm early every morning and smelled of goat all through class.

"Who is Ronald Cormac? Is he the village journalist?"

We smirked. On his first visit to our village, Ronald stopped by *Butterfingers* for tea and blueberry scones and was served by the baker herself. It was love at first bite. Patricia Cormac, pleased by the effect of her baking skills, grew to reciprocate the feelings of this broad, hulk of a man with slender hands. Ronald gave up big city lights for fresh baked bread, adopted Patricia's surname, and brought the village up to speed with his love of the very latest communication technologies. He made an energetic librarian. His nickname "the Boar" was inspired by his relentless energy to boar through the most challenging technical jargon or projects. Like Master Chef Patrick, Ronald the Boar had quite a following of people wanting to study with him.

"Ronald shot some footage of the Summer Full Moon Party. He will show us an edited version at the library tonight. Do join us, Anne!" She would get a broader introduction to village life. How very opportune.

Our village library was my father's pride and joy. This sprawling stone and wooden structure evolved over time into a conglomeration of rooms built in different periods and styles. Each structure was added on with more gusto than accuracy. The result is a formidable stew of architectural dabbling, cloaked, at least in part, with our own village style. The building and its contents have attracted many a puzzled architectural historian, and, like my father, numerous historians. I spent many hours there, but for quite a different reason—the seats.

The leather and wooden seats are dark with age, but the electric lighting is bright enough, replacing the candles and lamps of earlier times. Smaller rooms hold special collections that are of no interest to me. My father's favorite room contains old, undecipherable manuscripts. I prefer the most recent reading room, the great room with its new seating and fresh carpet.

Each of these seats can be heated with individual dials, making reading in inclement weather quite pleasurable.

When we arrived that evening, Tom Bates was sprawled out on one of these seats, snoring away. Our gathering became boisterous enough to wake him, so he managed to join us in the media room in time for the viewing. Sean and Megan did not attend, no doubt busy getting the affairs of *Chalice Lore*, the family store, in order. Horatio Caesar was no doubt taking care of his grandfather, no lover of new technologies. I invited Anne to sit next to me in order to whisper names to her.

Ronald had edited together brief segments of Bessy's poetic welcome, Jimmy Delane's gathering of birds, and Joanie MacLever's unruly pet goats, followed by Mary Lisa's sideways burst of mirth. Ronald used short clips of visitors and villagers alike to transition into the Hapless Hatless Potato Race. With the zoom lens on his camera, Ronald captured the general atmosphere of determination. It was quite funny to see the outward thrust of chins, clenched lips and sharp eyes of the contestants.

I smiled at Melissa's performance, and then grew still. A brief clip showed two people prone and entangled under the Kissing Bough. My downfall had been recorded for all to observe. My cheeks flushed. But that was not all. A jaunty reference to Sean's and my reunion later that evening included teasing hints about a shared future. Anne glanced at me, but said nothing. Looking around the room, I saw pairs of inquisitive eyes focused on me.

Life, as I had led it, was changing. Like a bear longing for hibernation, I was no longer certain that I wanted it to. For six years, I had managed my life and *Charmed Necessities* with Colleen's help and the support of good friends like Horatio Caesar. The look in Anne's eyes confirmed my suspicions. I was going to face change all right. My daydreams just might turn into reality.

IV.   Heavy Baskets

Monday and Tuesday passed by without a word from Sean. I could not endure his silence any longer. On Wednesday, I cornered Megan in *Chalice Lore*. In a subdued voice, she replied that Sean had had to return to the big city to finish his business.

"When will he be back?" I asked aiming for a casual tone.

"As soon as he can," was her only reply.

I tried to reason with myself. Megan's response was calm enough. He would return, the only question was when. If I cared about his return, then Megan did just as much. Megan adored her older brother. When I was still in school, Sean, four years my senior, left us for more education and other experiences. Megan would pass on occasional greetings, but gave no hint that Sean would ever return to us, except for the rare overnight visit. His ongoing absence seemed to indicate just how happy he was in the larger world. Recent events at our Summer Full Moon Party proved otherwise.

Once he had given us a taste of his company, we were both impatient for more. His words and kisses were laced with anticipation–both mine and his. Not knowing for how long I had to wait for his return was worse than drinking pure wine vinegar. My hands touched the old wood of the kitchen table as if seeking reassurance. Repressing tendrils of anxiety wasn't easy. My parents had not sat with me at this table for six long years.   The loss of Sean's company for an unknown duration hit a bit too close to home.

While anticipating his return with as much patience as I could muster, my waking hours were devoted to tending the needs of visitors and getting to know Anne Beauchamps. After Anne's furniture and belongings arrived from France, I paid her a visit with heavy baskets in hand.   Her grandmother, the admirable and on occasion unfathomable Mrs. Goodheart, would have wanted me to bring Anne some village specialties.

Mrs. Goodheart almost convinced me that the Mystical was a living being. 'Magic' had long graying hair, piercing yet kind grey-blue eyes, smelled of rosemary and lavender and had a kind smile. As I grew into 'nail-hood,' with my hammer in my back pocket at all times, the possibility that anything mystical could ever exist faded away, much to my relief.   Hard facts and hard nails informed my interactions. My visits to Mrs. Goodheart grew fewer and I grew to abhor all those related "M" words. So I was curious to return to the house where I had almost become a believer.

Like many of the dwellings in the village, her house is set away from the main streets. Whereas I live in the lower portion of our village not far from the green, Anne's house is situated in the upper part of the village. Curiosity can generate more power than the highest-octane fuel in a strong engine.   I made it there laden with two heavy baskets in record time.

On that sunny afternoon hovering between summer and autumn, bushes of herbs were flowering in profuse abandon on either side of the garden path. They enlivened the familiar facade of stone and wood. Vivid scents of lavenders and mints evoked fleeting childhood memories. I passed through them a buzz with whizzing bees unscathed.

Anne opened her front door before my knuckles hit the bright blue paint. I dropped my hand in embarrassment. She welcomed me inside with a soft smile. Baskets in hand, I crossed the threshold with undisguised eagerness.

At first, I did not recognize the room–the space was so bare. Mrs. Goodheart's cozy sofas and overstuffed armchairs had been replaced by just a few sleek pieces. No wonder Anne could move in to her grandmother's house with such speed, there was almost nothing there.

"I like the simplicity of modern lines," Anne explained. "Grandmother preferred this bareness as well, but she didn't want to take the time to replace her belongings."

My bemusement grew as Anne showed me from room to room. I compared Anne's appearance and demeanor with the furniture, quiet and understated. Anne's bland clothing, her round face free of any traces of make-up, and her blond shoulder-length hair matched her belongings, or rather, they matched her. If she sat on the beige chair with its straight lines, she would become almost invisible.

The kitchen was another revelation. Apart from a functional table made of light-colored wood surrounded by straight wooden chairs with padded seats, all sorts of things hung from the rafters. Along with gleaming stainless steel and copper pots and kitchen implements hung copious bundles of dried herbs.

I blurted out, "You know about herbs as well?"

"Grandmamma taught me."

I mulled this over as Anne pulled out the contents from my baskets one by one. Each piece seemed to fit into place. The white garden angel looked more whimsical in her new setting. The soaps and lotions resembled exotic flowers. The jams and spreads glowed like vivid jewels. Indeed, they were much more attractive on Anne's kitchen table than on the shelves and tables of *Charmed Necessities*.

An idea popped into my head. "Anne, would you be willing to help me rearrange my shop?"

She looked up startled, but gratified. "Why me?"

"I haven't rearranged anything, not a single thing in the last six years."

Anne's eyes sharpened.

"Colleen helps me restock shelves and tables, that's all. I would have done a better job at taking over the responsibility for a hardware store," I admitted.

"A hardware store?"

"Oh, yes," I replied, patting my trusty hammer by my back pocket. "And I can see how much better these items from *Charmed Necessities* look on your kitchen table. So, I would really like your input to help rearrange the whole store."

Her blue and hazel eyes lit up, the gold flecks gleamed. "That sounds like fun!" she exclaimed.

This idea born out of nowhere took considerable time and ingenuity to complete. I had plenty of the former, and Anne, the latter. Supported by Colleen's encouragement and my eagerness, Anne looked over *Charmed Necessities* with great care. She assessed at each shelf and table top, making lists of all the types of products, and under each heading, the range of products. For all my love of organization, I had never bothered to do this. I learned that the lists were longest in the categories "Beauty Products" and "Garden."

Colleen peered at the lists with a discerning eye and commented that we lacked items in the "Interior Décor" category. I promised to get the word out through the village grapevine that we needed more hand-made items for enhancing rooms, whether vases or placemats.

One of the obstacles, we all agreed, was the vast quantity and variety of shapes and sizes of the products. And all the patterns made the store feel a bit overwhelming.

A few days later, Anne returned with drawings of her suggestions. I was impressed. In one word, *Charmed Necessities* would feel "clean." I pinned her plans to the wall of the office. They looked a lot better than the many flyers. My mother, in her stately manner, had never pinned anything to the walls. When I took over, I couldn't resist this form of decorating.

Looking at Anne's designs for the new layout helped to take my mind off of Sean and my growing dejection about his role in my life. Sean's absence stretched into weeks. Megan only said that he was delayed, but would not give me any specifics. She looked as glum as I felt.

Just as I convinced myself that all the Summer Full Moon Party attentions were imagined, a giant postcard arrived, the kind that needs all sorts of extra stamps. The image was an abstraction with delicious, bright colors, and Sean's words written in bold letters–"I NEED A KISS."

With the colorful image pinned on the wall next to Anne's drawings, Sean's first missive to me, I began to daydream all over again. Sean would return soon. I was sure of it.

Horatio Caesar entered the office while I was daydreaming one afternoon and called me back to the unwelcome present. "Who is that from?" His finger pointed to the card; he looked ruffled.

"Why from Sean, of course!" I replied, jerking to my feet with such vigor that my trusty hammer banged into my chair.

"Sean is coming back?"

"As soon as he can."

Horatio Caesar peered at the image as if trying to gleam insights from the luminous colors. His glasses slid down his nose, and he pushed them back up with his middle finger while continuing to stare at the blobs.

"You want him to come back soon?" he queried without looking at me.

"The sooner, the better!"

His face and pose bespoke the unconvinced.

"Listen, ever since we were in school, Sean has been my secret hero. No one else has ever come close!" I blurted, incensed that he would even question my choices.

He eyed me as if I were a dubious and very smelly creature of the wilderness. "We always told each other our secrets, Barbara Mahoney," and left abruptly.

I had to go after him. I could count on one hand the number of times that Horatio Caesar called me by my full name, beginning when I was five and he caught me throwing mud pies at the geese.

Even more humiliating was when my determination to win the school prize for the most delicious cookie overcame any scruples. While she was out, I stole into Mrs. Goodheart's kitchen to find her book with a secret recipe that would persuade the judges in my favor. When Horatio Caesar saw my furtive behavior, he followed me.

He sneaked in just as I was reaching to pick the prized volume off its perch above the refrigerator, and yelled out "Barbara Mahoney! Put that book back!" I fell off the chair and landed in a heap. Disgruntled, he helped me up and dragged me all the way home. We never spoke about that incident again.

Leaving *Charmed Necessities* in Colleen's hands, I ran after him, but saw no sign of him in the street. I crossed the village green to the wooden bridge and followed the winding path down the creek toward the lake. Beyond the lake in the distance were old forests, and beyond that, way below in the vast plains, was the big city.

Many legends involved this large body of water. Mists and fog would form on the water and blanket the road up through the forests leading to the village, while we remained in sunshine. People said, no harm ever came to a person from the village. Those legends dealt with the fate of those from the outside worlds. Besides, I did not believe in those tales.

Water glistened between the trees, and soon I stood by the lake's edge looking out across the sunlit water. No sign of anyone. I stalked back toward the creek and up the meandering path and arrived at the green, somewhat out of breath.

"Barbara!"

Horatio Caesar ambled toward me. "What's the matter? Is everything O.K.? You look upset." His face looked like he was struggling. "I just had to think things through." Horatio Caesar added with obvious concern. "I didn't mean to pry."

I felt like a fast moving vehicle that had been shifted into reverse by an unskilled driver. In the time it would take to gain some skill with those gears, I regained my composure. And six lifetimes later, I was able to joke with Horatio Caesar.

"Owly," only my pet name for Horatio Caesar would do, "I was afraid I hurt your feelings so I went looking for you."

"But, BB!" Horatio Caesar whispered in my ear as he used to during the most boring classes. "You don't have *any* sense of direction! Remember the time you were supposed to pick apples in the West fields, and you went North instead, and ran into those wild dogs? They chased you all the way back to the village, and you had nightmares for weeks about being devoured by wild animals."

I grinned. "Well, it helped me improve my running time!"

Horatio Caesar grinned back, and we ambled back to the shop and to the ever-patient Colleen. What a dear friend he is; I never feel lonely when he is around.

Late that night, as I lay listening to the breeze in the trees outside my bedroom window, the face of Mr. Mostly-Green-Eyes surfaced in my mind, his jaw tight, his square face determined. I shot up in bed, that man had found me again. How dare he!

It was bad enough to have occasional, nostalgic memories surface of my mother's concern for my well-being, and my father's fond, if absent-minded gaze, as he taught me a new trick with my hammer, so that he could get on with the centuries that interested him the most. These memories left me missing them, a lot. But, at least, we shared a familial bond. To have a complete stranger intrude on my thoughts, and Sean not present to reassure me that his and my future would be shared, was the last straw. Something had to be done.

I did not believe in legends and old tales, but small fears rattled around inside anyway. Mrs. Goodheart's granddaughter seemed like the most fitting person to talk with. She could not believe the old tales; she had not grown up in the village. She would be my Voice of Reason.

V.   My Voice of Reason

Transforming *Charmed Necessities* into the new layout and design took longer than expected. Much as I admired Anne's plans, I lingered in my identity as the dutiful daughter and granddaughter upholding the dusty image of family tradition. Change crept up behind me and tapped me on the shoulder. I cringed and then made a change and then cringed again, as each design choice of my matrilineal ancestors was called into question.

It took weeks of Anne's gentle patience and my incessant hesitations to complete the task. Conversations took on a familiar pattern.

"Barbara, why don't we try putting one set of products, for example, a soap, a lotion and a scented oil out on this table, just to give your visitors an idea how they might combine your personal care products?"

"But my mother always told me that visitors liked the feeling of abundance. So we have to have piles of one product!" I exclaimed in a peevish tone.

"I am certain that she was and still is correct." Anne's voice was reflective, even pensive. "There is, however, a difference between an abundance of variety in what *Charmed Necessities* has to offer, and just an abundance in quantity."

Her quiet reasoning made sense, so I acquiesced. I liked the grouping so much that I followed her suggestion in other parts of the shop.

Other clusters of individual products appeared. The combinations were colorful, unique and plentiful.

Throughout that laborious process, there was no further word from Sean. Our encounters during and after the Summer Full Moon Party were shifting into the realm of the fantastical. Yet, my desire for our reunion continued to burn deep.

Anne's ideas for redecorating were fresh and unusual. A single lilac-colored garden angel looked out from its table perch. Others in different colorations stood behind it in a "v" formation. The bare wood of the table, darkened by age and oil, made the garden ornaments glow. Duplicate garden angels were stored in wooden chests under the table. Gone was the chintz effect, so beloved to my mother and grandmother. In its place was a sophisticated simplicity.

Removing the tablecloths made the shop seem larger. The scents of all the village-made candles and soaps no longer mingled with the smell of dust. Shelves, bare of runners, glowed with the colors of the products. As Anne pointed out, they needed no ornamentation to frame their beauty. Tablecloths and runners for purchase were placed in oval, hand-made baskets. The wind chimes by the front door were neatly arranged in a welcoming curve; visitors would no longer bump into them. Bouquets of dried flowers graced the counter. I had to agree with Anne; visitors would no longer be overwhelmed by quantities of each item and the multitude of conflicting patterns. Instead, the colors and the forms stood out against the old wood in a perfect marriage of the worn and the new.

To celebrate the completion of the transformation, we envisioned a More Charmed Necessities Party. Master Chef Patrick came up with a daring plan; he would make a replica of the old shop out of marzipan to be kept on display in the front window as a historic marker. My talk with Anne would have to wait until this momentous event took place.

Patrick popped by the shop almost every day "to get a better idea of the dimensions," he explained. He addressed his questions to Colleen, no doubt because I was busy with other preparations. Colleen's smile became mischievous, but her red locks swayed in denial when I asked her if Patrick was pestering her too often.

To avoid giving offense, I explained to willing ears at *Butter Fingers* bakery, at *The Abundant Basket*, my favorite source of fresh produce, and other shops that the purpose of this party was to acquaint out-of-town visitors with the new look. Colleen Shaw and Bossy Barbs shifted places. Colleen sat me down with invitations and envelopes to be addressed, and refused to allow me to be disturbed. I felt like a prodded cow, but murmured only occasional complaints.

Our party was only a few days off when Colleen cornered me. "Inviting your new relatives?" I stiffened. I hoped to keep them where they belonged, as a memory filled with the color blue. "Your parents would have wanted you to!"

I grumbled, but Colleen stared me down as only a former baby-sitter can, and I rummaged around for the card my "dear" relatives had handed me. The missing paper was under a jumble of others in my "take care of it later" drawer, perhaps better named the "take care of it never." Colleen kept on staring at me so I could not tear up the card and pretend that I had lost it. I picked up the phone and grumbled under my breath.

"We would love to come, my dear" Aunt Phoebe replied to my reluctant invitation. "I will check with Christopher's secretary and call you right back."

Colleen continued to stare at me. "Are they coming?"

"She will call me back," I murmured. Colleen was satisfied with my answer. My inner dog could now uncurl the tail tucked between its legs.

In order to accommodate more people, we decided to set up tables in the backyard under a canopy. Tom Bates, who never lost an opportunity to bait me (pun intended) had a little extra time the day before to help me set up. He emphasized "little." Since Tom was always behind schedule, I needed another source of brawn. Horatio Caesar offered a hand, but he could bring a tent down faster than anyone in the village.

Help came in a thrilling form. Megan provided me with very welcome news. She drifted into *Charmed Necessities* to inform me that Sean would attend the party, and he would even arrive the evening before. I glowed. At the back of my mind was one niggling question: Why had Sean not told *me* about his plans?

Just at closing, Tom Bates entered smiling. He had taken the time to brush his unruly flock of small black curls and put on a clean shirt. His smile became much wider when Anne arrived to help out. No wonder the promptness and the neat look!

Sean strode in on us as I was teetering on a ladder with a string of lights in one hand. He arrived just in time to catch, first the flying hammer, and then an inelegant me, as I lost my balance.

"I can see just how sorely your need me, Barbara Blue!" Sean helped me to my feet. I was flustered, happy and embarrassed.

"Sean, this is Anne Beauchamps, Mrs. Goodheart's granddaughter," I squeaked out to hide my confusion.

Sean leaned over and kissed Anne on both cheeks. "You are one of the family then. Welcome to our village!" The Sullivan charm was in full gale. Anne looked like she had been blown about a bit.

Any lingering wisps of resentment about Sean's abrupt departure and long silence melted away in the brilliance of his first smile. Somehow, the canopy was put in place, the lights hung, the tables readied, and we left the scene of the next day's party with relief. Sean pulled me aside and kissed me with tempting thoroughness and then ordered me to get a good night's sleep and strode off.

My body obeyed him. No memories of my parents or uneasy dreams appeared to haunt me, and the new day began with an abundance of happiness, the kind that begins with the first breath of wakefulness and lasts through all the subsequent chaos.

By the afternoon, Colleen had arranged fresh flowers everywhere. *Charmed Necessities* glowed. I hurried home to change. My dress was bland and blue; it was neither short, nor long, nor tight, nor loose. When I pulled my hair back from my face, I was ready.

My relatives arrived early on. Aunt Phoebe gave me a resounding hug. Uncle Christopher, ever the proper businessman, pumped my hand. I felt overpowered by their warmth. Aunt Phoebe took my arm and insisted on a guided tour of the shop. She paused only to examine the photo of my parents on my desk, taken when I was young enough to be tossed into the air. But she allowed me to lead her out back to the refreshments without further questioning.

Introductions were made all around. Anne was looking serene in pale ivory. Patrick's vest of burgundy brocade lacked its usual touches of flour. Even his hair was trimmed for the occasion. Sean waltzed in with Megan trailing behind him. With a flourish, he handed me a single red rose. *Charmed Necessities* and I were beaming, the former with chicness, and the latter with requited love.

After jovial toasts, Patrick unveiled his creation and we burst into applause. He had outdone himself. A miniature of the *Charmed Necessities* that my grandmother and mother had envisioned was composed out of colored marzipan, complete with objects on floral tablecloths, a marvelous tribute to those who had passed before me.

Sean entertained every one around him, including my relatives. Uncle Christopher's laugh boomed out above the chatter. I stifled a wish to have Sean to myself. He was back and that was all that mattered.

When Sean came by early next morning to help clean up, raindrops twirled around his light curls and then dropped onto his cheek and shirt. He lifted me up and twirled me around before he kissed me. Now that was the way to start the day! Breathless Barb would be more like it.

I studied him as we cleaned up. He had not inherited the stunning Sullivan looks that his sister had. In repose, his face was angular, with a sprinkling of freckles over his elfin nose. In fact, someone I did not want to remember had more regular features and was much better looking. But Sean's smile made me feel like the sun had burst open somewhere in my chest.

I was eleven and high up in a tree when I first felt the effect of his smile. Proud about having climbed so high, I gloated among the bird nests, happy to be above the world I knew. When I turned to climb down, I froze. There were only staggering drops. Like a cat, I clung to my spot and yelled for help. Sean appeared and smiled up at me: the sun had arrived and I was safe. As he helped me down, he did not make fun of my plight or laugh at me. He just hugged me until I stopped shaking. My heart was from then on no longer just my own.

With his agile hands and boundless energy, the shop had been restored to a spotless and inviting order. Before I could gloat, Sean told me that he had had an idea, and that it would involve my participation.

The successful businessman Sean announced that the Sullivan shop was going to be re-vamped with him in charge of the renovations and he was counting on my "advice." I suppressed a laugh, snorting instead, being the last person to give anyone that sort of counsel.

Sean then announced he would begin in a week when he returned from his final meetings in the big city and when he finished training his replacement, so I had better be ready for him. When he emphasized "final" and winked at me, that week seemed almost short enough.

When the opportunity arose for me to talk to Anne in her kitchen, I no longer had any questions. Sean had returned to us, and would be back in less than one week–he promised–and everything was perfect. A life together was a forgone conclusion. I had no questions or qualms, even though we hadn't talked about our future in detail. So far, my daydreams had come true, so how could they lie?

Congratulating me on the success of the More Charmed Necessities Party, Anne glowed when she spoke of Patrick's craftsmanship and of meeting so many lovely people. I even smiled when she spoke of Aunt Phoebe and Uncle Christopher and their kindness. I had almost resigned myself to their presence in my life, although I hoped they would remain at the perimeter. They reminded me too much of what I missed these last six years, and what I could never have again.

Anne began with innocuous question. "Barbara, who was the man you ran into at the Summer Full Moon Party?"

I stuttered, "You mean S...Sean?"

"No, not him," Anne replied, "The other man, who did not see you coming."

"Uh, I don't know." Her battery of questions caught me off guard.

I felt quite self-conscious. Amazing what a vicious circle that can be! I was turning pink from my exertions to run away from any mention of that man.

"What was it you fell under?"

"Uh, the Kissing Bough."

Anne was not giving up. "What is that?"

"Megan made it while she was growing up." Talk about evading the issue, I was becoming a pro.

"Why did she make it?" Anne was teaching me a new level of professionalism.

"It is a family custom."

"What is it used for?"

That did it. I could be evasive only for so long. After all, Anne could ask Megan and learn the whole story. It might as well be me.

"Ehem," I cleared my throat the way my father did countless times before beginning one of his rambling oral histories. "For generations, the Sullivan women have woven a Kissing Bough. It is supposed to bring them true love. Whoever they meet and kiss under the Kissing Bough is their destined partner for life."

"Then why was it hanging on the village green during the Summer Full Moon Party? Was Megan planning to meet her partner that evening?"

I sighed. "The legend extends to others in the village."

"So, if two people meet and kiss under the Kissing Bough, they will become life partners?"

"That's what some people say."

"Has this been the case in the past?"

"Well, it sort of seems to happen that way. But, when people believe in the power of an object or of a legend, then it will happen just as they expect it to, right?"

"You do not believe it to be true?" Anne countered.

"No, I do not! Of course not! No, and No. I hope it's not true," groaning at the thought. "Anyway, even if the legend is founded on some sort of similar chain of events, the supposed outcome is not clear cut in my situation," I clarified.

"First of all, I ran a stranger down under the Kissing Bough, but we did not kiss." My lip curled at the memory with some distaste. "He looked like he was going to after I told him what was hanging above us. But, he did not. So, you could say it was an accident, and neither person wanted to be there."

"You have no idea who he is?"

"No! And I don't want to know anything about him!"

Anne looked startled by my vehemence. "Have you ever seen him before?"

"No!" I all but shouted, and then remembered. "Uh–well, not before our Summer Full Moon Party. I bumped into his chair at the end of the opening ceremonies, which made him turn around and look at me." I remembered another detail. "He was with the pretty woman he sat next to. To be honest, I wasn't paying attention to any of the visitors until I bumped into his chair."

"Then you crashed into him twice?"

I winced. I preferred the term 'bumped.' "Well, yes, now that you mention it, I did. But we did not kiss under the Kissing Bough, and he was with that pretty woman." I tried to look and sound hopeful.

Anne blew some sense into me. "Would he have wanted to kiss you if he was involved with her?"

"Maybe he felt it was a sort of dare or challenge. He could tell that I did not like him." I felt hope ebb from me like a once proud flag in ever-calming wind.

My designated "Voice of Reason" looked more perplexed than I had hoped. "Did Sean kiss you under the Kissing Bough later on that evening?" she asked.

"Oh, Yes!" There was both longing and happiness in my face. I could feel them both, side by side.

"Sean seems very charming," Anne remarked as if she had not noticed that my face matched the color of the roses on her kitchen table.

"Oh yes, he is! And I am so, so glad that he is back," as my cheeks grew a deeper shade of pink.

Anne paused and looked me in the eye. "Would you like the legend of the Kissing Bough to be true, if it were to apply to Sean?"

"Yes!" This third "yes" was strong and hearty. There were no questions, no doubts. All the years of yearning united in one vision, one desire. Not even Sean's teasing could make me wonder about our compatibility, no—gulp—our love.

Anne, my dear 'Voice of Reason,' replied, "I see." And that was that.

VI.   If Vacations were Short and Sweet

When Sean returned in less than a week, any niggling doubts about his intentions, his constancy, would melt away in his presence. I did understand that he had to wrap up his current work. Training a replacement was the honorable thing to do. So while a part of me wished that one Barbara kiss would make him drop everything to be back by my side, I knew that it was unrealistic and unfair of me to ask that of him.

Meanwhile, the owner of my favorite village inn made an announcement that would affect us all. He was going to take a real vacation. Like the rest of us, the owner took a day or two, or the occasional week off. But this time, he meant Vacation, in other words, at least six months of travel and leisure in far flung locations around the world.

Named *Delights in Earthly Haven*, his inn is beloved by many. Each of the twenty-one rooms overflows with "uniqueness" and "character." With considerable historical accuracy, the rooms correspond to the first through the twenty-first centuries in Anno Domini. Each century is summarized in the rooms' decorations. The only compromise to historical fact is a smattering of creature comforts offered to those visitors who take rooms in the least comfortable centuries. The Eleventh Century Room, for example, offers a bit more than rushes on the floor and some hay in the corner to sleep on. But the amenities are disguised so they remain hidden from a casual perusal of the room.

No expense was spared to recreate each period. When some of the rooms were undergoing renovations, the owner consulted my father about details of the post-Roman through Medieval periods. He expounded at greater length than anticipated, but the owner of the inn delights in people's idiosyncrasies, and has a fondness for history. So he kept on inviting my father back for more history-over-ale sessions.

In keeping with its first incarnation as the main village hostelry, *Delights in Earthly Haven* boasts a small pub. Over the years, the current owner has served up his home brew Haven's Ale with such relentless gusto that he acquired a sizable girth. His character fits his physique; he is so cheery that he makes Santa Claus seem like the silent type. The only cause for embarrassment when growing up was the name his grandparents called him, Samuel P. McKnight, Esquire. With nary a single famous ancestor, at least none that he knew about, he was village born and bred. His family had owned *Delights in Earthly Haven* long enough to add three rooms, numbered nineteen, twenty and twenty-one. Wanting to generate more laughter and less embarrassment, he switched his name around and began introducing himself as Samuelesque P. McKnight. We shortened it to Samek.

While news of Samek's Vacation flew around the village, I knew better. The focus of his Vacation was *not* to recover from the accumulated fatigue of being so very jolly.

"Megan, Samek is finally going off on his Bride Quest," I blurted out, when she popped by.

Megan's mouth dropped open. Neither of us had thought that Samek would ever be able to leave his pride and joy, that quirky inn, for more than a week. "When is he off?"

"Next week!" My tone was abrupt. While I fully appreciated Samek's motive for his trip, I never liked it when friends left our village for a substantial duration.

"But who is going to manage the inn while he's gone?" It was Megan who thought of practicalities, for once.

"I have no idea, but Patrick is supposed to tell us, when he comes by this afternoon."

Megan smiled and I grinned at the image of Samek, who was almost forty, on a Bride Quest. I wanted her to use her special ability to see if Samek would be successful, but she said she was not "in the mood." If I had asked her about Samek's replacement, Megan might have obliged. This was of imminent concern. Samek's possible bride was too far in the future to interest her.

Patrick postponed his visit. He had caught a cold, and was nursing it along with crème brulée and chocolate mousse. When he walked in to *Charmed Necessities* two days later, he looked a bit pale and lost in layers of sweaters. Colleen fussed over him. I smirked. She even bossed me, Bossy Barbs herself, to place the spare electric heater next to the large office chair and make a pot of our Tea for Dreary Colds, which contains every known herb for cold care and some known only to our village herbalists. Echinacea, milk vetch root, and elderberry are only three of twenty ingredients. Colleen hovered around Patrick and he was enjoying every drip of her attentions.

This superb chef, who could bark out orders to large crews, command ceremonies, and was followed without question by his assistants and an assortment of children, transformed into a cozy bundle, making you want to just reach out and snuggle him. Colleen was doing just that.

Patrick looked like he had forgotten his latest flirtation at the Summer Full Moon Party. All recollections of Ms. Horizontal, our denizen of outrageous laughter, seemed to have faded from his mind. Poor Mary Lisa MaGuire, she was not even a memory now. Colleen's hazel eyes turned color and began to glow. Love was being birthed, all due to a cold and our tea. I would have lingered as Midwife to New Love, but Megan arrived, intent on finding out the latest news that Patrick shared with us.

Samek had chosen a cousin to take charge while he was on "Vacation."   His name was Michael Mathews. Yes, while he had grown up in nebulous parts of the big wide world, he had been to the village before. Samek had invited him to the Summer Full Moon Party. He had? Yes, Michael sat in the third row at the opening ceremonies, along with his sister, in seats reserved for them by Samek.

I had been sitting next to Horatio Caesar in the fourth row.   Michael Mathews and his sister were sitting in the row in front of me.   But it could not be the man I bumped into–no way. Mr. Mostly Green Eyes had no charm, no jolliness, no roundness, in fact none of the qualities needed to take over Samek's pride and joy.

What did Michael look like? He was rather tall and slender. I paled, but stopped myself from reacting further.   While Mr. Mostly Green Eyes fit that description, so did many men at the village party.

Patrick continued with his revelations. Samek did not want to limit his Bride Quest, which he still persisted in calling his "Vacation," with a definitive return date.   Michael Mathews, hopefully not Mr. Mostly Green Eyes, would take charge of *Delights in Earthly Haven* for the next six months "at least."

At Samek's request, Patrick was charged with inviting all of us to welcome Michael Mathews, in the pub room of the *Delights in Earthly Haven* on Saturday night. I would know then for certain.

Under any other circumstance, I would have been delighted. Apart from satisfying my thirst for information and for Haven's Ale, a visit to the pub meant, in some very private part of my heart, reconnecting with my father. The suit of armor near the pub's entrance was thought to be 16th century German, but my father was able to prove with a tremendous wealth of detail that it was in fact late 15th century French, and had been worn in the Burgundian Wars.

It would be just my luck to have Mr. Mostly Green Eyes show up, when my childhood dreams about Sean–if only he were here this very moment–

were becoming a reality. My dismay could not be concealed. If this person was indeed Mr. Mostly Green Eyes, he would not only be back in my life, but he had a name–Michael Mathews–and he was going to live in my village for at least six months. I flipped from dismay, to incredulity, to stewing. Budding Love evaporated into a seething field of orange and red. I stalked out past my puzzled friends, fuming.

The Kissing Bough incident was just a legend. But this man would have a definite connection to the village, he was not "just a visitor."

I came to a complete standstill. If he was the man whose chair I bumped into, then the pretty woman next to him was not his girlfriend, but his sister. His subsequent behavior toward me under the Kissing Bough would be that of an unattached male.

All rational arguments, and I used them all, failed to lift my spirits. I even reminded myself that the antics at the Summer Full Moon Party took place over two months ago, and so much could have changed for everyone. Look how much my own life had changed! Autumn was upon us, with the changing colors of leaves, the different smells, cooler weather. Change was everywhere, but to no avail.

Doom hung over me like a leering gargoyle, and Sean was too far away to rescue me. I chased after sleep, to no avail.

VII.   The Ale of Haven

By Saturday, the dark circles under my eyes lent considerable definition to my face. Colleen did not ask any questions, whether out of consideration for me or out of oblivion. She was engrossed in her own New Love.

Megan, bless her, did not ask any questions either, although this might have been because she caught Patrick's cold. She sniffled away in the shop next door, grateful for my pot of Tea for Dreary Colds. When she mentioned Saturday night's invitation in passing, she assumed that I would attend.

After much sleeplessness, which I described to myself as "periods of reflection," I decided to attend the gathering at the pub. I just had to go. I could not use illness as an excuse. No one would believe me; I was never sick.

The support Samek had shown my father in his pursuit of his life-long passion could not be ignored. In good conscience, I could not refuse Samek's invitation.

Just popping by was impossible. Samek could deter an early departure just by grabbing my arm. He had a rather un-jolly grip. I could neither sneak in, nor hide behind the suit of armor, being too tall and big; my mother endowed me with her blue eyes and also her sturdy build, and the 15th century had not bred enormous French knights.

As I tossed and turned under my comforter in the wee hours of Saturday morning, I reminded myself that Sean and I were going to spend our lives together. As soon as he trained his replacement in the business that he did marketing for, he would be back with us, with me. His wink told me so. We had not yet had the time to talk about the details, but it was as real as all the events in my past had been. We would live in this house of mine, with Megan and whomever she chose as her partner staying on in the Sullivan house nearby.

I decided that I did not believe in legends anyway, and any Special Powers such as that that dreaded "M" word, the one I could not bring myself to say, even in my mind, just did not exist in my pragmatic world of hammer and nails. As long as I denied their existence, they would not exist.

Yet after several hours, tiny doubts wiggled back in my mind. I could never disprove the existence of all things Magical—woops!—the forbidden word. Banish it! My parents, no doubt recognizing my independent mind early on, kept their beliefs to themselves.

Megan was a believer, while Sean ignored and even despised all talk of that "M" word. I smiled; ever since I could remember, I agreed with Sean about this. His years away from our village must have only reinforced his aversion. Big City Life and "M" could never mesh. My smile broadened. Sean was returning, not in time for Samek's final gathering at the pub, but soon enough to make me feel oh so much better.

By lunchtime, I was feeling grim again. When Anne dropped by, I dragged her out back and poured out the whole story. Her face was inscrutable. She listened, nodded and asked some questions. She mentioned that Samek had invited her as well.

"So you will come, Anne? Please do! It would make me feel so much better."

Anne looked at me with such a steadfast gaze that I wondered whether my face had morphed into a meditation object, such as an unwavering candle with a plume of mysterious colors.

"I will attend, of course, but if Samek's cousin is the man you bumped into, I can't help you. I cannot prevent you from meeting him, but I will stay by your side."

My heart sank. My secret hope was to hide behind her somehow, just in case. And she guessed it. Phooey.

When Horatio Caesar bumbled through the wood and glass-paned front door of *Charmed Necessities* and into the office, we were in our post-lunch lull. I looked tired, and felt even more worn down than I looked. My trusty hammer lay on the desk in the office. Horatio Caesar didn't notice my looks or demeanor, but he saw the hammer.

"Let's go together to the gathering tonight, BB!"

Horatio Caesar qualifies for admission into the ranks of the guardian spirits; the term "guardian angel" would offend his manly pride. Although silent by nature, living a shy life with thoughts imbedded in his private world, he has a knack of showing up just when I need the most support. For all his physical awkwardness, Horatio Caesar has a tender side to him that endeared me to him when I first began to run around on stout and determined legs. Bless him.

Since Sean was not present to be my boyfriend for real, Horatio Caesar would make a bona fide substitute. At the opening ceremonies of the Summer Full Moon Party, we sat together just behind Mr. Mostly Green Eyes and his sister. I was armed, with my true friend, Horatio Caesar.

When he collected me at my house, he wore his grandfather's jacket. It was a bit too long and big, but it was presentable, if a little musty. His grandfather, that crusty gentleman of the old school, must have given him "instructions" about his appearance.

My looks complimented his. I was respectable and even prim in my white button down shirt and baggy pants. The only visible flesh was about the amount allowed of a nun in the Carmelite order. And my hair was pulled back in a firm tail.

As we walked through little mounds of fallen leaves up the streets to the inn, we spoke little. In the light of dusk, the scent of mist mingled with dying leaves made my mood of impending doom complete. Not even the cheerful glow from the window of *Butter Fingers*, with its display of village-made mugs, teacups and plates for pastries and cookies, brought a smile to my face.

In an effort to distract myself, I asked Horatio why the plates were decorated with slivers of a crescent moon rather than with mythic motifs, or elves and fairies and other 'hidden folk.' He looked blank. He had never noticed the plate decorations, only what was placed on them.

The warmth of the pub of *Delights in Earthly Haven* radiated out into the street. The reassuring smells of fresh beer and pub food floated out to embrace us. My heart began to pound. I may be doomed, but my ammunition was abundant and kind; I had Horatio Caesar with me.

Samek greeted us with gusto, looking more rounded than ever. His bride-to-be would have to develop a fondness for fun-loving and very well-fed koala bears. Samek whisked us past the suit of armor and handed us brimming glasses of Haven's Ale. I forgot my foreboding as we all smiled at each other, toasting Samek, his achievements and his delicious brew.

The effects of Haven's Ale were marked. Within minutes, Horatio Caesar started telling jokes, quite funny ones. As others entered the pub, a few picked up on the punch lines, even before Horatio Caesar got to them, which somehow added to the general hilarity. Patrick's deep chest heaved with booming laughs, while Colleen giggled and Megan, who resembled a water nymph in shades of green and blue, sparkled.

After our second pints of Haven's Ale, Samek announced that his replacement would be arriving in a few minutes. The questions poured forth. Who was this person? Where had he grown up? And what was his occupation?

With pride, Samek expounded about his cousin Michael Mathews. I didn't force myself to listen; if he proved to be Mr. Mostly Green Eyes, knowledge would be a good defense.

Samek's cousin had been raised in France and the Americas, with sojourns in Ireland and Switzerland.

"Michael trained as a veterinarian. But for a few summers, he learned about hotel management at a resort in the Swiss Alps, so he will be a little bit familiar with some of the aspects of running all this." Samek made a grand gesture with his robust arms.

"But," Samek grew quite serious, "Michael doesn't know much about our village customs and practices, so he may need guidance and help from all of you." Samek looked at each of us with mournful eyes. "Please, help him," Samek pleaded, "Help me."

Guilt permeated my heart. I owed Samek a great deal more support than just showing up for his invitations. When he asked us for help, he touched my sense of family honor. Since my new relatives had only visited, it was up to me to uphold the family honor as the last Mahoney living in the village. As I stood there, petrified, I imagined little cherubic angels, looking down at me from their heavenly perch and chortling, "Well, she's in a pickle, now!"

Responding to his plea with "Of course we will, Samek," Anne caught me by my arm, and whisked me toward the back of the pub. Amidst the chorus of angelic voices in my head, I wondered if Anne could read my mind, and see those impish angels.

"It will be all right, Barbara. He will treat you with perfect courtesy."

"But how do you know he will?" I blurted out.

"There are many villagers here tonight. He may need their counsel in the future. For us, this is a party. For him, this is where he will be working." Rock solid common sense, yet I still could not trust it, or his good behavior.

"But what about the ah–legend?" I asked craven. I know, I know. I don't believe in any of them, but I had heard a bit too much growing up.

"You will not be trapped into doing anything you do not want to do."

Anne touched the very core of my fears. I did *not* want to be forced by any village Magic, woops, legend, into anything. Although touched by Anne's benevolent show of support, I couldn't see how she could help me. I tried to camouflage my disbelief, but my face, to my disgust, has always been transparent.

Anne smiled. "My grandmother taught me some things."

My mind went wild. Mrs. Goodheart, one of our wisest inhabitants, was able to work miracles. To be sure, Anne learned how to make herbal preparations from her grandmother, and could therefore do some healing work. But, Anne had given me no inkling that she possessed any of her grandmother's other talents or knowledge.

To be fair, I hadn't asked. How could I just blurt out, "Do you have any of your grandmother's special skills?"

Then I would have had to explain what they were, and I would much rather not talk about Mrs. Goodheart and her wise ways. My transparent face must have given me away again.

"I haven't been here very long." Anne replied to my unspoken question about why she hadn't mentioned her grandmother's legacy.

My mind raced on. What a fool I had been! Fool, double fool, triple fool! Welcoming visitors and even new inhabitants to our village is one thing I'm good at and enjoy. But I had chosen Anne to be my friend soon after meeting her, which is rare for me to do.

In my moment of self-reckoning, it became clear that Mrs. Goodheart would have handpicked her successor, not only for her house, but also for her life's work. She must have taught her granddaughter all sorts of things during those frequent trips to France.

I was so busy placing all the pieces together that the official arrival of Michael Mathews went unnoticed. I was in the middle of realizing that Anne was not at all what she at first appeared to be, and that she could be a rather awe-inspiring friend.

I was even wondering whether I should be a little afraid of her, when she touched my elbow, and said in her calm way, "This is my friend Barbara Mahoney, and my name is Anne Beauchamps."

Without thinking, I held out my hand and felt it being squeezed as I looked straight up into a serious pair of mostly green eyes.

My mind went blank and my tongue followed suit. Anne's quiet voice smoothed things over; "We were just discussing village affairs when you walked in. Welcome to our village, Michael."

As she held out her own hand, mine was freed from bondage. All he did was murmur something polite to us both and move on.

After a few breaths, my tongue began to reawaken. "That's him, Anne! Did he squeeze your hand as hard as he did mine?"

Anne's face acquired a few dimples as she looked at me.

"Are you trying to tell me something?" I demanded.

Anne replied with her usual calm. "I only just met him, Barbara. He seems polite enough to have good manners."

What a dissatisfactory answer. But no intelligent repartees came to mind. Meanwhile, Michael, as I must now learn to call him, continued making the rounds, unaware of my scrutiny.

My attention was diverted from the newcomer in our midst when Horatio Caesar drew close and began casting surreptitious glances at Anne. Joining us in hurry, Tom Bates tried to get Anne's attention. She turned and asked Horatio Caesar questions about the inn. He stuttered, but responded to her inquiries with a daunting flood of information. Tom turned to me, instead, and began a familiar argument about the advantages of screws over nails.

Our bride seeker called for our attention. First, Samek made certain that we all had enough ale and then raised his glass to toast us all, and then Michael Mathews. After we drank a bit, Patrick raised his glass to wish our host a successful Vacation. He added that we all looked forward to meeting Samek's success in person. We all laughed and hooted, as our host squirmed as much as man of his size could.

Michael diverted our attention with a little speech. "I'm looking forward to helping out with the management of such an illustrious destination in the village and carrying on the proper traditions." There were smiles all around at that.

He continued. "I will be grateful for any and all advice that any and all of you can give me over the coming weeks." His politeness was tinged with more humility than expected. "I have much to learn from all of you," He concluded.

By the time we left, Haven's Ale had produced a most amicable atmosphere. The hops grown around our village added the perfect balance of bitterness to the ale. As Horatio Caesar walked me back home, we teased each other about childhood mishaps.

It was only later in bed when Haven's Ale had lost its advantage that I puzzled over some of the evening's events. It was like watching a movie unroll as a secondary character. Given the amount of stuttering, Horatio Caesar must be quite taken with Anne. Tom Bates tried to be attentive to her, as well. Mr. Mostly Green Eyes paid only polite attention to me. He had not approached me again, nor had he sent me meaningful glances. He seemed focused on taking over the management of *Delights in Earthly Haven*. It was as if my previous encounters with him were part of another, very separate movie. One movie did not fit with the other.

One detail of the evening's events kept popping up in my mind. When Mr. Mostly Green Eyes greeted each person, there was one person, to whom he paid special attention. I couldn't hear their words, but it was clear from his laughter that he was very happy with her company. And the woman seemed just as pleased, although I couldn't see her face. I recognized her blond tresses, her posture and gestures; it was feminine and dreamy Megan.

VIII. If Goodbye meant Until Tomorrow

'I was free. I am free. I will always be free.' Repeating these words under my breath made me feel better during the idle moments of shop tending in the days that followed. Lingering on visions of Sean and me together, blissful at last, I smiled to myself.

Interrupting this delightful reverie, my dear friend Megan burst in through the front door of *Charmed Necessities*. The adjacent wind chimes jingled with such vehemence that the sounds were dissonant.

Megan never rushes. She resembles a nimble fairy clothed in flowing garments found in those ancient fairytale books, the ones with faded black and white engravings. Her two years of seniority made her wiser and much more feminine when I was exploring just what a hammer and nails could do. Since I took over *Charmed Necessities*, we began to have what might be called a more "equal" relationship. Even fairies need hammers.

Megan dragged me into the office, slammed the door and pushed me into my chair. I could only gawk up at her.

"Sean," she uttered trying to regain her breath, "It's about Sean!" Megan's eyes held tears and her cheeks were moist.

I paled. Sean was injured. No, Sean was very ill, or even at death's door. He lay lifeless in some strange city. He...

"Sean may never come ba..aack," Megan wailed.

"What???"

"Sean's been asked to manage the marketing for a company in," Megan gulped for a moment and then blurted, "in Arg..en..tina."

My mouth dropped open.

Megan wailed some more and then manages to regain some control over her quavering voice.

"Of course, it is..." she gulped trying to find the right words, " It's a great honor to be asked at his age."

I could only stare. My limbs grew cold and damp.

"He speaks the right languages."

"But..."

"And he gets on very well with people, even difficult ones."

I nodded just once.

"But there is one stipulation. He has to leave for Argentina today."

"WHAT??" My turn to gulp. "Why the rush? Why today? That's insane!"

"He's replacing a much more senior person, who just had a heart attack." Megan paused for a breath, while I tried very hard brush this all away. "Sean has to go take this man's place immediately."

"He's not coming back, not even to say..." I just couldn't find the words–what could he ever say to me? To Megan?

She shook her head.

"But he *must* be returning soon!" This was a living nightmare.

Megan's bleak face said it all. "Sean had to commit to staying on for several years."

I rallied. "He can't go! He belongs here, with us!"

Megan nodded, then flopped on the floor, put her head on her knees and began to sob with her whole body.

"I just don't believe it!"

Megan lifted her head long enough to murmur. "He said to tell you that he'll be calling you in a few hours from the airport."

As I stared at the photograph of my parents on my desk, my affirmations about freedom seemed hollow and meaningless. How free was I, when the man, whom I had idolized since childhood, would now be far from my world and my life? My body ached with growing sadness. I was not free, not free from grief.

By the time the call came through, I had gone through countless memories of my parents. Gripping the arms of my chair in an effort to get a grip on my emotions, I imagined what they might say or do.

My mother would abandon her regal posture and hold me tight, like she did when I scraped my knees yet again.

My father would pat me on the arm and give me lots of sympathetic glances in between launching into exactly which historic narrative my situation reminded him of and why. Let's see, perhaps Tristan and Isolde. No, no, that would be too dramatic. The outcome of my own dilemma was not yet clear.

The phone rang. Sean began talking into my reluctant ear with airport noise in the background.

"All this came about today. I had no idea that I would ever be considered for the position." He sounded excited and tense.

"Sean, what about us?" I could not bring myself to say "me."

"That's my Barbie, she always goes right to the point," he laughed in a nervous manner and then got serious.

"Barbie, I want you to come and join me. I want you with me."

His words came toward me, shocking me cold.

"But Sean, you know I have the shop and my parent's legacy to carry on."

He paused before he answered. "Colleen could manage it for you, Barbie. She would do a grand job of it, too. It would only be for a couple of years."

I was silent. These thoughts had never entered my mind. They were too unfamiliar to respond to.

Sean sensed my uncertainty. "Think it over, Barbie. I know this is a shock for you, it was a great surprise for me."

I was still silent.

"I will find a lovely place for us to live and tell you all about it next week. I will call you on Sunday around 5 in the afternoon if you like, or another time if that is better for you."

I was still silent.

"Barbara Blue, I need you,"

I was still silent.

He whispered, cupping his other hand around the phone, so that only I could hear, "I love you."

I stopped breathing.

"I have to go, they just called my flight. Don't forget what I said."

I managed a shaky good bye, put my head on my folded arms, and made my desk wet with tears. The joy of hearing him say those three precious words, the yearning for him to be present when he said them, mingled with grief over his departure and the shock over his proposal.

After what felt like four years later, I managed to wash the tears from my face, wipe off the desk and pretend that I was still Bossy Barbs, the owner of *Charmed Necessities*, whose hammer could wield a mighty wallop.

IX.   The Twenty-First Century Room

The knock on my back door brought me to the present. I welcomed the radiant winner of the Hapless Hatless Potato Race at our Summer Full Moon Party. Sweet Melissa, my would-be younger sister with all the graces and beauty that I lacked, held out a bouquet of flowers from neighboring fields. The colors were lush, with all the vibrancy of the autumn, with yellows, purples and shades of orange. This offering was filled with all the life I had lost that afternoon.

Flowers and their power hit me in full force. Until Melissa handed me that bouquet, I took flowers for granted. I promised myself that I would never again take another bloom for granted.

We walked hand in hand up the street to *Butter Fingers*. The aroma of fresh Abundant Pantry Cookies welcomed us into its enticing embrace. While crisp and yet chewy toward the center, these cookies included whatever was in the pantry, such as chocolate chips, several times of nuts, and then pureed fruit swirled in. You never knew which exact flavor you would get.

We ordered mugs of hot chocolate and then picked one of the tiny metal tables by the far wall. With great care and a straight back, Melissa sat down in her chair. I plopped into mine, making sure, just in time, that my hammer didn't bang the chair. A few visitors were having a late afternoon tea, and looked us over with curiosity.

Our hot chocolates arrived brimming with frothy whipped cream. The owner Patricia, finished with all the preparations for the next day's baking, brought them to our table herself. We expressed our appreciation and she looked pleased in spite of her fatigue. She pushed back her short, brown curls, and smiling left to go to bed early to be baking by three the next morning.

The door opened, bringing some welcome faces into the bakery. More distractions, just what I needed! We smiled and waved. Anne and Horatio Caesar gathered their share of cookies at the counter and joined us. Soon to be thirteen Melissa was shy at first, but was soon smiling and laughing with the rest of us.

I looked at Horatio Caesar's plate. It was piled high with a small mountain of cookies. Melissa eyed it too, and blurted out, "You're going to eat all *that*?"

He flushed and mumbled something about how she was welcome to have as many as she wanted, and then, glancing at Anne, added that all of us were welcome to dive into his plate. Melissa looked somewhat mollified. We sipped and nibbled away, like merry mice at a sugar-laden feast.

In the middle of our pleasures, Michael Mathews entered the bakery. My heart braced itself and found nothing to push against. The events of that afternoon had drained all my reserves and I could no longer fight anything or anyone. Mr. Mostly Green Eyes walked in unscathed.

I had not seen him since the Haven's Ale toasting party. In the warm light of *Butter Fingers*, he appeared like another person altogether. Gone was Samek's charming replacement. He was subdued, with eyebrows drawn together in lines of worry.

Anne glanced at me, and then called to him, inviting him to our table. He looked taken aback, but joined us with a cookie in hand. Anne made the round of introductions. He was polite enough, but appeared so preoccupied that Anne asked if something was bothering him. He paused and said that he needed some hot chocolate first.

Hot chocolate did not fit my image of him. He should have ordered spiked espresso or some other fiery substance. Under his distracted gaze, we renewed exchanging pleasantries.

Melissa had us giggling over some of her ideas for Halloween costumes. When she mentioned that she wanted to be a toad, I snickered. Anne intervened and suggested that she could be an exotic flower, which Melissa thought was much too mundane.

Horatio Caesar chimed in. "What about a wall-flower?"

"What would her costume look like?" I asked, skeptical about how to make his suggestion a reality.

"Well, she could make a giant flower and wear it as a hat and paint cardboard to look like a grey stone wall and attach pieces of it to her sleeves and clothes." Horatio Caesar explained.

An unexpected chuckle came from where Mr. Mostly Green Eyes was sitting.

"Isn't that a bit too literal?" he said to Horatio Caesar. "What about wearing a mask painted with down-cast eyes and clothing as colorful as flowers?"

Melissa smiled at his suggestion. "I like that." It *was* a good suggestion.

Anne chimed in and asked me, of all people, "What are you going to dress up as?"

I stuttered and mumbled something about how I hadn't yet thought about it. To my intense embarrassment, my friends decided that this was the perfect moment to be helpful, and began to call out ideas.

"A butterfly!" Melissa said with glee.

"A pirate!" Contributed Horatio Caesar.

"A Tree Guardian." Anne called out. How did she know that I had a secret admiration for trees?

"But what would she wear?" Horatio Caesar puzzled, yet game enough to entertain Anne's idea.

"She could wear bits of tree moss and mistletoe pinned to a dark green and brown dress and small branches in her hair," Michael Mathews answered before Anne could reply, with his hot chocolate in hand.

We all turned toward him with some surprise. He looked rather startled himself, as if his own thoughts should have engrossed him, but hadn't.

I squirmed at all the attention, but had to admit that his costume suggestions weren't half bad. "Thank you," I managed without looking him in the eye.

Anne changed the subject by asking whether there was anything in his new job that we could help him with.

"I seem to have run into some staffing problems." Michael replied with a rueful grimace. "I just don't understand how so few people can manage to clean all twenty-one rooms, in addition to handling breakfast and maintaining all the common rooms. I must be miscalculating the workload."

"Have there been many complaints?" Anne inquired with a sympathetic tone.

"Well, no, but we haven't had a full house, yet. I'm concerned about Halloween weekend. Every room is already booked, even the room number twenty-one got booked up just after I arrived. I thought it would be the last room go."

Affronted at his implied condemnation of my favorite room, I lost sight of the issue. "But that room is so much fun with all those gadgets and bright colors!"

Michael looked me straight in the eye, green transmitting a sense of re-appraisal to blue, and replied in a mild tone, "I didn't know that it's a favorite of yours. Most visitors come to the village for its links to olden times."

He was right and I was mollified. The Twenty-First Century Room was often in less demand than the others, even though it boasted a touchscreen for operating such delights as mood lighting, streaming music and the Jacuzzi. Brightly colored globs made of plastics and other new materials, festooned the walls and composed furniture. Colorful, bright, airy, loud and loaded with technology, the room was my favorite. As the only child of a historian, I was a bit ashamed of my preference. How could I like anything quite so new?

Anne asked whether he had spoken to the inn's staff about his concerns.

"Not yet," he replied, "I only just found out about the bookings."

"They may have some suggestions for you. Some people like to work very hard and don't find the extra labor a burden." Anne's voice was her own, but the phrase came straight from her grandmother.

Michael's face was a study in conflicting emotions from mild derision at the simplicity of her words and disbelief that she could have any inkling of what he was talking about. I smiled to myself. Mrs. Goodheart was always right; Anne would be, too.

Horatio Caesar spoke up. "Samek's staff has always been very good. They have special talents."

Anne smiled at him and nodded. I cringed at the inevitable question, but Mr. Mostly Green Eyes only said, "Well, I'll follow your advice," nodding to Anne, "I'll talk to the staff." With that, he pulled back from the table, said good-bye and walked out the door with firmer strides.

"He seems serious about his responsibilities." I said in all fairness after the bakery door closed behind him. "He'll follow your suggestion, Anne, even though he thought you were being too simplistic."

We all nodded. Anne's advice was good. On some unspoken level, we all knew just how wise, even if Mr. Mostly Green Eyes did not.

"While replacing Samek, he'll learn a great deal about others," Anne concluded. "And about himself. Now Barbara, may I walk with you to your house? I'd like to talk over something with you."

I left in far better spirits. Oh, the power of Abundant Pantry Cookies and hot chocolate, and friends.

After chatting about the forthcoming Halloween Party as we walked, Anne asked how my afternoon had gone. I stopped in mid-stride, pulling her to a standstill.

"How did you know?" I blurted.

"Megan told me that you might need someone to talk to, someone who isn't involved in the situation."

Poor Anne. I flooded her with details about Sean's sudden change of plans, his last-minute phone call and what he wanted me to do.

Anne linked arms with me and started walking me toward my house, while I continued to vent.

When we arrived at my front door, I had a brief glimpse of myself as a child running back home after some momentous occurrence, and being folded up into the loving embrace of the ancient dwelling and the comforting presence of my parents.

The house reverted back to mere wood and stone as we entered the front door. The front hallway was lined with aged wood, repaired by generations of family. Most of the hooks for jackets and coats were empty and the bench sheltered just one pair of boots.

The kitchen windows looked out onto the garden and fields, just discernable in the twilight. Lights on the walls blessed the room with cheer and distracted from the bareness of the countertops. When my parents and grandmother were alive, these flat surfaces were filled with various foods in chaotic states of preparation.

Anne admired the long table, uneven with age, its surface marred by loving histories. She stroked it with long fingers and then sat down as I made tea. It seemed so natural and effortless, as if I had known her for much of my life.

After we sipped some tea and settled into the quiet, Anne asked me an unusual question.

"Barbara, are you happy when you leave the village?"

I had to think about how to phrase my answer. In my heart, the feelings were clear-cut, but to negotiate the right words in their place, that took some effort.

"Most of us leave the village from time to time on errands or short excursions. Some, like Samek, go on extended trips to find someone to bring back to live with them here in the village."

I thought about the trips taken with and without my parents. "But every time I leave, I yearn to come back. Some villagers leave and never return. But I find it very hard to imagine ever leaving for long."

"Do you feel you are missing out on something by living here in the village?" Anne continued.

"No, oh no. I *never* have. Yup that sums it up!" I grinned.

Then took a moment to think it over. "I always knew I would manage the store one day, I never considered another occupation. Well, except being a carpenter."

Anne smiled, and I just had to smile back.

"What do you think, Anne? Can you see me leave the village for a longer period?"

"You mean, say, for two years?"

"Yes," I nodded, "yes, about two years." Was she able to read my mind, or was that just a lucky guess? I had interpreted Sean's "several years" as implying two.

"Before I respond, let me ask you," Anne replied, "Can you imagine a life in the village without Sean?"

Darn. I was being forced to think about this, willy-nilly. Better now, than later on, and by myself. "I don't know, Anne. It may sound weird, but until our Summer Full Moon Party, I never thought that Sean would ever see me as his girlfriend or even consider sharing his life with me. And now that he does, it's driving me crazy!"

Woops, too much melodrama. Try again, Barbara Blue.

"Sean is four years older and so he wanted different things. But I followed him everywhere I could. He was always my secret hero, even when he teased me. When he did notice me, he acted like I was part cousin and part sister."

"That must have been frustrating for you," Anne murmured.

I grimaced. "He traveled a lot growing up, often for months at a time. Of course, I missed him, but I always knew he would come back home, sooner or later. When he left our village for college and then work, he conveyed sporadic messages through Megan. The last time I really saw him was when he came back for my parents' memorial service. He was so very kind to me then, I'll never forget it."

"That must mean a great deal to you," Anne replied.

I nodded. "But it was only at our Summer Full Moon Party that my secret dreams came true." I couldn't help smiling; it seemed too wonderful.

Anne continued to watch me, so I felt compelled to continue. "Sean says he would enjoy living in the village again. But I'm not so sure anymore." My voice wobbled a little. "He chose to take up that job offer in Argentina over moving back here to be with me; that says something."

Anne nodded, her face serious.

"Perhaps he'd be happiest spending part of the time here and part of the time somewhere else." This was an option that came to me in the middle of the night.

Anne looked at me with kindness, so I continued.

"But I'm not sure whether I'd be happy leading such divided a life, one minute he's here and the next he's gone. Or, if I went with him and left the store in good hands, whether I'd be happy traveling so much, even with him. But maybe, I'm just being too narrow-minded." This was a valid point. Hammers had never appealed to me, until I tried a few out and learned how to use them.

Anne's face remained as bland as banana rice pudding for babies. I felt forced to continue.

"And yet, I've never dreamed about sharing my life with anyone else. So, if I don't join Sean soon, I'll remain alone."

Anne's voice was quiet, yet firm. "I'm sure that some of the children in the village would love to adopt you as an older sister or favorite aunt. Melissa seems very fond of you!"

That was a new and welcome concept. My inner tension eased up a bit.

"So tell me Anne, can you see me leave the village for several years to join Sean in Argentina?" I asked again. "And can you see us forge a life together somehow?"

"Perhaps you should consider the choice that makes you feel the most free."

What on earth did she mean by that? I didn't have a clue.

Anne rose to her feet. I received a warm hug, and was left to prepare a simple dinner. Her words rattled around in my hazy brain, as I sliced tomatoes to put on my salad.

What was freedom anyway? Why was it so important that it had to be the basis of my decision? Why had I begun that day with an affirmation about my own freedom? It looked like I was in for some sleepless nights in order to get a glimmer of a clear answer.

X. If All Answers were Nails

Sean was true to his word. He called me from Argentina the following week and then again every couple of weeks after that at around the same time, just as he said he would. Each conversation ran along similar lines.

"Barbie, you can get Colleen to take over the shop, she's a natural." How could I argue with that?

"I've found a great apartment for us." He described the rooms and the adjacent garden at length. I looked around the home of my ancestors, as he spoke of its location on the 11th floor, and felt depressed.

"Everything is arranged, Barbie, so all you have to do is pack some clothes and come." He made it sound so simple, so easy.

Sean described the languages, the people, the food, the wines, and his marketing job. He sounded happy and confident. All the arrangements he made to welcome me, his eagerness for my arrival moved me. And he made his new life sound enticing, exciting and he knew–we were neighbors after all growing up–he knew just what I would like.

I almost blurted out "Yes, I'll come as soon as I can make arrangements!" But his enthusiasm about his new surroundings emphasized his lack of interest in village affairs. I withdrew, silent and very confused.

I didn't ask Anne for her opinion again. She would defer the answer to my own heart. My sneaking wish was, though, that someone wiser than myself would tell me what to do.

Colleen, with all the tact and charm of her sparkling presence, didn't complain about my moods. If only she would be less cheerful and more somber, more like the way I was feeling.

My nights were restless and my sleep was fitful. In the middle of one night, I woke up drenched with sweat after a dream about Sean turning toward some other woman. A wall descended between us and I couldn't shout loud enough for him to hear me yelling, "Wait for me!"

As I lay in bed wide-awake after that dream and propped up by all my pillows, I willed my mind to try to think of something else, such as our next village party, or Patrick's Halloween costume. I kept on reverting to that horrific dream.

I forced myself to think of something even more horrific. The worst memory of all was seeing my parents' lifeless bodies under a fallen beam in the barn. This worked, but the details kept fading. I was back in my bedroom, which had not been painted since I was small.

As I contemplated the murky paint, I gasped. My mouth dropped open and I froze as Brigit Boyle Mahoney, my mother, tall and majestic, appeared at the foot of my bed, her eyes brimming with concern. Then my father shimmered next to her, his pale face serious as he gazed down at me. If they spoke, I couldn't hear them. I bawled; "Go away!" and they vanished.

For days afterward, I tried not to recall this sudden apparition. Nothing like this had *ever* happened to me. Was it even "real," whatever that means? Was I somehow still in that other dream, the one with Sean? Was I really wide-awake in the middle of the night?

And if it were a *real* manifestation of their spirits? No, I would not go there. It was just too much to take in. But I continued to gnaw away at it anyway.

Why then had I pushed away my mother and my father, even in their ghostly appearance, and even if it was part of a dream? Was it just the shock of seeing them like that? The last six years without them were hard enough. Was I trying to punish them in some way for leaving me like that? Or better yet, for being so aloof (my mother) or for being so good at delegating all repairs (my father)?

If I had nothing to forgive them for, then why had they chosen that precise moment to appear to me? Why not soon after their death when I was in such a state of shock that reassurance of some kind, any kind, would have been so helpful?

Horatio Caesar succeeded in making me laugh when I told him about the whole weird experience. First of all, he made the apparition sound commonplace.

"But Owly!" I began in protest.

Then he pointed out that Bossy Barbs would prefer to have a vision at her own request, better yet, command. Unbidden visions did not suit her love of organization. I laughed; I couldn't help it. Horatio Caesar was quite right.

Well, it was time for Bossy Barbs to open up to new possibilities. If another apparition occurred in a dream, daydream, or, shudder, a waking state, I would try to keep an open mind and be a bit more welcoming.

On the afternoon following my resolve, I heard a knock on the back door of *Charmed Necessities*. The knocking was hesitant, as if the person was unsure of being welcomed. There stood Michael Mathews, better known to me as Mr. Mostly Green Eyes, his back curved, his demeanor serious.

My astonishment made him stumble a bit over his first words.

"Ah, I wondered, ehem," He cleared his throat and began again. "We wondered whether we may ask you for your help."

The words "Of course" slipped out from habit.

"We are having some unusual problems."

I raised one almost black eyebrow.

"Some annoying things have been occurring."

I raised both eyebrows. The ploy worked, he stumbled on.

"Three of the rooms are posing some difficulties."

My eyebrows stayed up.

"Members of the staff, uh, thought that you might be able to help."

"Well, I don't know why!" How strange, and why did they think I could help? "I am rather good with a hammer and nails and that is about it." This odd request demanded modesty.

"Would you be willing to come with me now? We are expecting a full house for the Halloween Party, and I am responsible." He brought that last word out with obvious effort.

Better to satisfy my curiosity and head up to the Inn than sit wallowing about the Unavailable or Unattainable Sean.

On the way there, Megan hailed us. Michael smiled at her, and Megan beamed up at him. Bossy Barbs was an outsider to their conversation.

As we walked together toward *Delights in Earthly Haven*, the old oak trees that lined the street seemed more fragile. Their leaves were bursting with gold, but the trees appeared smaller and careworn.

When Megan left us at the corner, the trees grew stronger. I closed my eyes and shook my head. This could not be real. No, it was my eyes playing tricks on me.

Searching for another topic to distract my errant vision, I asked Michael, whether he had made many friends in the village.

"Not enough," He replied with a rueful grimace. "Animals are so much easier than people."

I didn't have a clue what he meant, but remembered Samek explaining that his cousin Michael had trained as a vet.

"Do you have a private practice to return to?"

"I've worked in several large practices specializing in small animals, but haven't wanted to start my own. You can't leave your own practice."

"Because you'd lose a lot of income?" Was I being cynical, or what?

"Well, no, although what you say has some truth to it. I was thinking more about letting the animals down, by not being there for them. Most of the time, they don't like being checked out or receiving shots or other treatments. But it's easier for them if they sense a familiar touch or smell, which they associate with kindness."

His point of view took me by such surprise that I stumbled over my feet. I was still digesting his comments, when we walked through the large double doors of *Delights in Earthly Haven* and into the wood-paneled pub. Michael pulled down some smaller glasses suitable for an afternoon drink, and then handed me a brimming glass of Haven's Ale. I took some gulps but otherwise kept my mouth shut.

"Samek told me to turn to you and Megan." With what sweetness he said her name. "She's very been helpful." I felt put out. I can be helpful, too.

"In this particular situation, the cook thought you'd be most helpful." Now this was news to me. True, I almost always joined my father on his visits. But I was only my father's shadow.

"She mentioned that your father helped identify and date some objects. And that he corrected inaccuracies in the furnishings of some rooms."

"Quite right," I murmured after another gulp. The ale was smooth, refreshing and familiar. My hammer hung by my side. I felt prepared. But I didn't know for what.

Michael looked like he would much prefer to tend to an ailing creature than tell me about the problem at the inn. "Soon after I took over the management of this pub and inn," he gestured around, "I noticed that something would fall apart just as I was leaving three of the guest rooms."

My mouth dropped open. "What do you mean by fall apart?"

"Well, a painting would fall off the wall." His voice was apologetic and perplexed. "Or a part from a piece of furniture would fall off."

"Like a chair leg?"

"Yes." He looked relieved that I got it.

"And," he added, "the staff would repair it, and when I visited that room again, the same thing would happen."

"To the same pieces?"

"Yes."

Wanting to get all the facts, I dug deeper. "Did you say this happens in just a few of the rooms?"

"Yeah." His brow furrowed again. "This only happens in three of the guest rooms, and the same thing always occurs in the same room."

"And this happens every single time you leave each of those rooms?"

He nodded. "I just had the latest round of repairs done, so we can go to the rooms and observe what happens."

"Before we go, I just want to make certain that I understand the situation. If you do not go into these rooms after all repairs are completed, then nothing falls apart or off the walls?"

"Yes."

"Then why can't you just avoid going into those rooms during the days around Halloween?" The Ever-Practical Barbara presents her case.

He looked at me with some derision. "I have to help any guest that needs assistance. I can't make a lame excuse to the occupants of those three rooms about being unavailable!"

I was inclined to think that the guests would like some mysterious behavior during Halloween weekend and a good story to take back home. But, he looked so upset it seemed pointless to divulge my inclination.

It was time to take charge, even though I had no idea what I could do to help out. Bossy Barbs was back in full force. I pulled back my chair and stood up and said in a loud tone, "Shall we?"

Michael jumped up, and led the way up the creaking staircase to the guest rooms.

We passed by the doors from the tenth on down to the second centuries. He stopped before the last door, labeled Century I in hammered metal to indicate the first century room. He looked at me, and said "Watch this."

He opened the door and walked into surroundings reminiscent of an imperial palace room in Ancient Rome, at least that was my father's contention. As I toddled behind my father, wide-eyed on his frequent visits to the inn, he had indoctrinated me on the contents of every room.   This one was spotless, light and airy. A pair of gilded stools faced each other on either side of a table on which rested a board game.

Michael turned around and walked toward the door. He opened it and stepped over the threshold into the corridor. "Crack!" a leg popped off one of the stools, which collapsed.

I rushed over to inspect the damage, and sure enough, the leg lay there like an outcast, separated from the rest of the stool.   The leg was neither splintered nor scuffed. Examining the stool, I could tell that the leg had been re-glued quite a number of times.

I pondered the outcast. My hammer lay heavy against my right hip. I turned back to Michael and asked him for some nails.

He scurried off, as I puzzled over the pieces. The situation made no sense. But as I held the leg in one hand and the rest of the stool in the other, I felt an odd sensation of warmth.

If I were at all prone to indulge in my imagination, I would say that the stool was glad that it was in my hands. I continued to hold the separated parts. All of sudden, I knew what to do.

Michael strode in and handed me a box of nails. I sat on the floor, cradling each piece in my lap, and picked out a slender nail and placed it just above the joint. The nail moved just a little bit under my fingers. I pulled my hammer out of my back packet and gave it a sharp whack. The nail slid in to the wood as if greased, and with one more whack it was in place.

To be certain that the nail would hold, I began to pick out another nail. But I felt a strong pressure on my arm; I was not to do so. One nail would be enough. I don't know how I knew it, but I did.

Michael looked at me with some respect tinged with skepticism. "That one nail is all that's needed?"

"Yes." I replied while placing the stool in its rightful location. "Now, please leave the room."

Startled, Michael walked in slow motion over the threshold. No crack, the leg held. Nothing moved. The room was whole again.

Michael expressed his gratitude while leading me upstairs to the Fifteenth Century Room. As he opened the door, familiar sights and smells greeted me.

This sumptuous room could have been part of the Palazzo Vecchio or Palazzo Medici in Florence, as my father pointed out to me in great detail. The vaulted ceiling and walls glittered with golden fleur-de-lis, the Florentine Lily, on a celestial blue ground. The curtains, bedclothes and covers were made of silks and velvets in rich hues. On the wall away from the paned windows hung some excellent copies of the early work of Sandro Botticelli and his teacher Fra Filippo Lippi. My father would mutter that they seemed like originals.

Michael walked around the room and turned to leave, crossing the threshold. Crack! My favorite painting crashed to the floor.

I rushed over to assess the damage. To my intense relief, the painted surface was unmarred and the gilded frame only scuffed. The hooks that it had been hanging on lay under the bed like exhausted veterans of an improbable war. This Botticelli portrait of a young man coupled the delicacy of boyish features and translucent skin with a mocking, inner strength.

Michael returned to my side, his face pinched, as if he were taking this incident as a fall from grace. On the surface, it appeared to be his "fault." After all, the painting only fell when he was leaving the room. But quibbling over whose fault it was offered no solutions. I examined the wall instead. The holes for the hooks looked normal enough, there were no cracks in the wall itself. No logical explanations for the crash came to mind. It was as if the hooks had been ejected with considerable force from their home in the wall.

When I pointed this out, Michael looked unnerved. Mind you, I understood his point of view. To cause some unknown force to eject hooks from a wall so that a painting crashes to the floor would never raise my self-esteem.

I did not allow my mind to dwell on the tricky question of what that unknown force might be. My job was simple. Repair it!

I asked Michael for some new hooks.

When he left the room, I sat on the floor, holding the portrait with all the tenderness of a reformed Bossy Barbs. The portrait came alive for a moment, the eyes looked at me, and one of them winked. I shook my head. I must be going through severe caffeine deprivation or Haven's Ale delusion. Wake up, Barbs, think of a solution!

It came in a flash. I was to put the new right hook a smidgen to the left of the present hole. That was all. When Michael returned and handed me a box of hooks, I picked out ones that looked just like their predecessors, only without the battle fatigue. The left one went in with ease and held firm, the right one got its new hole and held fast. The painting was back on the new hooks, and Michael walked out the door without a crash.

As I closed the door behind me, Michael murmured, "Thank you. This means a lot." What surprising praise. Bossy Barbs became as awkward as a basset hound puppy with overlong ears.

I glanced down the hall and stiffened. Emerging from the Sixteenth Century Room were my newfound relatives. They embraced me with way too much vigor.

"We wanted to surprise you for the Halloween festivities, my dear," said Aunt Phoebe with considerable satisfaction. After all, they *had* succeeded–my surprise was genuine. Uncle Christopher's self-congratulatory air was the business deal special–with a slight forward twist of his ample girth.

When I introduced my relatives to Michael, he transformed into the host of the Inn. I preferred him without the smirk.   Concern suited him better.   I brushed past my relatives with the promise to be in my shop first thing in the morning.

Michael opened the door of the final room. With dubious relief, I traded my Aunt's gushing pleasure at seeing me for the ornate Eighteenth Century room with its abundance of cherubic gold. This was without doubt one of my least favorite rooms at *Delights in Earthly Haven*.   The profuse ornamentation of the rococo made me feel like a stiff figurine plopped on top of a fluffy, pink and white cake. There was just too much icing all around.

However, the ample icing was quite popular with visitors. Even Horatio Caesar liked this display of gold and white frills. I admitted that my relatives had had the good taste to pick a room of a more austere century. My family's love of simplicity prevailed over this sort of ostentation. Woops, I admitted that Aunt Phoebe and Uncle Christopher were family.

When Michael turned and left the room, the loudest crash of all left me breathless. The bedpost nearest to me tipped over like a drunken mast and hit the floor in a resounding smack. The huge bed sagged in distress. The slant transformed any attempt at sleep into a slippery daydream. While the other rooms had problems, this room had THE problem.

With lots of huffing and puffing, we removed the mattress so that I could examine each part of the massive frame. Its construction was sound; a young elephant could have lain on the bed in splendor without a creak of protest from the frame. But the breaks were uncanny.   The repair jobs had been masterful. Why the frame had not held was a mystery to me.

As I pondered the problem, I sensed Michael's keen unhappiness boring into my back. I, too, would feel quite unnerved if my departure caused such a monstrous bed to collapse.   His unspoken rawness was understandable, but didn't offer a solution.

As I examined each part of the frame and post, I waited for any tingling in my hands that would show me the right way to repair the bed. I sensed nothing.

Michael must have noticed my glumness and decided it was time to cheer me up. Since I was sitting on the floor by the broken bed, all he could reach was my right shoulder. Putting his hand there, he said with some difficulty, "This is an impossible task. It's unfair of me to ask you for your help with it. The frame is beyond..."

He was about to say, "repair," when I jerked away from his touch. I had had the oddest impression. While his hand was on my shoulder, my arm glowed, my hand tingled, my fingers itched, and I knew.

My face beamed. "I know what to do, but this time, I will need your help." A mystified Michael nodded. If this didn't work, I was going to look very, very foolish.

I explained what I wanted him to do. Looking skeptical, Michael crouched down holding the bedpost on one shoulder and one hand holding up half of the frame. He then placed his other hand on my right shoulder.

I felt an instant surge of energy through my arm. My fingers worked without thinking. The box of nails offered up the ones that felt right. Nails slid in like silk. Both sides of the frame were done with a speed worthy of Bossy Barbs at her best.

I let go of the frame; Michael let go of the post and me. The bed held, looking robust and expectant. We hoisted the mattress back in place. And the frame held, too. We both took turns sitting on it without causing a squeak; even bouncing up and down was soundless. The final test remained.

Without a word from me, Michael walked out the door. I stayed seated on the bed. Nothing happened. Beaming, I hopped off the bed to my feet. Michael walked back in, relieved and impressed.

"You did it!" he exclaimed. "You really did it!"

"We did it!" I yelled back.

He gave me a quick hug. I was so happy that I hugged him, too. And that was that.

My attitude softened under the benign influence of my overwhelming success. I preened. Even Uncle Christopher and Aunt Phoebe couldn't disturb my sense of wellbeing. I overlooked their pointed questions about Sean and about the new manager of their favorite inn, answering with facts and left it at that.

After morning tea and a tour of the shop, they left laden with smiles and herb bouquets. Uncle Christopher uttered one phrase, just for my ears, as he walked out the door, "I like him." He meant Sean, of course.

My state of contentment spread through the rest of the week. I had completed the task that I had been asked to do, and I had done it well. Questions about how I was able to know what to do, and the cause of these mysterious happenings at *Delights in Earthly Haven*, had no room to blossom in my mind.

Our Halloween Festivities were a huge success. The village was brimming with excited visitors.

In place of Bossy Barbs was something altogether different. I transformed my appearance, inspired by my Third-Favorite Oak Tree, no longer caring that suggestions for the costume came from Mr. Mostly Green Eyes. I rustled my limbs. Pretty cool, if I may say so myself.

Michael became a minstrel in green carrying a lute. The special smile on his face was for Megan, who wore the rich blue gown of a medieval lady, her blond hair in braids wrapped around her head.

They spent much of the evening together. When they danced, their costumes matched, and they moved as one. Watching them, I felt something indescribable. Of course, it couldn't be envy.

When Michael asked me to dance, I was so surprised I agreed. In spite of dancing with a tree, he turned out to be nimble, and amused by my clumsy movements. He laughed when his hands got caught in my branches. The dance was over and he reverted back to being polite again, instead of fun.

Then I danced, or rather shuffled, with the Book-Worm, better known as Horatio Caesar, stomped with the Black Pirate, also known as my Uncle Christopher, and twirled with Patrick, the Whipped Cream Chocolate Moose. Food puns are the worst.

His antlers and my branches stayed a respectful distance apart.

For that evening, Sean remained forgotten in Argentina. I forgot my hammer, my cares, and the decision yet to make. I felt free.

XI.   The Crimson Dress and My Hammer

So this is what freedom felt like. I savored the expansiveness; it was like taking long breaths of fresh morning air on a sunny day. Or like a light and airy feather duster that cleans away all the specks of debris. The happenings around me no longer seemed so dire. Problems became transparent and melted away, and solutions popped up in their place. This was time for something momentous to occur. And it did.

Holding my beloved hammer in my hands, I did the unimaginable. For the first time since childhood, I put my hammer down, laying it on a piece of red velvet in the top right drawer of my office desk. No need to wear my trusted friend, my shiny and weighty hammer. My best friend lay at peace on cloth the color of royalty, a fitting honor for such a proven warrior.

My pants hung empty. I felt lopsided, and shifted my weight from one foot to the other, seeking a new sense of balance. My hips moved now that they were freed from the extra weight and responsibility.

I looked down at my pants. They looked back at me, wrinkled, worn, faded and so, so comfy. These sturdy pants were cut to carry that warrior hammer. And now, they lost their function.

"What if," I began, talking to my reflection in the wavy bathroom mirror. "What if I no longer wore my beloved pants?"

Sacrilege! Then again, so was putting my best friend to rest.

I grinned. My mother wanted me to change my style of clothing when I began acquiring small curves. But baggy pants and crumpled shirts, in dark colors and tans that never showed stains, defined The Keeper of Practical Order.

The Free Barbara had earned the right to choose: to choose what was right for *her*, and her alone.

So why not try on–gasp–a skirt or two, or even a dress? Just for a moment, I could almost feel Brigit Boyle Mahoney breathing a sigh of relief; her daughter was seeing reason at last.

My mother's closet was filled with colorful garments, a few of which she had never worn. For the first time since her death, I opened her armoire door and smelled the lingering scent of my mother without that familiar pain of loss. This was indeed true freedom, to smell her and feel only familiarity and no pain.

In a spurt of whimsy that Bossy Barbs would never express, I pulled out a crimson dress that my mother hadn't worn and put it on. After I buttoned a long row of tiny, silver buttons, I stood gazing into the armoire mirror. There stood The Free Barbara, dressed in fine crimson, allowing the curves to emerge. Not bad, not bad at all.

Just for a second, I thought I saw my mother wearing the same dress. She felt so close that I almost reached out to touch her.

When I wore the dress to *Charmed Necessities*, Colleen stubbed her toe against some planters in her enthusiasm. When I walked next door, Megan's voice tinkled out like a silver bell, a sign of her delight. Patrick gave me a resounding hug. Horatio Caesar's cheeks became almost as red as the dress, and his expression was tinged with awe. Anne, the quiet one, laughed and twirled me around. Melissa's youthful gaze was filled with new respect.

All this attention made me squirm; I wanted to run back and pull on my old pants and baggy shirt. But The Free Barbara had courage, I reminded myself.

And I thought I sensed my mother's relentless spirit prodding me forward.

Others continued to shower me with enthusiasm. Patricia gave me a free serving of chocolate and cookies at *Butter Fingers*. Tom Bates goggled, his eyes glinting as if really seeing me for the first time. Did he want my hammer, I wondered? When I ran into Michael at *Treats and Sweets*, the centuries old chocolate shop with its sagging wooden floor, he mouthed an "Oh." He gathered himself together and stated, "Red suits you."

The one person I didn't tell was Sean. How could I ever explain? And talking with him only reminded me of the choice I had yet to make. I wasn't ready, and knew it. I wanted just to revel in being The Free Barbara a bit longer and then decide.

The Free Barbara began rethinking the condition of her ancestral home. The small house exuded comfort in abundance, but not freshness. I had kept it in good order, of course, but that was all.

With Anne's unerring eye for interior space, and Horatio Caesar's back, we began. My small bedroom, the only one that I had ever known, was in dire need of refreshment. Musty walls and faded colors were familiar, but not inspiring.

Rather than just apply a fresh coat of color everywhere I could, I made a radical decision. Let's transform this familiarity into a room with ample space for projects and enjoying the sheer pleasure of playing with different materials.

"What a marvelous idea!" Anne enthused.

"Your bedroom should be your parents' bedroom, BB," Horatio added, avoiding my shocked expression with care.

"But it's *their* room!"

"Was." Ah, the bluntness of former schoolmates.

My plan was to sleep in my grandmother's room. Owly was right, of course. The Free Barbara was free to choose her own bedroom now.

My parents' bed was a sturdy piece that had been in the family for generations. Panting with consolidated effort, Horatio Caesar and I, with Colleen and Anne's extra support, pushed it against the North wall, so that I would be able to lie in bed and look out the windows toward the warm South light. Almost three times the size of my former bedroom, the new Barbara Room was airy with windows on three sides.

With my helpers' advice, I even sorted through my mother's clothing. A surprising number of garments suited and fit me. It was a bit uncanny. Her initials BBM could also stand for Bossy Barbs Mahoney or better yet, Brave Barbara Mahoney, so garments with her initials were included in my new wardrobe.

After all the moving and sorting, we considered the walls of each room. They looked dingy from more than twenty-two years of neglect. We painted them in vivid colors: persimmon, sunshine yellow, and periwinkle.

From the walls out, each room began to vibrate. New light and a fresh perspective bloomed everywhere we looked, even with the approaching dark days of winter. The deciduous oaks were bare, and the evergreens tightened up in preparation for the cold and damp weather. But the house welcomed all who came to admire the progress we were making.

Friends supplied encouragement and much needed assistance. Even Michael dropped by although he was very busy. Since my Visit of Mercy to the inn and the Halloween Party, most of the rooms of *Delights in Earthly Haven* had been occupied. Visitors chose our village as the best place to shop and gather strength for the holidays. For many, our Winter Solstice Celebration was worth booking rooms at least one, if not several, years in advance.

Michael brought some flowers whose perfume was intense enough to mask some of the remaining paint fumes. Stripping off his jacket, he offered his assistance. Patrick arrived in time to help us move my former bed from the New Projects Room into my grandmother's bedroom, which transformed into a guestroom for two.

Everyone was in a generous and expansive mood. Michael and Anne began to tell each other jokes. Their silliness made the rest of us exuberant, even if we didn't grasp the subtleties of their banter.

Megan brought over the Sullivan specialty, delicate cinnamon cakes. With tea mugs in one hand and cakes in the other, we gathered around the kitchen table.   Hands were spattered with paint, and our clothes dusty. It didn't matter. We were creating a new beginning in this old and well-loved house.

Near the stove, I thought I saw my mother and grandmother breaking into smiles, blue eyes intent on me.   I shook my head, and then remembered my resolve to welcome any visions. They were gone.

Michael and Megan sat close together. Anne watched them with an amused expression, while Patrick and Horatio Caesar stared at Anne. I watched as well, until I had to rush over to *Charmed Necessities* to receive another call from Argentina in the privacy of my office.   I could feel inquiring eyes, including Michael's mostly green eyes, follow my retreat.

When Sean asked about my wellbeing, I described in a wealth of detail how we had rearranged and brightened the rooms. Sean responded with a damp quiet, so unlike his cheerful self.

"So, you aren't coming before the Winter Solstice?"

It hit me then. My enthusiasm for all the changes was an answer, the one he didn't want to hear. In a muffled voice, I could only whisper, "Oh, Sean."

"I'll call you soon. Bye…" His voice was terse and dismissive, a first for Sean Sullivan, Mr. Charmer Man.

I opened the top desk drawer and pulled out my hammer. It felt good, solid, comfortable and comforting. As I held it, aching for some kind of reassurance, I glanced at the photograph of my parents. It was a candid shot of them at the kitchen table.

My mother was looking at my father; her majestic posture relaxed into the eagerness of a younger woman. My father was gazing with pride at the photographer, their only child. He held up a piece of my mother's special desert, an "Everything Fruit and More Tart," which changed toppings depending on the variety of fruits and vegetables at hand. The physical distance between them was immaterial. They sat without touching, but they were united. I longed for Sean and I to sit together just like that.

I glanced down at the paint blotches on my hands. They looked just right. My broad hands were colored with good intentions and good cheer.

If I went to be with Sean, I would adapt to all those big adventures and Sean would try to make every hurdle seem easy, delightful even. He would beguile me with his smile and wit, while part of me might withdraw behind locked doors. I wondered whether I would ever feel as free in his world. And whether it could ever fully become our world instead of just his.

With fresh eyes, I looked at my life, the life that was changing, because I was changing. Part of me knew with absolute certainty that I belonged here in the village, not because I had to be here to fulfill inherited responsibilities, but because I could be free in this village in a way I had never experienced in the lands beyond us. Sean's exotic world and life would hold many adventures for us both, with extravagant and unknown beauties and discoveries. Maybe I would find another place that would adopt me, as my village had embraced me all my life.

I don't know for how long I sat there.

Colleen knocked at the door. When she saw my face, she gave me the warmest hug, much like she did when I was nine and stricken by my first wave of Seanitis.

After holding me for a moment, she let go and smiled. "We have a surprise for you, Barbie. Do come back home!"

Home, where the women in my family had created a living with beauty around them for generations. Home that welcomed me and held so many memories. Home that kept my parents' energies close around me. Yes, I wanted to go home.

XII.   Fresh Paint and Heart Pangs

All through our holiday season, I kept so busy that little time remained for personal reflection. Our Winter Solstice Festival is the highlight, representing the new light emerging from the darkness of winter on the shortest day of the year. Since the village also celebrates all the winter holidays including Christmas and New Year's Eve, we are busy with bonfires, ceremonies, singing and merry-making for almost two full weeks. Our village remains filled to the brim for the whole holiday season.

Sean continued to press me. "Barbara Blue, this land is meant for you."

"You know how much I love the trees here."

"There are many new kinds of trees for you to explore here!" He countered.

I had to admit he was quite clever. That argument about trees stirred up some curiosity. He also tried wit, humor, and cajoling. I slammed the phone down, and worked off my frustration by chopping up some firewood. I just wasn't ready–he would have to wait. Love, my long standing, and only recently requited, love for Sean, or my love for my home–which would win out?

For the first time, I sent holiday presents to relatives. Deciding what to give Aunt Phoebe and Uncle Christopher proved to be an easy task. Our holiday cake is so filled with fruits and nuts that it holds its shape in all sorts of different molds. Bells decorated with big, blue bows covered in thick icing would be the perfect gift for them.

Aunt Phoebe called to thank me, and couldn't resist asking all sorts of prying questions. No one was spared: Patrick, Megan, Colleen, Anne, Michael.

Even Horatio Caesar got his share of speculative questions. He had lost quite a bit of weight, what was his secret? I stifled a grin. Was this Aunt Phoebe wanting to find out why he lost the weight, or how? The former was easy to answer: Anne. And the how? Maybe Melissa had had a say there in pointing out his excessive cookie consumption. Also, he did a lot of heavy physical labor in the rooms of my house, in between caring for his aging grandfather, who was mentally alert, but physically challenged.

Sean was mentioned, but without great curiosity. Sean was not in the village, and that was all that mattered to Aunt Phoebe. For better or for worse, Aunt Phoebe had become absorbed, if not obsessed, by our village life. I groaned.

Aunt Phoebe hadn't seen the transformation of Bossy Barbs, the All-Round-Handy-Person, into the Free Barbara. I didn't mention any changes to my appearance or the house. We villagers have our pride; we do keep *some* secrets.

Uncle Christopher and Aunt Phoebe returned the favor and sent me a holiday present, their first one to me as well. It took my breath away. Had Aunt Phoebe somehow guessed? Wrapped in gold tissue was a sumptuous and tight-fighting dress made of royal blue velvet. It just hid my knees scarred from many flawed attempts to bicycle through the woods and village streets at the hardy age of eight. I had never worn anything like it. My awkwardness returned and I tripped. Transformations have a price. Mine was a bruised shin.

When I showed up for a holiday gathering, Horatio Caesar all but drooled in his eagerness to tell me how great I looked. I returned the favor and pointed out that he was no longer clumsy, and his new glasses and hair cut looked great on him. He turned pink and we sort of beamed at each other, like two fledgling birds just leaving the nest.

Patrick gave me such a congratulatory bear hug that it took me a few moments to regain my breath. Tom Bates made a long and low whistling sound when he saw me. Anne and Michael, who were standing together in earnest discussion, broke off in mid-sentence. Both called out words in French that too many of the surrounding visitors understood. "Magnifique! Très belle!" All this teasing, was it worth it?

Megan smiled with a bit of wistfulness. All she said was, "If only Sean could see you now..." I froze, having shoved him, as best I could, onto the back burner of my heart.

After the holiday crowds had left the village in early January, Sean called me as usual, but with a twist. He was so excited that he forgot to ask how I was. In a voice reverberating with enthusiasm, he announced that he was being promoted. He added that he would be too busy to call me in the following weeks. Overall, he sounded so very pleased with himself. I congratulated him and bit down hard on unhappy thoughts.

There was no doubt about it. Bossy Barbs may have become Barbara in the Blue Velvet, but I still clung to familiar desires. My wistfulness defied all logic and reason, but it was there, lodged in my body, and it was palpable.

Several weeks after Sean's promotion, Anne joined me for tea in my kitchen, now painted two shades of yellow, first a golden sunshine, and then sponged over with a lighter lemon shade. The fresh paint brightened the winter afternoon. We talked as the light faded about forthcoming events. Less than two months remained to prepare for the Spring Equinox Celebrations, one of the most joyous festivals in our village.

Anne changed the subject without warning. "Have you found your sense of freedom, Barbara?"

"Oh. Well, I thought I had."

Anne observed my expression with care. "You don't seem quite as happy as you were when you repainted the rooms in your house."

"I, ah, I am MUCH happier!" I wanted everyone and everything to hear this, most of all myself.

Silence.

"Well, I am happier most of the time," I amended.

Anne looked down at her fingers as if she were searching for the right touch. "What about your heart, Barbara?"

I had never thought about my heart as an isolated organ. It always seemed so connected to everything else in my body. "It beats as it should."

Anne smiled, "I meant your feelings for Sean."

That did it. She opened up the dam, and recriminations poured out.

"...And he has no sense of what his promotion means to me! He didn't even ask me how I felt about it. And he hasn't called since then. His work seems so much more important to him than I am!" I exclaimed, rebuke dripping from every word. "It's not that I feel his work should be unimportant. I work as well. But he's making choices that seem to exclude me from his future. And he makes them without even thinking twice about them. He only cares about career success!" I choked with bitterness.

"What would you like him to do?" Anne's tone was mild and calm.

"I want him to quit his job and move back home where he grew up, and spend the rest of his life here with me!" I yelled. At last, I said it, my heart's desire, not just Sean for the rest of my life, but also living in our village.

"And no, I've never told Sean, not in such a direct manner." I was quick to add.

Anne's face made the next suggestion. "Well, it said, why don't you?" At any other time, this silent conversation would be rather fun, but I wanted action. There was little point in calling Sean. He was so very busy with new responsibilities, and I just couldn't leave a voice message about this. I ground my teeth. I would have to wait for the right time to talk to him in person.

I cleared my thoughts and started on a happier track. "Have you heard that Samek found a bride at last?"

"How wonderful! When will they be returning? I wonder what Michael will do when Samek returns with his bride. Michael seems quite at home in the village." Anne was not in the least put out by my shift of topic.

"I suppose he will leave after Samek gets back." After all, I reminded myself, he had only come to help out his cousin.

"Or, he might find something else that he would like to do in the village," Anne suggested.

Anne's words struck a nerve. Without being aware of it, I had come to take Michael's presence for granted. That Menace to My Peace of Mind, that Mr. Mostly Green Eyes, showed a genuine interest in village life.

Although Michael complimented me on my change of dress and helped move furniture, he never approached me except that one time to ask for help on a ticklish matter at the inn. He was neither aggressive, nor intrusive. Although he danced with me and appeared to enjoy himself, his personal attentions were directed toward my next-door neighbor.

It was hard to stuff both Mr. Mostly Green Eyes, whom I knocked down under the Kissing Bough, and Michael Mathews, Manager of *Delights in Earthly Haven,* who overcame the occasional hurdle at the inn, into the same body. Honesty compelled me to admit that there was only one Michael, and that I had become accustomed to his presence in our village life.

Before the Winter Solstice Festival, Michael presented a holiday treat to each of us. I peeked; his presents were not identical. Michael gave Megan a whimsical holly bush pruned liked a topiary into a pyramid. Colleen received a book of infamous jokes that each ethnic group told about its neighbors. She repeated them to visitors at *Charmed Necessities*, producing appreciative groans from all of us.

Michael must have wormed out my secret fondness for meringues from the cook. In a large cookie tin, meringue drops spelled out the words, "thank you" in a tribute to helping solve his problem with broken furniture and fallen paintings. At the austere age of eleven, the Smitten with Sean Barbara decided to give up all meringues, in order to become more appealing to the object of her young love. The cook, who used to ply me with as many as I could eat—a lot—had promised to never offer them to me again. Just how Michael was able to persuade the cook to divulge my secret vice was a puzzle. Or, was it just a lucky guess?

Michael continued to have a special smile for Megan. They gravitated toward each other at village gatherings. Wafting was no longer Megan's style. She fluttered. Around him, she fluttered more than ever. It had to be flattering, all this fluttering. He might want to stay on in the village just because of her.

I didn't feel like asking Megan any personal questions. Her relationship with Michael was none of my business, and furthermore, I couldn't express to her just how upset I was by Sean's promotion. In spite of her desire for her brother's return, she was very proud of his advancement. And she wanted Sean to get everything he desired. How could I explain to her, the adoring sister, that my sense of freedom was linked to this village, and not to exploring the greater world under her brother's tutelage?

On Valentine's Day, we held an afternoon party around my kitchen table in honor of Melissa's thirteenth birthday. A much more slender and fit Horatio Caesar arrived and presented her with a large bouquet of red flowers. Melissa was enchanted. Reverting to his usual manner, he patted her on the back. Patrick brought over a glorious cake in the shape of a ballerina decorated in a red dress and red ballet shoes.

To my dismay, I had to return to the shop to find her present. While I searched for the small, bright red package, the phone rang.

It wasn't Sunday, but it was Sean. He showered me with apologies for being too busy with his new job to call me, and wished me a happy Valentine's. His gift was on the way. He promised undying love, before I could get one word in.

When he whispered, "I love you," my whole body quivered.

"Sean, I want to talk, but we are having a birthday party for Melissa at the house."

"She can wait, Barbara Blue," he crooned. "'It's the day of red hearts, it's Valentine's Day and I just told you now much I love you. What are you going to say to me?"

When asked point blank, my heart spoke. "Sean, I want you to come back home so that we can spend the rest of our life together here, here where we both belong."

Sean sucked in his breath and stayed silent.

"It'll be a wonderful life together. All the villagers will welcome you back home with open arms. They care about you, Sean. Your family loves you, Megan needs you."

Sean continued his reign of silence.

"I feel free here, Sean, the way I don't feel free anywhere else."

His answer was abrupt. "You haven't been many places, Barbara Blue. How can you be so sure about that? I used to think that way, too, until I began traveling and found all these great opportunities."

"Sean, what would there be for me to do away from the village? You have your work. What would I do?"

"What would I do in the village?" he countered.

"Live like Megan does."

"But I want big challenges, I want to succeed."

"Sean, I just don't want to live anywhere else. I love it HERE."

"Alright, my Barbie, calm down, calm down. Let's think about this, shall we? Just keep dreaming of me, that is all I ask." Sean replied in his most charming voice.

My confidence ebbed.

My eye caught the color red, peeking out from under a stack of papers. I leaped up, and ran back to the party, gift in hand. What a Valentine's Day!

XIII. If All Changes could be of My Own Choosing

Sean's Valentine present launched my Self-Knighthood in the Holy War for My Own Freedom. He had had the audacity to send me a flimsy night garment, the kind that never had, and never would, have any function in my life.

This lacy object was an offending black, a color that could only remind me of my parents' funeral. It looked tiny and cheap, although with Sean's predilection for making dramatic statements, it must have been very, very expensive.

What did he think I would do with it? Stare at it and desire him? Use it as a dust cloth? Drape it over my hammer? That last possibility conjured up an unintended chuckle.

Holding this piece of transparent cloth between my callused fingers, I brooded. I even wondered whether Sean knew me as well as I thought he did, or, even whether he wanted me to be like someone else.

In a kinder moment, I thought that it might just be an outrageous way to tease me. And it also may be a way to tell me once and for all that he no longer viewed me as a second sister or a cousin. Well, he had my attention all right, but not in the way he bargained. I began to harbor rather an unkind feeling or two about Mr. Argentina-Loverman.

Whatever his motives, I didn't want to be treated like someone I could never become. Whatever his fantasies were, I didn't share them. He would either see me as Barbie, the hammer-laden girl he had grown up with, or as the new Free Barbara, but not as the Object-of-His-Passion-in-a-Skimpy-Black-Morsel.

At night, when I had no control over my thoughts, my dreams alternated between longing for Sean and fear that he had found someone else. Daylight brought the fears to fore, and the longings receded.

His post-Valentine phone call was tight and tense. I didn't withhold my censure and he flustered and blustered. So much for hoping that his gift was a joke! He had been serious after all.

During the following weeks, my heart armored itself. After each conversation with Sean, another bit of heart-metal fell into place. It became a challenge to hide all that necessary protection. In spite of my best efforts to dissemble, all those around me must have felt my determination and my resentment edged with fears and longing.

Happily, distractions always work. We immersed ourselves in preparations for our Spring Equinox Celebration, which involved planning decorations and equipment to reconfigure our village green, and the creation of circular benches for viewers to sit on. Every year, new embellishments are added to some of the previous ones. Everyone in the village is involved, young and old, some in making garlands of fresh spring greens and flowers, others in drawing characters on large sheets of paper to be fastened to the trees. These vivid drawings of nature spirits and creatures of the forest are filled with color and whimsy. Fairy-like creatures might sport four pairs of wings, not just on their backs, but also on their ankles, like Hermes, at their hands and behind their ears.

In the midst of gathering materials and supplies, we heard that Samek had completed his quest. He had even married her. He would be bringing his bride back to her new home, our village, in the week before the Equinox Celebrations.

Michael detailed Samek's wishes for his bride's welcome as we gathered around the big table in the pub with glasses of Haven's Ale. They included one more event for me to organize. And since I was in the mood to work hard to redirect all my conflicting emotions about Sean, I was more than happy to contemplate evenings filled with all sorts of preparations.

We plied Michael with questions about Samek's bride. We heard "petite and blonde" and "appealing." Much younger than Samek, and a few years older than I, Jeanne was born and raised in Brittany. Growing up near venerable stone circles gave her high marks on our village rating scale. We would welcome her with open hearts, no doubt.

From where I sat at that round table, I espied the suit of armor and thought how much my father would have enjoyed sitting here with us. Since he had been a newcomer in his day, every new inhabitant merited particular consideration and welcoming in his eyes.

I could imagine him wanting to ask the questions about Jeanne. Such as, what are her interests, her skills and occupation? We only learned that Jeanne's family owned a small inn. So, she would be a true helpmate for Samek.

I drifted into reverie, helped by Haven's Ale. We could tell her wonderful stories about each room in *Delights in Earthy Haven*, and even about the adventures of guests with a ghost or two.

What about the time that Great Aunt Hopie suggested to visiting friends that they ask to stay in Room Number 13? Having heard about some of the features of the inn, they assumed that they were going to be lodged in a rustic room surrounded by gruesome apparatuses. Much to the amusement of Great Aunt Hopie, they arrived in clothing appropriate for a 13th century Medieval English farm with thick, scruffy boots.

When Great Aunt Hopie led them to their room and opened the door, they gasped and turned to flee. She laughed so hard that she knocked her head against the doorframe, and had to be helped to one of the silk-covered divans.

Much to her friends' dismay, Room Number 13 embodies a romantic version of an Islamic Sultan's suite, replete with poems by the thirteenth century Sufi poet Rumi inscribed on the walls. The silk curtains, covers and pillows are lavish and in brilliant hues, in contrast to the rich dark wood and the patterned mosaics on the walls and the small fountain near the entrance to the room. A room of exquisite refinement and culture.

Her friends were not at all amused and refused to stay in such luxurious surroundings. Room Number 11 appeased them; they wanted hay on the floor.

A recent tale I could share with Samek's bride might be about those unusual repairs. No one else knew about them, not even Horatio or Megan or Anne. I glanced at Michael, wondering if he ever thought about those strange events. He was fully absorbed in conversation with Megan.

That evening, Michael was receiving plenty of attention. Megan was entranced by every word he uttered. On his other side, Anne radiated contentment, but when did she not? Horatio Caesar kept his eyes glued on Anne's face. Patrick, looking very pleased, sat next to Colleen, who bubbled up with more mirth than the froth on just-poured beer.

Disregarding the overt coupling phenomena, I concluded that Samek would be proud of us. He could introduce his bride to us with impunity and we would help her feel welcome. Since his departure over six months ago, we had evolved into a more harmonious state. There were no sore edges sticking out.

With good will and effervescent cheer, Samek would accept all the changes since his departure. He would delight in my new appearance, enjoy talking with Anne about any problem that arose, and share some funny jokes in stumbling French with Anne and Michael. He might even speak le français with a decent accent. A miracle indeed! His French guests would always cringe at his hearty and loud mispronunciations.   They forbore to correct him; he beamed at them with too much good will.

During a lull in the conversation, Anne queried Michael about his plans after Samek's return.   His unconcerned reply made me think that he *had* thought quite a lot about it.   He caught my skeptical gaze and smiled with a hint of an apology as if to say, "Sorry, I can't tell you yet."

Megan looked quite upset, which was so unlike her.   Yes, it was time to break down my reticence. Megan needed someone to talk to.   To give her the opportunity   to   unburden   her   heart–that   was something I could and should do.   I hesitated only because, if she asked me, I would have to divulge how Sean's Valentine offering made me feel.

But with all the preparations for our Equinox Celebration and Samek's return, I was too busy to sit Megan   down   at   my   kitchen   table   and   force   a conversation.   Our village was always inundated with visitors for the Spring   Equinox, our   second most popular event of the year.

Nature mimicked our hectic behavior, or rather we tried to mimic the vitality and speed of spring growth.   The bulbs planted by my forebears were showing off with tiny blooms in shades of purple and yellow as Spring burst forth in all its power.   Even I, who witnessed this display every year, was impressed.

Aunt   Phoebe   and   Uncle   Christopher announced an extended visit.   I felt obligated to offer Aunt Phoebe the newly renovated guestroom in my house.

"No, No, dear.   That's very sweet of you, to be sure.   We appreciate your offer and your kindness to us.   But we want to stay at our favorite inn.   We want to be there when Samek returns with his bride."

Aunt Phoebe's devotion to the goings-on in our village life even exceeded my own.   In an uncharitable moment, I wondered if her life in the big city was a bit too ordinary.   Like my father, Aunt Phoebe must have penchant for the unusual.   Perhaps unknown to her husband and even to herself, Aunt Phoebe longed for the sense of community that we created so easily in our village.

To my relief, they had managed to book their favorite room. Aunt Phoebe concluded, "Michael was very accommodating. What a nice young man."

My response was non-committal and I turned my attention back to restocking the shop in preparation for the deluge of visitors. All the fresh teas, potpourris, and herb bundles lent the shop aromas of enticing abundance and effervescence. *Charmed Necessities* was living up to its name.

In spare evenings, I cleaned my house. Using Michael as intermediary, Samek had asked me to host an afternoon tea party to welcome Jeanne. Dust and dirt were neither welcoming nor relaxing, so I banned them from all the rooms.

In a stilted conversation, I told Sean when he called about Samek's imminent return. He only said "oh really" and switched topics to his latest marketing coup and the praise he received not only from his boss, but the head office. His voice took on a tinge of awe. While I was happy for him, I was secretly unimpressed.

Michael popped by *Charmed Necessities* a few times with further requests from Samek, who was making an inordinate fuss about his bride's welcome. In each phone conversation with Michael, Samek detailed not only each food item he wanted to have presented to his bride, but which flowers should go where.

The day before Samek's return, Sean called again and began chattering about all his business achievements, when I interrupted him. It was now or never.

"Sean, you love your work and your new life just as much as I love my life here. You aren't interested in our lives here anymore. Our daily activities have lost meaning. I accept that. But, they mean everything to me. I really don't want to leave our village. And I don't think you would be happy moving back here to live. Not even after two years in Argentina."

"But I want you, too," he began.

Well, I could understand that. I wanted Sean too, skimpy black morsel aside. But there was one point that puzzled me. Did I have the nerve to ask?

"But why do you want *me*?"

"Because I've known you all my life, and we grew up next to each other." This was not the answer I wanted to hear.

Even for Bossy Barbs, Sean's reasons defied the poetic. The truth was as crisp and clear as fresh snow on evergreen trees against a blue sky. It was not just my personality or my person that attracted Sean, but my familiarity. He had been searching for a means to connect his past with his present. And I was available.

Being considered a tool did nothing for my self-esteem. But I held back from voicing my hurt. I forced myself to remember the Sean I had loved all my life.

"You need someone who would be happy to go with you anywhere, someone who doesn't have strong ties to our village, or any specific place," I murmured.

Sean cut off the conversation, and I was left, once again, with misery as my companion. I felt little better than a half-squished earthworm.

The knock at the door and Colleen appeared before me, her eyes filled with concern. Without a word, she just came and held me, much as she had long ago when she babysat me. Her reassurance filled my ache and after a while I poured out my story to her. She sat back, her eyes serious.

"Sounds like he didn't listen to you, Barbie, not deep down."

"His reasons for wanting me in his life are just so practical, so planned. It's like I'm an item on a business agenda." It was hard to keep the bitterness out of my voice.

Colleen wrinkled her brow and put her fingers to her chin in thought. Then she smiled. "Sounds a bit like you, Barbie. You're very practical."

That did it. She hit the nail on the head. And that pun is one that I, as Barbara, the Hammer Queen, find quite appropriate.

"Well, I don't like it! It's fine to be practical, and to be realistic and, and…" Words failed me, as the Ultimate Hammer Queen gave way. "But it's not enough. I don't want to be just prosaic and pedestrian."

Colleen's mouth puckered. "Well, well, what have we here? This is a new Barbara indeed."

"It's not new! It 's just, well, that I got used to hiding my desires." Brave words, yes, and I meant them.

"Oh yes," Colleen replied, "I can see how you had no other choice. But I still get a sense that what you are looking for now is different from what you wanted in the past."

How could I argue with my invaluable store manager with six shared years of life experience, not counting all those babysitting years? I kept my mutterings to myself. She wasn't right, of course. I was the same Barbara underneath, and my longings were the same.

By next morning, my thoughts were diverted by happier events. The day began cool and crisp with thick sweaters and jackets. But the sky was a fresh-washed blue, and the morning light clear and crisp. Nature was conspiring to make Samek's return and his bride's welcome quite scenic.

Samek had planned to drive his bride up the main street around mid-morning. How wise of him! Just as we were opening our shops, we heard shouts that Samek was about to drive by, so we popped outside to wave.

Samek's grin was wider than I remembered, and his girth much reduced. His vehicle crawled up the street as he yelled out personal greetings. His bride sat next to him, her posture demure. Next to me, Horatio Caesar pointed out that she looked like a precious doll, one of those collectable ones.

On the way to *Delights in Earthy Haven* for the lunch to welcome Jeanne, we gathered up Megan.

"What did you think of Jeanne?" I asked as we walked.

"She appears to be shy, yet she'll twist Samek around her little finger." Was this Megan's special ability kicking in? Or was it pure speculation?

"But she seems so quiet and small next to him!" I countered.

"Yes, but she'll seduce him into making changes."

"What changes?"

"I don't know," Megan began, "But there will be changes."

"Not to the rooms!" I cringed at the thought of modifications to the inn.

"Perhaps not," Megan conceded, hesitating for a moment. "Everything runs so well. But somehow," she paused, "there *will* be changes."

My pale blue dress and the absence of hammer were noticeable, even to a recent bridegroom. After looking me over, Samek gave me a resounding hug and boomed into my ear," You look GREAT!"

He turned to his diminutive bride and began, "Let me introduce Barbara Mahoney to you, ma chérie (he made it sound like 'my cherry'). Her mother's ancestors helped found our village."

Taking my hand between her two, like dove wings embracing a horse's hoof, Jeanne reached up to kiss me on both cheeks. "I am delighted to meet you!"

I smiled and felt gauche and murmured something polite. As others arrived and were introduced, I continued to observe her. Jeanne's appeal lay in her heartfelt sincerity. Dwarfed by most of the villagers, she overcame her diminutive size by her attentiveness. Her waist was about half the size of mine. But her shoulders were broad enough, as if she were accustomed to exert herself.

Michael acted like a guest. He stood in the background, no longer the active host. Samek exclaimed over and over how well-kept the lobby and the whole pub looked. Samek had only words of praise for Michael. Michael praised Samek's staff.

The chef had prepared a hearty, country lunch with a number of dishes from Brittany. Quite clever, I thought. Jeanne murmured "très bon," at frequent intervals. Sidling over like a dorky donkey to Michael's side, I asked him in an undertone, whose idea the menu had been.

He glanced at me and hesitated. "I thought she would feel more at home with food she's used to." His tone was defensive.

"No, no," I was horrified that he had misunderstood my question, "I was only admiring the sensitivity of choosing these dishes! What a great idea!" I was so appalled that he mistook my question for direct criticism that I touched his sleeve in a friendly gesture.

He jerked away, and I pushed through the crowded room, bumping hard into Horatio Caesar. His plate of food samples for Anne spilled all over his front and my own. We were quite a sight. So much for my pale blue dress! It was turning shades of purple (beets) and brown (gravy) and orange (carrots).

Attentive Anne rushed to our rescue with napkins and began helping us sort ourselves out. Horatio Caesar didn't utter one word of censure–he was enjoying Anne's attentions too much. My face, which had turned almost the color of the beets, returned to its normal sallow shade. The star of the lunch advanced with a glass of water and cloth napkin to press on the stains. She was kindness incarnate.

Jeanne neither made me feel like the clumsy fool I was, nor treated me with unwanted maternal mutterings. She smiled and said that a similar mishap happened to her after their wedding.

As I made futile stabs at the stains with her napkin, she regaled us with the story of her wedding day fiasco. Her cousins were teasing her about marrying and moving away from her village and her country. She tried to escape them by running in her wedding dress. But in her eagerness to get away, she stumbled and collapsed into a fellow guest carrying a full plate of food and the inevitable happened.

"Oh, mon Dieu," she said laughing, "I was full of color then!"

I liked her. In fact, I liked her quite a lot. Samek, pulling Michael behind him, joined our merry little post-staining party.

Samek laughed at my mishap and boomed out, "Welcome to the club, dear friends!" Casting a fond glance at his young wife, he boomed again. "We decided that it must be a sign of good luck to gather a festive stain or two!"

Anne nodded, Megan smiled, and Michael's eyes glinted, although he forbore to laugh outright. I chose to look the other way and regain my precious dignity.

As we were leaving, Anne took my arm saying she would like to talk with me. I was rather pleased by this reversal of roles.

Horatio Caesar joined us as we walked. He tended to follow Anne around like a pet sheep. When she spoke to him, his eyes glazed over, with stars glistening in his pupils.

With obvious reluctance, Horatio Caesar left us near my house. His grandfather was expecting him for an afternoon of chess and he had to change his clothing before his grandfather saw that sartorial mess.

"Please understand, Barbara, I do not wish to interfere. However, there is a situation that seems out of balance, and I am a bit concerned about what might happen."

Out of balance? Anne had never used those words. She spoke of harmony when she redecorated my shop, but about a situation? And then to say that she was concerned? She appeared to be the strongest woman I knew, apart from her grandmother!

Anne did not mince words. "Megan needs a friend to talk to, an old friend."

Just what I had been feeling, but Anne's urgency startled me.

"With her brother not returning to live in the village the way she hoped," Anne continued, "Megan has pinned her desire for family, for companionship onto someone else."

It took me only a fraction of a second to guess the identity of that "someone else."

"She may be very hurt."

"So, he's leaving soon?" I asked, not even bothering to put a name to the "he."

"I do not know his plans for certain." An enigmatic answer, indeed.

Well, maybe Anne did know his plans, and just couldn't tell me in so many words.

I felt a ball develop in my stomach, a dark, heavy one. I did not relish telling Megan bad news.

"She will understand better coming from you," Anne explained. "You have not gotten your heart's desire either."

Here I was, Barbara Mahoney, Pillar of the Community. The Former Hammer Queen, who had chosen to remain behind and not join her life-long love, giving up forever the opportunity to be united with him, out of love and loyalty toward the village and its inhabitants. Hey, I was getting into this. My self-pity quotient spiked and I felt ready to tell Megan anything.

Colleen agreed to watch over *Charmed Necessities*, while I bumbled over to Megan's shop, my face graven with gloom. Megan was in her office.

Not looking up from her accounts and not noticing my demeanor, Megan asked, "Well, how do you like her?"

Megan meant our latest inhabitant, the New Bride from Brittany.

I stopped short, shifted gears, and mustered "She's seems really nice!"

Megan glanced up at my stained front peeking out from my jacket. "You had better go home and change, Barbie. Those stains will be fierce unless you soak them in cold water as soon as possible." She stared at her accounts again.

I called on my overload of self-pity to come to my aid.

"Megan, I need to talk to you. *Now.*"

Startled, Megan looked up. Our positions were in reverse, the one in control exchanging places with the emotional hot plate. Megan closed the door to her office behind us. We were private enough now, sitting there together.

"I had a really tough talk with Sean," I groaned.

Megan replied, "Yes, I know. He called. He was very upset."

"He told you?" I was on my feet.

Megan smirked a bit. "Yes, he often talks to me after he calls you."

I flopped into my chair, bewildered. Why had Sean not told me? That Sean was telling his sister about our conversations didn't bother me. He just should have told me that he was relating the gist of our discussions to Megan–that was all.

I took my courage in my hands and began. "Megan, I cannot leave our village. I cannot join Sean in Argentina."

Leaving her metaphorical fairy wings aside, Megan looked me over the way a scientist looks at microbes. "Are you *sure*, Barbie?"

"Yes. I've thought about it for months now. You understand, don't you?" Her reassurance would be oh, so welcome.

Megan's tone was firm, no wafting. "I would follow the man in my heart anywhere."

I looked at her in bewilderment. Megan had always been scornful of villagers who left. She loved our community and our way of life.

She must have read my unspoken thoughts as if I were a cartoon figure with a visible thought-cloud rising above me. "I realize now that love is more important."

"Megan, it is not a question of not loving Sean enough. But *this* is my life. My sense of the rightness of things is here, with you, with everything." I gestured around.

"Even your parents' accident?" Megan glanced at me sideways.

I winced. "I still don't understand why it happened, why it had to happen. But, there's an explanation; I know there is. I just can't see it."

She looked me over as if I were still in elementary school. "You're a fool to believe that! You just don't love Sean enough, Barbie, it's as simple as that. And because you don't, he'll never come back."

With that, Megan burst into tears and refused any comfort. There was a wall between us that had a fresh layer of plaster on it. Conversation seemed pointless. She could no longer hear, nor begin to understand my point of view.

I left her crying. I felt miserable. My actions (inactions?) were causing my dear friend and neighbor such pain. I dared not broach the topic of Michael's departure. If Megan had changed to the point of being willing to leave our village for love, then she must be so smitten that no words of mine would help her. Besides, Michael would very much like to take her with him when he left. I felt certain about that. Harmony would be restored the minute Michael asked her to join him.

That thought lingered after I returned to *Charmed Necessities* dressed in a fresh shirt and skirt. I still felt miserable, but not unhopeful that Megan would find happiness soon.

Colleen was answering some probing questions. No, we do not run around naked as part of our Spring Equinox Ceremony. No, we do not cast spells on the people who attend. No, we do not curse anyone or anything, ever. Colleen handled one outrageous question after another with far greater tact than I would have. I begin to huff and puff when people hint at orgies and black magic.

Retreating to my desk with the office door closed, I tried to regain some composure. Since Sean's last kiss, he had become ever more remote. First, by placing his career in distant lands above caring for his sister and family, or caring for my needs. Second, by becoming so prosaic. Sean, My Childhood Hero, turned out to be but a distant relative of the Sean Who Kissed Me.

The phone rang. Colleen was busy giving those inquisitive visitors a list of the forthcoming events. It was unfair to ask her to answer.

"Barbara? Michael speaking."

I dropped the phone. Our village habit was to visit each other, not to call, except in a crisis. Michael had never before transgressed that unwritten code.

"What's the matter?" This must be big.

"I apologize for calling you, but I have a favor to ask you and need an immediate answer. My sister just contacted me."

"Your sister?"

"Yes, Isabelle. She's been traveling in Europe on business. She wants to come up to the village tomorrow. I wondered..." he began and then stopped.

"Yes, what Michael?"

"May I bring her to your party for Samek and Jeanne tomorrow?"

"Oh. Well, if she's not bored at the thought of meeting so many strangers all at once, of course she's welcome. Why, yes. Why not?"

Life was providing me with a lot of quirkiness. First, Samek's bride Jeanne appeared as soft as a dove, yet as funny as any professional standup comedian. Second, in the name of Love, Megan had reversed her life-long position about never leaving our village. Third, the object of Megan's desires would be introducing his sister to all of us, including Megan, tomorrow.

My new-found order was filling up with bits of chaos again. I pulled open the top desk drawer and picked up my hammer, trying to gain the assurance that I wasn't going crazy. As I held it, my parents' photo shimmered in my field of vision. I closed my eyes, leaned back in my chair, cradling my beloved hammer. Quiet, silence, peace. I opened my eyes and turned to glance at the announcements on the office wall.

In front of the wall hovered Brigit and James Mahoney. My jaw dropped open. All breath left me. My mind screamed "it's daytime, it's not a dream." I could not utter a syllable.

My father was the first to 'speak,' although I am unclear whether I heard him with my ears or with my mind.

His words were simple, "You're doing just fine."

My mother added in her majestic manner, "We are proud of you."

Even in my stunned state, the comfort of their personalities, with all their quirkiness, was palpable. I blinked and they were gone.

Uncanny though this event–whatever it was– had been, I stayed put, not moving and just taking long, slow breaths, over and over again.

I shook my head hard trying to gain some clarity. The Free Barbara was a new person that I was still getting to know. Perhaps she had the imagination that Bossy Barbs lacked. The Spring Equinox was welcoming in some unexpected new beginnings.

XIV.   If Only I Knew Her Name

"Barbara!" Colleen called out from the counter of *Charmed Necessities*.

I sat up at my desk in the office, took in a firm breath and rose to answer her appeal for help.

Visitors had carried an injured dog into the shop.   Curled in their arms, the little dog looked starved and forlorn.   They had found it lying by the side of the road on the steep, windy road up to our village.

Growing up, I was always stumbling over some creature or other around our house.   Other family members opened their hearts to hurt animals.   But that nurturing gene had skipped my generation.   I preferred tools to pets.

I was just about to tell the rescuers to take this bedraggled creature up to our animal clinic, when it opened its large, liquid brown eyes and gazed straight at me.   Maybe The New Barbara had more in common with her elders than Bossy Barbs, or maybe this particular canine specimen was an expert at emotional blackmail.   My phrase of referral expired under the roof of my closed mouth.   I gulped and managed to utter, "Let's take it into the office."

Colleen was delighted.   With her ongoing devotion to small creatures, she puzzled over my indifference.   So I put her to work, getting this miserable creature some food and water, while I knelt down and stroked the matted fur. It looked up at me. Emotional blackmail in full force.

Since my family members relied on their own skill and knowledge to heal the injured creatures found on or near our doorstep, I was not about to call the animal clinic for help. Yet, when this bundle of fur staggered to its feet to lap some water and gulp down some scraps, it seemed too frail to be left to my neophyte care.

"Colleen, what should we do?"

"Well, what about calling Michael?" Colleen understood the Mahoney Pride.

I stared at her, my mind blank.

"Michael trained as a veterinarian." Colleen reminded me.

A dim memory surfaced. It would not hurt to ask him for advice. He was an outsider. He had just asked me for a favor, so my family pride would remain intact. Besides, it was my turn to break the village code and call him.

When he answered, "This is Michael Mathews of *Delights in Earthly Haven* speaking," it was as if Samek had not returned.

"Ah, Michael, sorry to b...bother you." I stuttered, my resolution wavering for a moment.

"I have a rather unusual question to ask you. You have had experience with animals, as I remember," trying to sound as vague as possible so as not to emphasize my imperfect recall. "Some visitors brought in a starved and feeble dog. I'm concerned that it might be injured in some way. What do I need to look for?"

Michael's response was brisk. "I'll be off work in half an hour. I would be happy to come take a look, if you wish."

"Oh, no. I wouldn't think of bothering you."

"It would be nice to get back into my own line of work." With that he hung up, assuming my acquiescence.

My new, four-legged acquaintance looked so exhausted from its efforts to absorb some nourishment that resistance to any concrete offer of help bordered on heartlessness.

When Michael strode in, he was carrying a black bag rather like an old-fashioned doctor's kit. Gone were his showy clothes. He wore old jeans and a sweater, which, oddly enough, suited him better.

He went straight for the sick one. Colleen and I became part of the furniture, as he focused his complete attention on the dog. It responded to his touch, but made no attempt to bite or snap. In a comforting monotone voice, Michael addressed both it and us in one stream.

"This little one is about two years old. She must have been well cared for at some point. She was struck by something, but no bones were broken. Her wounds have healed quite well on their own, but you'll need to apply an ointment twice a day to these areas." He pointed out tender skin. "She needs small amounts of food and drink at regular intervals until she's stronger. And let Anne have a look at her."

Michael stood up with his eyes still on the little dog. He must have guessed my reluctance to take on this new responsibility, one that I had no experience with, let alone talent for.

Without looking at me, he said, "It will be hard to trace her owners. She has been in the woods for some time. She may have jumped out of a parked car to follow a scent and never made it back. She will need quite a bit of care over the coming weeks, but she will recover and will make you a very loyal and loving companion, Barbara."

I bristled. A companion. For me. I was not amused.

"You'll give her the home she needs and she will thrive under your care." With that prophetic announcement, he turned to go, refusing all payment, and only promising to check in on her later, whenever that was.

Colleen offered to help out. Why not? She was a good babysitter to me and she would be a good one for this frail bundle of matted fur. Together, we managed to bathe her in warm water, without too many yelps. At the very end, my hand got a few cautious licks. And those brown eyes, how they continued to watch me!

Colleen's only comment, apart from reassuring me about my ability to take care of this little one, was to appreciate Michael's care of her. She was impressed.

I wrinkled my nose. He hadn't said when he was going to return.

When Anne arrived, we stood staring down at the dog, now fast asleep. Anne nodded when I repeated Michael's words. "Good. He will continue to watch her."

In my blunt manner, I asked Anne why Michael wanted her to come over. Her grandmother, the Wise Mrs. Goodheart, never took care of animals.

Anne looked me over. She must have felt comfortable with what she saw, because she began to talk about things that I had refused to listen to from my own family, and indeed, from anyone in our village.

"Mysticism, some prefer the word Magic, takes many forms." I cringed, that dreadful "M" word again.

"In some cultures, Magic is called by many other names, such as the Power of Love, or the Law of Attraction, where like attracts like, when we call into our lives what we need at any given time."

When she paused, I mulled over her words. This was a new interpretation for me. I much preferred the Law of Attraction to any hocus pocus.

"Magic and miracles are often the same, just as healing and achieving harmony or balance are often synonymous."

I nodded with some caution. Her words made a certain amount of sense, at least the healing and harmony part did.

"And insight or intuition or even telepathy," my back stiffened, but Anne continued. "That inner knowing, not just of a person's thoughts and feelings, but those of an animal or even," Anne gazed at me with a thoughtful air, "those of a tree."

I almost choked on my own intake of air.

"Our ancestors and members of our village, have studied and understood the powers of nature, and used them to heal themselves, as well as creatures of all kinds, and live in harmony with nature."

Was there any air left in the room?

Anne's face remained serious. "Through our heritage, all of us were given the talent and ability to use some form of intuition or magic or telepathy. Some of us have been reluctant to train or to even use their own abilities."

I quailed. I felt like a five-year old getting a long overdue scold.

"Now, it is time to use your own abilities, Barbara."

"I don't have any!"

"Just try. This is for the benefit of another being, Barbara," Anne countered with unrelenting firmness.

I looked down at the still unnamed little one, and began to feel my body soften, even though my mind and heart were reluctant.

Anne whispered, "It begins with her name...."

The pathetic state of this particular animal moved me; there was no time to waste. Under Anne's benefic presence, I began to take deep breaths and then, sinking to sit on the floor, I felt my body and mind enter a state of deep relaxation, and my heart opening.

As I stared down at the little one, I felt a bubble rise up from my belly and it came out of my mouth as a word. "Blarna, that's her name!" When I said it, the dog opened her eyes and looked at me.

I began to speak words I never knew that I knew. I called Blarna into a state of healing, and began to remove unknown things that I somehow sensed in her body. My fingers reached to pull out these things, like pulling out weeds from the soil. My hands kept sensing these congested areas and pulling them out.

When my hands glided above her body to check her; these unwanted things, these knots of heat and of cold, had dissipated. When her body felt clear, my hands reached way above her and brought energy from above down into her. Blarna stretched out, happy and content.

I was a little embarrassed that Anne should witness my first attempts at whatever it was, for want of a better word, at 'healing.' But my self-consciousness dissolved when we stood up and gazed down at a happy dog.

Anne touched my arm and exclaimed with radiance lighting up her entire face, "That was just wonderful!"

With a party to host in less than twenty-four hours, I bustled around making preparations. That night was not one for sleep. I got up every few hours to check on Blarna. She responded to my touch with gratitude, licking my hand until it was damp.

There was no moment of solitude and quiet to reflect upon the utter folly of my actions. I had used some unfamiliar form of something—I shall just say 'energy'–to help her. It just could not be! That I had ever allowed strange energies to come through my own hands!

By the time the guests arrived the next afternoon, Blarna looked stronger. Now clean and brushed, she sported a neck-bow of bright red velvet with dignity, and yet spoiled all that when she grinned at me.

Blarna greeted each guest with a certain reserve, sizing up each human. With two of the guests, however, she lost all sense of decorum.

When Michael arrived, Blarna didn't even give him an opportunity to introduce his sister; she pawed at his pant legs and wagged her tail many times faster than the ticking grandmother clock.

He laughed, bent down and patted her, while I introduced myself to his sister.

"Welcome to our celebration, I'm Barbara," I held out my hand to a dainty blond woman with short, chic hair and sensitive lips parted in a winsome smile.

"Please call me Isabelle, Barbara. It was so kind of you to include me in your party. Michael has often spoken of you."

He had? This dainty creature embodied the familiar flavor of an unusual tea consumed at a friend's house. I had seen her with Michael so long ago that it seemed like another existence, at the Full Summer Moon Party where so much had happened to Barbara, the Keeper of Practical Order.

Now, looking at her with unbiased eyes, I saw touches of a family resemblance. Both brother and sister had delicate lips. Her eyes were a vivid blue in contrast to his more subtle green, and she was quite pretty, lovely even, whereas Michael had a bit closer to average looks. I glanced at his face smiling down at an eager Blarna. Well, perhaps his looks weren't quite that average when he smiled.

The next guest to elicit Blarna's euphoric behavior was Patrick. He must be clothed in all manner of delectable scents, Isabelle pointed out. Patrick's entry was impressive; he was laden with goodies for our party. His canine hostess could not stop sniffing and wagging, and Patrick could not stop chuckling down at her. It was all very busy, the patting, the sniffing, the laughing.

When Patrick glanced up to say hello to me, his human hostess, his gaze swerved past my face to Isabelle and stopped in a sort of stunned appreciation. The chef had encountered yet another muse. It was as if Colleen no longer existed in his universe. My introductions were unnecessary and I turned to tend the other guests.

Anne was amused by Patrick's defection. Colleen, however, was not. She looked close to tears.

But that just would not do, not for this celebration. So I asked Colleen for help with the food and drink. She gained control over her emotions and helped out with a semblance of her habitual generosity.

When Samek arrived with his arm draped over Jeanne's shoulders, we all whistled and shouted out "Welcome!" Jeanne's self-consciousness dwindled when Horatio Caesar stumbled over Blarna, who received this battery with only a mild yelp. Horatio

Caesar didn't land on the cake, but caught himself, for once, on the buffet table. Catastrophe averted!

Megan tried to approach Isabelle. But Patrick was not allowing anyone near his prize. His way of guarding his quarry resembled the way a celebrated chef guards a favorite recipe. Perhaps his life would be filled with a succession of favored recipes, a succession of Annes, Colleens and Isabelles, to guard with care until the next one appeared.

Anne whispered to me. "One day, he will find his favorite and not ever let her go." It's uncanny the way she reads my mind.

Tom Bates arrived, holding two bouquets. Tom? He handed one to Jeanne, and one to me. To me? He said that he wanted to wish me a happy spring. Bossy Barbs was speechless. He smiled down at me, and then turned to Samek and began talking about a project for the inn.

I grabbed Horatio Caesar, pulled him aside, and told him about the second apparition of my parents, as well as my doubts about the veracity of the whole event.

He beamed at me, as if I were his prize student. I bristled.

He chuckled; "BB, what great news! Sounds just like them! Now that you can see and hear them, you won't miss them so much!"

In some sneaky way, I always felt a bit superior to Horatio Caesar; he was clumsy, I was deft. Now he was acting more like my teacher. My world was turning upside down.

Jeanne was grateful to those who spoke some French with her. Even Blarna began to preen at phrases such as "comme elle est belle."

Blarna returned to her duties as co-hostess, making the round of legs, sniffing each one as a potential bearer of exotic delicacies.

Colleen found a number of welcome distractions from guests who appreciated her ready smile and wit.

Michael drifted away from Megan. And Megan looked affronted.

Anne and I intervened. We took Megan aside. She pouted, but both brother and sister were otherwise engaged.

Megan looked me straight in the eyes. "I wish you would say 'yes' to Sean, Barbie! He has been unbearable."

I gasped. Saying "yes" under Sean's conditions was no longer an option. I had made that clear to her, I thought. Composing myself, I affirmed in an almost steady voice, "Sean and I will only be together if he moves back here."

"How can you say that! He's been so loyal to you all these months! You are cruel and unfeeling!" Megan's voice was getting louder. "You are being disloyal to the Sullivan family. After all that we have done for you! After all the friendship we've shown you. You repay this by rejecting Sean! How can you!" And she burst into gulping sobs.

I am not very good at coping with deep woe. I stood there, helpless and hurt. Her words cut deep, even though part of me realized that all Megan's pent up frustration about Michael's uncertain future was being transferred onto me.

Anne put an arm around Megan and spoke into her ear. "It will feel better to cry, my dear. All will work out for the best. You will see."

As Megan's tears slowed, she regained some composure and hunted for something to wipe her cheeks. I handed her a napkin. I am much better at handing over nails. My gesture was clumsy, but effective. Megan managed an awkward apology.

Horatio Caesar approached and led me away to get a drink. "It will be alright," he whispered in an uncanny replay of Anne's words to Megan. Teacher Horatio Caesar was at it again. His eyes were as sincere as any Father Christmas, and just as benevolent.

We had all changed. But who were we now?

Questions opened up further questions. I had seen two apparitions. I had put aside a lifelong resistance to special skills or working with energy, which some call by that M word. Horatio Caesar seemed now to be the wise one. I had adopted a dog. If I no longer knew Sean, or Megan, then did I know myself?

The rest of the party passed in a blur. Anne stayed by me, so of course, Horatio Caesar followed suit. My guardians took care of me, while Blarna distracted us all with her playfulness.

When the guests turned to leave, I was still half-numb. Isabelle thanked me for including her and invited me to have breakfast with her at *Butter Fingers*. Michael held out his hand to shake mine, an unfamiliar gesture. His hand felt warm, reassuring. His gaze was penetrating. I looked down.

By the time most of the guests had gone, my body released its rigid stance, muscles relaxed and I regained some awareness of the trunk of my body, my breath, my heartbeat.

Anne and Horatio Caesar completed my composure by helping me wash all the dishes. They never once mentioned Sean or Megan. The object of their attentions, other than the cutlery and dishes, was Blarna, who was determined to help us. She sniffed our heels, even licking that ticklish patch near our ankles.

My guardians left me dozing in a chair with Blarna in my lap. I fell into a dream, one that was so vivid I could almost smell it.

I was standing by the lake. The rain began to fall in a light sprinkle. I knew that Sean was on the other side, waiting for me to cross over to him. A sturdy boat hovered by the shore for me to climb into. Blarna didn't want to go. Every time I put a foot into the boat, she jumped away and began to bark. I tried to pick her up to put her in the boat, but she squirmed out of my arms and jumped back to shore. She even grabbed my clothing and dug her feet in the dirt, growling as she hung on. I asked her to let go, and she did, but she began barking and barking, and would not stop. I woke up to her barking at the phone that was ringing and ringing.

XV.   When I Picked Up the Phone

I never sleep during the day. No naps for Bossy
Barbs. I like to keep busy. This departure from my
routine was odd. Rather than being refreshed by my
post-party nap, I felt weighty and sluggish. I had no
desire to move, but Blarna's bark was insistent. So, I
rubbed my face and eyes, and pulled myself to my feet.
I shuffled to the phone, and lifted it to my ear.

Sean's voice glared at me. "We need to talk."

I shook my head to clear it and just managed to
agree.

"You've changed," he commented after an
awkward silence.

"In what way?"

"Megan told me what you are wearing. You
never liked dresses." So they had talked about me
while I was caught in my dream by the lake. No
wonder he knew where to reach me; Megan told him.
He always called me in the office. I was indifferent to
it all now.

"And where is your hammer?"

"It's in the office desk."

"Don't you wear it?"

"Sometimes."

"When did you start wearing dresses?"

"A while back." I was not very forthcoming.

"Megan told me how different your house
looks."

"I moved furniture around, and repainted the
rooms, as you may remember from our conversations."

Sean took a deep breath. "While I'm away from the village, your house, my family's house and store, none of that seems real. My new life does. My work, my boss, my company. The village just seems like such a sleepy little town living in the past with very little going for it."

I inhaled fast.

Sean resumed before I could defend our village. "It's a thrill to wake up in the morning and not know what the day will bring. I have no idea what my boss will ask me to do. I may be speaking one language at ten and another at eleven. My job is to meet with many different people. I enjoy the challenge. I can see their reluctance to deal with me, and then bit by bit, I break down that barrier and they are willing to do business with me, and with the company."

Sean would be good at this form of communication and seduction. I could see it. This was not a pejorative statement. I had a fleeting vision of Sean opening up minds to new ideas. It may be in the service of his company, but he was still opening up people's minds.

"Your family and friends are proud of you for that," I replied in all fairness.

"Well, I enjoy it!" He paused. "The thing is, the village is part of me, too. When I go back, I always wonder why I ever want to leave it. But I know that sooner or later I will."

Yes, it seemed inevitable. He would leave, always. And I would stay, always.

In adopting Blarna, I didn't make a conscious commitment to stay put. I must have made that decision long before her dramatic entry into my life, even before Sean kissed me at that fateful Full Summer Moon Party. In all probability, I had made that commitment when my parents died.

The man of my dreams waited for some sort of answer. Did he want me to reject my life and all that was dear to me to follow him? My body held a mixture of secret hopes and unspoken regrets. I remained silent.

"And you have changed, Barbara Blue," he continued. "So, I don't know what to think. I don't know you very well now. I would like to get to know you better, but I doubt whether you'll give me the chance."

"I have not changed that much!" I rushed into the fray, unwilling to admit that he was right. I was so irritated by his superior knowledge that I wanted to prove that I was indeed the same person, the girl who trailed after him all through school, who adored him and who was kissed by him not so long ago.

Looking down into Blarna's anxious eyes, I realized that persuading Sean was unfair, because it was untrue. "You are right," I admitted in a small voice, "I have changed a bit."

In the silence that followed, I felt the character, the essential nature of the man I loved. The same fifteen-year old, who smiled up at a frightened eleven-year old Barbara stuck in a tree, was there, deep inside, but laid over that essence was a whole succession of choices that he had made to change his destiny.

Sean sought the kind of challenges that he would never find here in our village. And in his searching, his quest, he had learned many new skills, seen different lands and cultures and become enthralled with them. He knew a yearning, a questing that I did not possess. I knew a contentment that would be elusive to him. We were poles apart.

In those moments, I felt very mature, very wise and very clear. The Wise and Clear-Sighted-Barbara spoke to her Long Beloved. "I have been in love with you since I was four. I trailed after you, giving you little or no peace. You laughed at me for hanging around you. But I adored you anyway, and loved your family. What was there not to love? Your sense of joy in life, your wit and delight. The Sullivan family has more of these qualities than most of the rest of us do."

I smiled just thinking about each Sullivan, and all but heard Sean listening to me.

"But you've made choices, and they've changed you. Not who you are deep down, but what you want. We picked different life paths, but they suit us."

I paused to gather more strength. "If you had asked me to follow you six years ago, who knows where we'd be now. I would have gone with you and perhaps become quite different from the person I am now."

Sean grunted. Was that a 'yes' or a 'no'?

"It's unfair of me to ask you to be the person you were six years ago, and start all over again."

Sean listened; he really listened. "Well, if you moved here, I would have both worlds. And, I would feel better about leaving Megan in charge of the store." His reply rang of truth.

It was my turn to be just as honest. "We both wanted the other to fulfill our yearnings. After my parents died, I wanted you to be my family."

"We all miss them, Barbie."

Silence, blessed silence.

"I will explain all this to Megan," Sean offered to my profound relief. "She doesn't seem happy. Our decision will not make her feel any better."

I could not agree more. Was there anything I could do to help her?

"Sean, may I make a suggestion? Why don't you invite Megan for a visit? She may need to get away for a while."

"Why would she need to get away?"

What could I say that would not be an assumption on my part, and yet be helpful to her? After all, I had failed as her confidante.

"I think she might be interested in someone."

"What do you mean by interested?

"She likes someone, a lot."

"She never said anything to me." Her brother's tone of voice was full of bristles.

"They haven't made any joint plans, as far as I know."

Sean, Mr. Know-it-all-Charm-Man, cut close to the bone. "You mean she's in love with a man who's not in love with her?"

"Oh, he likes her, likes her a lot, but he is in a similar position to you, Sean; he is probably going to leave soon."

Sean growled. I returned to tact.

"She just seems unhappy, but refuses to talk to me about it. She may talk to you."

"But if she comes for a visit, she'll need to find a replacement to run *Chalice Lore*."

"Yes, just as I would have had to for *Charmed Necessities*!" I retorted. Sometimes people can be so dense. "Once she puts the word out, she'll find someone. She's always lucky," which was true. Megan attracted luck like the way I attract nails.

"Will she enjoy visiting me?" he asked with a whiff of anxiety.

"A brief change of scene might do the trick."
Blarna jumped to her feet. Sean stalled me with one final question.

"So, who is it?"

A direct query is hard to parry. Nevertheless I was reluctant to answer him. After all, I had not discussed the matter with Megan.

My response was measured and tentative. "I am guessing here," I began. "I'm not sure, but the object of her affections may be Michael Mathews."

"The man who replaced Samek? But he sounds so dull!"

I flushed. "He is not! He is much liked by the guests."

"But he doesn't love my Megan?" Sean demanded with gathering wrath.

"He has a special smile for her, and they spend a lot of time together at village gatherings."

"So what's the problem?"

"He may leave soon, and Megan looks so wistful," was my only reply. Blarna cocked her head at me and looked a bit anxious.

What had I let out, when I picked up the phone?

XVI. The Hammer in My Mouth

Why, oh why was I such a blunt female? Several months ago, I put my hammer in its place of honor on red velvet. But for all intents and purposes, I still carried it, in my head, in my mouth, in my speech.

After Sean hung up, my conscience kicked into high gear. What had I divulged about Megan? Was it indeed true? I had told Sean about my own conclusions, but was I being fair to all parties?

As a matter of plain fact, I didn't have the slightest idea about Michael's feelings. His amorous gestures towards me, without doubt the fruit of my over-active imagination, were part of a mythical past. Since his arrival, he showed Megan a great deal of warmth and attention.

As night cloaked the village in light fog, I made a conscious effort to remember different occasions when Megan and Michael were together. They made a striking couple. Both tall and slender, his brown hair and mostly green eyes made an excellent foil for her long blond hair and grey eyes. And he showed every sign of enjoying her company. At every event, Michael gravitated to Megan.

A much more probable scenario was that Michael was smitten with Megan. Until he knew where his future lay, it was unfair to tell her. When Anne asked me to speak to Megan, she implied that Michael would be leaving our village soon. She did not imply that he was indifferent to Megan. Since

Megan had such a profound change of heart, saying that she would move away from our beloved village for love, Anne's concerns became irrelevant.

The fog had become thick. No one would be able to enter or leave the village that night. All of nature was still, except my mind and my conscience.

Blarna demanded my attention. I had held off on her sleeping on top of my bed next to me. But my resistance was ebbing. Soon, her soothing warmth allowed me to drift into sleep. Images of a tearful Megan and wrathful Michael flitted through my dreams. Sean was in them, too, but I refused to remember the roles he played.

In the morning, Blarna stayed put, but managed a frown on her otherwise happy face when I walked out the front door. Looking damp and unfinished, I scurried off to meet Isabelle at *Butter Fingers*, remembering just in time to tuck in my shirt before opening the bakery door.

Isabelle thanked me for including her in my tea party. She exuded charm, the way I exude practical competence. She knew, I wondered how, that my day would be hectic and thought that treating me to a good breakfast might help. She agreed to come by *Charmed Necessities* for a tour just after lunch. I sped off to get Blarna and open shop.

When Isabelle walked past the front door chimes, her brother followed her. Colleen stiffened, but relaxed when she saw Michael.

While Michael checked up on Blarna, I showed Isabelle around. She was quite delighted with the lamps and table coverings. She gushed about the little hand blown glass flowers in jewel-like colors, which she was convinced would make the perfect table decorations for a dinner party. She asked so many questions that Colleen, who trailed behind us, began to answer them out of habit.

Isabelle, we found out, had been the buyer for an exclusive French boutique. When asked what she was doing now, she admitted to "looking."

"Where?" I asked.

"Everywhere," Isabelle replied.

Colleen looked askance. By definition, everywhere could also include our village, and Patrick had been far too attentive to Isabelle for Colleen's liking.

"We lead very simple lives," I warned her.

Isabelle nodded, "I like that. The clothing bored me. It was all the same. Chic, chic, chic." She shrugged her shoulders and let out a sigh. I forbore to point out that Isabelle was clothed in chic.

My loyalty toward Colleen warred with my favorable impression of Isabelle.

"Would you consider working in the village for a while, Isabelle?" Colleen stiffened.

"Perhaps." Enigmatic reply, hmmm. Food for thought.

Michael joined us and informed me that Blarna was recovering with admirable speed. He looked pleased by Isabelle's interest in *Charmed Necessities*.

"Are you planning to stay on in our village, Michael?" I tried for a causal, even languid, tone of voice. Megan's happiness depended on his answer.

"For now," he replied, looking at Isabelle rather than me.

That was not an answer, and we both knew it. I gritted my teeth. But it was hard to press him further.

After they left, Colleen admitted that Isabelle seemed quite nice. And that Michael was cagey. It left us both feeling a bit dissatisfied and unsettled.

Out of the blue, Colleen gave me a warm hug and whispered in my ear, "I think you made the right decision." Her words battled my gloom over lost dreams.

An hour later, Jeanne made a pretty picture when she entered the store. I showed her around, ignoring visitors. Jeanne had lost any trace of shyness. Before she left, she gave me an unexpected present, a wish.

"It is so beautiful to be in love and be loved. Ahh, l'amour. I wish that for you very much, Barbara." And with that reached up and kissed me on both cheeks and departed. A Bemused Barbara stared at her receding back.

When Megan popped over just at closing, she dragged me into the office, closing the door.

"Sean told me that he'd changed his mind about you."

That rankled, but, in all fairness, Sean picked the most effective way to inform his doting sister.

Megan was nice enough to ask whether I was coping with his shift in intentions. When I nodded, she proceeded to relay Sean's invitation.

"What did you tell him?"

"Well, at first, I didn't want to leave. But he said something mysterious about absence making the heart grow fonder, which made me think a bit..." her voice trailed off. In a resolute tone, she continued, "I promised him that I would fly out as soon as possible. Help me, Barbie! Who can look after *Chalice Lore*?"

I pondered the immediate solution. That very afternoon, Isabelle seemed at loose ends. Her prior experience was fortuitous. By giving Isabelle a reason to stay on in the village, Patrick might abandon Colleen for good. On the other hand, if Isabelle managed *Chalice Lore*, it would solve Megan's dilemma and Michael would be grateful on his sister's behalf. So whose interests did I choose to further?

XVII.   What Birds and Friends have in Common

Anne and I tried out her new herbal tea blend in my kitchen after *Charmed Necessities* closed.   The last rays of afternoon sun were sending warm golden shafts into the room.   Her tea contained hints of lavender and stevia leaf that added a sweet bouquet to the spring air wafting in through the open window.   It calmed me, my body relaxed.

I hadn't known dogs could possess any tact. Blarna lay by the front door.   She was giving Anne and me some privacy.   Tact in a canine is an admirable trait.

When I finished my tale about Sean's and my mutual, albeit very reluctant, decision, Anne nodded. For the first time since his last phone call, I felt a tiny sense of relief.   For too long, I had carried the burden of indecision that grew out of my longing for Sean. Now that a final decision had been made, I could go on with my life, I hoped.   Part of me remained unhurt by Sean's actions; we had both been self-serving.

Drawing a deep breath, I relayed my conflict about helping Megan, at the expense of protecting Colleen and her interests.   There was a long pause. The pause lengthened and passed over my threshold into discomfort, as I stared first into Anne's blank face and then down at my broad fingers.   They were capable hands, I reassured myself.   Had they not wielded a hammer with deft precision for years?

Anne stood up from the table, her movements abrupt rather than graceful. As she placed her empty teacup by the sink, she stared out the window. Birds of all sizes were flocking to the feeders in the garden. She turned back to me and asked me a single question.

"What do you see out there?"

"Wha…What did you say?"

"What do you see out the window?" Anne gestured to the comfortable view.

What I saw out that window was the need for more birdseed and or some pruning. Let's face it. I looked out that window for chores to be done.

But referring to the prosaic was not like Anne. I had better find out what she meant. So, I stood up and joined her.

We watched, as first a pair of small birds flitted in and out again with agility and speed, followed by birds of different sizes and colors. Some sat for a while and peered around between pecks of seed. Others chirped from their perch on the feeder. We stood there watching for over ten minutes. We were silent, but the birds were not.

None of this made any sense to me. And yet, as I stood first on one foot then the other, I became aware of a sort of shuffle between the different birds. Not being much of a bird watcher, I didn't know any of their names or the exact species. Nor could I tell whether the same pairings kept coming together.

After a while their movements wove a pattern in my mind, yes, a dance, not unlike our own village dances. As I observed these feathered creatures in the quiet of Anne's presence, the pattern began to make more sense. An unfamiliar bird, or so it seemed to this amateur's eyes, joined in from time to time, almost like another thread added to the pattern. Some of the birds ceased to feed. Perhaps they had eaten all they needed. The pattern continued, but just as a new thread was added, others were dropped. And it was really quite marvelous, all of this twitting about!

When I turned and looked at my friend, Anne's face was no longer blank. A faint smile hovered

around her lips.   When she turned toward me, her
eyes were questioning.

"So, it's the pattern that counts," I replied at
last.

Dimples appeared on Anne's cheeks.

"And so it doesn't really...." I hesitated because
this seemed so far-fetched, even for The Free Barbara,
"...matter."

My words tried to catch up with the complexity
of my thoughts. "If Isabelle agrees to stay on and help
Megan out, she adds another thread to the pattern,
while Megan leaves the pattern for awhile with Sean.
And that unfamiliar bird is like Isabelle, or better yet,
Jeanne, who is here to stay."

Anne nodded. "How do you feel now about
helping Colleen versus Megan?"

I began to sputter that this bird pattern was not
at all relevant, and then paused.

Even if I prevented Isabelle from minding
Megan's store, by not telling her about this
opportunity, she could find another job in the village.
However inspired my own idea was, it would not be
the only opportunity for her.

And Patrick, food-lover that he was, he had to
decide whether he was going to make one woman after
another fall for him, as he pursued first one then
another, or, whether there was one woman above all
others who would become a more enduring flirtation.
Who was to say that if Isabelle left the village today,
tomorrow a Flavia would not turn up and turn
Patrick's head?   Would he make Colleen miserable
now or later? I could not prevent her pain.

"Fine, now. Thank you, Anne." My tone was
lighter and more certain. "I will help them both, when
I'm able to."

Anne laughed and gave me a warm quick hug.
Blarna rushed in and barked, her tail wagging with
excitement.

What on earth would this pattern bring for us
all? One thing was certain; the pattern that Blarna
wove with her tail was boisterous.

XVIII. Mayhem Rules

Events pushed all of us forward with the speed of a soaring hawk on the hunt. Spring showered us with new colors of small flowers and tiny leaves. The pattern continued to be woven. I did nothing to stop it.

Isabelle was pleased to find a temporary occupation in the village. Her prior experience made her a good fit for Megan. Also, Isabelle's brother had managed *Delights in Earthly Haven* in Samek's absence, which proved that Isabelle could manage *Chalice Lore,* and get along well with visitors and villagers alike.

Megan was delighted to find such a speedy solution to her dilemma. I was once again her best friend.

The prospect of Isabelle managing the store next door upset Colleen. Mind you, I saw her point of view. The threat to her love for Patrick Doweran was no longer ephemeral, an afternoon's dalliance, but working and living in close proximity to *Charmed Necessities.*

Yet Megan's obvious delight over the arrangement was hard to resist. It's not easy to remain disturbed in the presence of so much gratitude.

With rare tact, Isabelle asked Colleen for advice. Soon, Colleen was talking up a storm, explaining some of the finer points of shop tending and village customs. Her lilting charm shone forth, in spite of her dread of being supplanted.

After Isabelle left, Colleen pulled me into the office. She was about to give me a scold; she had that former babysitter's look about her. I sat down on the edge of my seat.

"It is a marvelous thing you did, Barbie, putting Sean in his place. It would never have worked out between you two. Never. I bit my tongue so often, it turned red and then blue. But you had to see it for yourself, for you were always a stubborn one."

I gawked. All right. I *am* stubborn; I admit it. How else do you get a nail in just right?

"And it's high time you let go of all those crazy ideas that Sean had of you leaving us. It would never have suited you to leave all this behind. You are always craving to get back home from any trip you take, Barbie, and you know that in your bones."

She had a point, but then again, I didn't make a habit of listening to my bones.

"And furthermore, it's high time that you looked around here and settled down with someone who wants to stay here. This is where you belong, and you know it. There are some nice possibilities shaping up."

Some possibilities? The only person I could think of was Horatio Caesar. But Horatio Caesar was just a friend, a dear friend, a special friend. I have always been fond of him, but he was too much my would-be-brother. Besides, he was smitten with Anne. And Patrick had never glanced my way. I was not feminine enough. And as for Tom Bates, I snorted. We liked the same things, carpentry tools, but we spent a lot of time arguing. It was sort of fun, I admitted. And began to wonder a bit more about Tom. I had just never considered him as a man, with potential to be *my* man.

Before I could question Colleen any further, the banging on the front door got us moving; we greeted the impatient visitors, and soon thereafter my relatives who dragged some new acquaintances from the inn with them.

Uncle Christopher, that successful and sharp-eyed businessman, unbent for a stray dog. He was soon to be found in my office, sitting in the chair with a very self-satisfied Blarna on his lap. The little one grinned as he stroked her lean body, her ears and even her paws.

Aunt Phoebe pored over the shop, yet again, and followed Colleen's advice for the many gifts she purchased. She even began explaining some of the products to her inn acquaintances, becoming in short order an unofficial shop assistant. As I sped between customers, I was pleased that a certain harmony prevailed throughout *Charmed Necessities*.

I tried not to gawk when I peeked in the office. Blarna was in bliss, and Uncle Christopher was as close to a similar state as a man of his stature and life experience could ever be.

Patrick, like the rest of us, was overloaded as the Equinox festivities approached. Nevertheless, he popped by with some lemon meringue bars, which we devoured. He also visited *Chalice Lore* to wish Megan a safe journey, and welcome Isabelle as the temporary manager.

Megan was so preoccupied with departure plans that she overlooked Patrick's kindness; she had only two days to prepare for her trip, train a new manager, arrange her affairs and depart. She made no mention of Michael, which was odd. In her manner, she seemed to have already left us behind and was soaring off to her beloved brother.

For the first time in her life, Megan would miss our Spring Equinox Celebration. When I thought about her pending departure, our long-awaited festivities lost some of their luster. I was missing her, even before she left.

With Colleen at the helm, Aunt Phoebe in tow and Blarna on Uncle Christopher's spacious lap, I slipped away from *Charmed Necessities* for a couple of hours to help Megan pack.

The Sullivan family home, much larger than my own, was in considerable disarray. When Megan and Sean's parents decided to enjoy their early retirement, they became pleasant, vague and erratic. More often than not, they were off in the mountains with no regard to schedules, house repairs or bank balance, and leaving no way to contact them. They left for months at a time, we never knew when to expect them next. The old house showed their lack of concern. Dust lingered and curtains took on a grey tinge.

Mama and Papa Sullivan were off on another one of their post-retirement honeymoons, oblivious to Megan's forthcoming trip to visit her brother. However, until Megan's return, Isabelle promised to live in the house, while I agreed to check on practical matters, whenever Isabelle felt the need for any assistance.

Megan's room overlooked the front door. On other occasions, she would see me coming up the garden path and waft her way down to greet me. This time, however, I let myself in and ran up the spiraling stairs, the wood creaking under my vigorous steps. After a quick hug, Megan put me to work making lists of all the things to pack.

Her desk was old and scarred from generations of Sullivans, but the paper was crisp and white, and the pen in good working order. I began with the usual items, the toiletries and such. I had no idea what she would need. Party clothes? Hiking gear? What would Megan do while her brother worked? How would they spend evenings and weekends? I made a stab at guessing and left the number of items blank.

"How many shirts and tops are you planning to take, Megan?"

"Oh, I don't know," Megan replied, hovering between dresser and closet. "What do you think, Barbie?"

"Well, it sort of depends how long you are planning to stay," I responded with uncharacteristic discretion. "Then again, you could have your things washed and cleaned."

Megan halted and stared at me. Her voice became light and breathless. "I will be gone for, ah, for six weeks. Sean wants me to stay longer."

Six weeks was a long time for Megan to be away. On the other hand, she could have chosen to leave for as long as Samek. What was bringing her back?

"Are you concerned that Isabelle might do a poor job at *Chalice Lore*?" At times, I have the delicacy of a bullfrog.

"Oh, no, not at all. She seems very..." Megan paused as if to search for the right word, "...competent."

No, it is just that," And she stopped, looking off in the distance, and began picking each word with care. "I want to see, I want to talk to Michael."

"Talk to Michael?"

Megan shook out her long blond hair so that it framed her face. Her dreamy eyes darkened. Her voice shook a bit. "Yes, I told him about my feelings, my feelings for him."

"What are your feelings for him?" The bullfrog croaked.

"I want to marry him!" No signs of Wafting Megan now, she radiated determination with her hands and jaw clenched. A New Megan that took my breath away.

I sucked in my breath and my gut. My observations about her feelings for Michael had been more than accurate; Megan not only liked Michael, but also loved him enough to desire a life together. My heart split; one part was in that happy state of self-congratulation at its acumen, the other part was frozen. My brain followed my heart.

"You had the temerity to tell him that?" My voice rose up one whole octave to meet the occasion.

"No, oh no. I could never use those words, but he understood." Megan replied with a tiny smile on her lips.

"What were your exact words?" An image of ethereal Megan making a direct statement to Michael about her heartfelt wishes was impossible to conjure up. I shook my head to clear away that frozen sensation.

Megan's face betrayed her. Frown lines formed. My questions were unnecessary since the answers were so obvious to everyone but me. Megan and I were in Communication-Gap-City.

"I told him that I hoped he would decide to stay on in our village," Megan explained with exemplary patience.

I digested this, or at least, I tried to. "When did you tell him this?" My thirst for details remained unquenched.

"After Isabelle agreed to take care of the shop." Megan replied in a 'well, it's all so very obvious' tone of voice. To be fair, I deserved her contempt. This bullfrog was being very dense.

"Why did you tell him then?" I persisted.

"Oh, Barbie. Isn't it obvious?" I moved my head once to the left and then to the right. The bullfrog needed a special tutorial; I was swamped with thick fog.

Megan hitched her shoulder, another unfamiliar gesture, then descended to my level. "It occurred to me that Isabelle might make a wonderful partner for the *Chalice Lore*, Barbie. She seems so competent and efficient. And we would compliment each other so well."

Megan had more practical wisdom than I gave her credit for. Her sensibility coupled with Isabelle's skills would make *Chalice Lore* into the lovely shop it had been, before the Sullivan parents lost interest and dumped the management onto Megan's slender shoulders.

But Megan was not finished. "And if Isabelle agrees to become my partner in the shop, it would be a long-term agreement. Then maybe Michael would be more willing to take on more permanent work and commit to staying on in our village."

I gawked at her. She had a solution all sketched out, and such a neat one, too.

"But what would Michael do in our village?" I was still at a loss. There were other inns, but nothing to compare with *Delights in Earthly Haven*.

"Oh, Barbie, I happened to overhear a conversation." Megan whispered bending over near my ear so I caught every word. Wafting Megan would never have eavesdropped; she lived in her own world. She always left that sort of activity to me.   All this shifting of roles was making me dizzy.

"Anne offered him the opportunity to work with her.   While she helps people, he could work on animals." My jaw dropped. "He's a good veterinarian, you know."   Megan said to the Five-Year-Old-Pea-Brained-Barbie, who was also her life-long friend.

I knew, yes, I knew Michael was good.   For all my so-called handiwork, Blarna was flourishing under his care.   But I was hurt.   Anne hadn't mentioned a word about any of this to me.   And Michael had not told me, either.   At the very least, I presumed to be a good enough friend for Anne to tell me about her plans.

Megan applied a salve to my hurt pride.   "I doubt anyone else knows about her offer.   They stood apart and spoke in soft tones."

How had Megan overheard them then?   Why not me?   A spurt of envy came between us.

"Anne explained to Michael that she had observed how well he took care of Blarna." Megan added, seeing my grimace.

"Anne made him the offer after he treated Blarna?"

"Oh Yes, she did."

So, the offer was that recent.   And when I last met with Anne, my thoughts were filled with the pattern that I had not begun to see.   My heart and mind united in a more reasonable state, although hurt lingered in small wisps.   The bullfrog's curiosity heightened.   Bullfrogs are never silenced by ruffled pride.

"Well, what was Michael's answer?"

Megan turned away, brushing her blond hair from her left shoulder. "Well, he didn't say very much, just something like, thank you, or some such phrase."

"And that was the end of your conversation?"   I persisted.

"Well, I told him that I would talk with Isabelle about the possibility of her becoming my partner in the shop when I return.   My parents will never return to live here in this house," Megan's arms gestured to all the old and careworn Sullivan objects that I loved for the comfort of their familiarity.

Megan broke through my nostalgia. "They will never manage *Chalice Lore* again, nor will Sean. So, it occurred to me that another kind of partner might be best. And Isabelle is here now. So, it must mean that she would be the perfect person. That is, of course, if Isabelle likes managing the store."

That sounded more like the Megan I knew, seeing events as signs of significance. I caught myself from huffing in disgust at this hint of synchronicity. I reminded myself that I liked, better yet, that I loved the Familiar Megan.

"And what did Michael reply?" This bullfrog was determined to find out all the details.

"He looked a bit funny, but didn't say anything. Except, he thanked me again for giving Isabelle the opportunity to work in the village."

"He said nothing else?"

"Such as?"

"His feelings for you, Megan!"

"Oh, he had no time to do so, Isabelle joined us." Megan's countenance was serene and assured.

I was still perplexed. For all I knew, Michael was very much in love with Megan and was waiting for his future work to fall into place in order to make his life with Megan a reality. But I would have been happier if he had wrapped her in his arms and kissed her then and there. Now, that would have been a statement!

As Megan's life-long friend, I needed a bit more clarity. Yes, that was it. I needed more reassurance. So I stood up. Standing up felt good. I put my hands on her shoulders.

"Megan! What does your intuition, your sight tell you?"

"My sight doesn't tell me a thing! It's all cloudy. Every time I try, all I see is dense fog, Barbie. You know that my sight never works for anything that I desire." Megan whimpered.

Since I ignored this phenomenon in Megan or anyone else whenever possible, I didn't know. It seemed a bit unfair. If you have this skill, why can't you use it for yourself? But I was getting off track.

"Megan, you have so much to offer, so much to give. Are you quite certain that Michael is the right man for you?"

"Oh, yes. I think so." Her smile was dreamy.

"You think so? You aren't certain?"

"Oh Barbie, he's wonderful, just wonderful. I dream about him night after night. He is so very fine. He has such beautiful eyes and hands. He is so good with people and with animals. He is, oh, you know him, you must understand!"

What a scold. The implication that I didn't understand her love made me feel like a lousy friend and unappreciative of all Michael had done for Blarna.

It was just that, well, maybe Megan was wrong, maybe I didn't know Michael. I suppressed a tiny voice inside that said, "Yes, you do, just open your eyes." I was appalled, what a thing to think. I blinded myself.

"Does he feel the same way about you?"

Megan tried pulling away. "Oh, Barbie, just because you and Sean didn't succeed in getting together, does not mean that I can't!"

I clung to her, this was too important. "Has he ever kissed you, or told you that he cared about you?"

Megan looked shocked. I was being very, very nosy. At the very least, I deserved a glass of ice-cold water in my face.

"He tried many times to kiss me, but we were always interrupted!"

I pulled away. Knowledge can be a good thing, or a sharp, painful thing that sits brooding like a panther on a limb.

Michael must like her. He really must like her, he must even love her, and I mean, really love her.

All I wanted was to sink into a deep, dark hole in the ground and curl up there for a good while. A nice dark, cozy space, where I would hear nothing and see nothing. Numbness sounded oh, so good.

To top it all, my best friend Megan was leaving for over six weeks. And all these changes were happening. And I couldn't control a thing!

Meanwhile, I wasn't of much help to Megan. I handed her a pile of socks when she asked for shirts.

Megan chatted away about all the plans Sean was making for her. He was taking some of his saved-up vacation days to go on four-day trips with her. Red carpet treatment for his beloved sister. And me, all alone at home, I sulked.

When I returned to *Charmed Necessities*, mayhem ruled. My new canine friend was no longer on Uncle Christopher's lap. When he had had to excuse himself, Blarna sneaked out of the office into the shop. A rather plump lady was so startled to see Blarna appear out of nowhere that she bumped into a stacked tower of hand-blown glass ornaments. Several of these village-crafted gems landed on adjacent garden angels anointing them with glittering halos. Others were not so fortunate and shattered on the wooden floor. Nearby visitors began picking up the tiny fragments in the most helpful manner. But the mayhem did not stop there.

Blarna must have felt under attack. She jumped into the nearest available container, a large hand-made basket that had come down in my family for an impressive number of generations. It held pillows in vivid colors with silk tassels and beadwork. No doubt Blarna was hoping to find a haven. Instead, the basket toppled over, and pillows scattered in all directions, adding bright patches of color to the wooden floor.

Blarna remained hidden behind basket weave. But the room filled with voices. My errant Uncle was calling out to Blarna. The rather plump lady huffed and puffed that she was not responsible for the breakage. Colleen was trying to get a broom and dustpan over to the broken glass, saying "Excuse me, excuse me" as she wove her way over arms and legs.

Aunt Phoebe stopped other visitors from either stepping on the pillows or trying to help out, and paved the way for me by saying, "The owner, Barbara

Mahoney, will take care of all this. If you could just please stay put."

I was able to step over body parts and puffy spots of color, pick up an embarrassed Blarna, and carry her squirming to my Uncle's willing arms, and then return to put pillows and basket in proper order. By the time all the glass splinters were picked or swept up and the tower of ornaments reassembled, the plump lady no longer sputtered and all the helpful hands were thanked.

I opened a box of chocolates made by Cerise Duvet, our matron of chocolates, and passed them around to all the visitors, relatives included. We had a Communal Chocolate Bliss Experience, as only Cerise Duvet can devise.

After closing, Aunt Phoebe and Uncle Christopher joined me around the kitchen table for a cup of tea with cookies and a biscuit for the smallest of us. Uncle Christopher snickered as we remembered odd clips of Blarna's misadventure. Blarna looked pleased by our merriment, or perhaps by the gourmet flavor of her biscuit, and cocked her head at the mention of her name.

After enough mirth to make clowns jealous, Aunt Phoebe inquired about Megan and her preparations. It all flooded back, all the chaos, all the uncertainty, all the hurt.

At first I was non-committal, but Aunt Phoebe could have sat on a tribunal. She could even pass as one of us. She had my directness, or maybe I had hers? I saw no other resemblance, but then, I had been blind about so many things, including myself. Blarna was living proof of the inexplicable developments in a rather stubborn human being's existence.

Aunt Phoebe dismissed Megan with a summary, "It will do her the world of good to get away for a while and be with her beloved brother." She sighed and added, "I wish that I could have visited my brother and watched you grow up, my dear."

I began to squirm. This was a bit too much sentiment for me. Besides, my father had never mentioned his half-sister, so her interest must not have been reciprocated.

Uncle Christopher patted his wife's arm. "Now, now my dear, we must be going. Barbara has had a very full day, and has much to prepare for the upcoming festivities."

His good sense and ease of manner made me glad we were also related. Blarna and I showed them out, only to return to the kitchen for a quick bite for me, and a proper dinner for my chaos-maker.

The knock on the front door was gentle, yet insistent. My last bite was in my mouth as I walked to the door. Could it be Megan, or Anne, or even Michael to check up on Blarna?

It was Isabelle. She held out a huge bouquet of flowers with scented freesias and tulips in a rainbow of vibrant colors to thank me for helping her find such an interesting job.

Of course, I invited her in. Isabelle noticed the worn wood, the fresh paint and the warm light in the kitchen. She noticed Blarna, who received a few pats. Blarna sniffed back and began wagging her tail.

As I put Isabelle's offering in a seldom-used vase, she sat down at the table. Blarna tried to jump up onto her lap. Laughing, Isabelle picked her up. By the time the pot of tea was ready, they had bonded in the way that dogs, warm laps, spare hands to stroke, and hot cups of tea in-the-making, do.

In honor of this display of burgeoning affection, I got out the old family china. While we sipped tea from porcelain cups, I relayed the finer points of Blarna's misadventure that afternoon. Blarna basked in our undivided attention. That Princess of Emotional Blackmail.

Isabelle spoke about her first day at *Chalice Lore* with pleasure. How could she look so poised and relaxed in a new job, and furthermore, at such a busy time of the year? Our Equinox Celebration was only six days away.

Isabelle must have an inordinate talent for fitting into new situations. A streak of envy crept into my heart.   I squashed it.   Isabelle was too accommodating to deserve any form of resentment.

I could feel her unspoken questions hover between us. So I plunged in. "Can I help you in any way?"

Isabelle's delicate lips curved, her eyes glinted. "You guessed that I need your advice?"

I nodded, offering her a plate of cookies.

She took one and glanced down at Blarna. Without looking up, she asked, "Tell me, Barbara, what is this thing I hear about, this Energy, this Magic?"

Surprises never cease. I was not the person to tell her, no question about that. "I would ask Anne, if I were you."

"It's not easy to talk about then?"

Should I tell her? Her blue eyes had tiny gold flecks in them that made her eyes glow. They shone without pretence, without guile. I might just be able to trust those unfamiliar eyes. Well then, why not?

"It's a rather long story, but as I was growing up, I wanted nothing to do with those powers, what some people call Magic, others call Energy. My mother and grandmother would invoke this energy, but I didn't believe in it. It just didn't exist for me. Anyway, I knew that I had no such power in me. But last week, Anne showed me that I was wrong." Isabelle's eyes remained blue and gold and guileless.

I leaned over and patted the panting canine on her smooth head. "It was after your brother checked out this little one's injuries. Anne came over and, with her encouragement, I somehow knew that her name was Blarna." At that, Blarna barked, and we laughed.

"And then Anne somehow guided me to move my hands over all the hurts in her body." This was getting uncomfortable.

"But that's wonderful!"

"I don't know how it works, or why, or even when, or what it is." I shook my head. "But Blarna looked a bit better when I finished."

"Yes, my brother was amazed by the speed of her recovery."

"It was, well, I don't understand what it was. Ask Anne."

Isabelle ignored my disclaimer and pursued her own train of thought. "My brother also told me that you helped him at the inn. It quite astonished him. He doesn't understand how you did it, but you knew just what to do. That could have been this Energy, too." she mused.

I felt the blood leave my cheeks. I hadn't thought about the repairs in those three rooms of the inn—a mystery to me, even now.

While part of me was flattered that Michael had mentioned my help to his sister in such glowing terms, it was a bit of a letdown. The whole affair seemed private, just between Michael and myself.

And that a special power might have been at work was a very unpleasant notion. It had all happened without my invoking it. I felt superseded, and even a bit used. I was no longer in control. My skill with a hammer hadn't solved those strange problems, something else had.

Isabelle reached over and patted my arm. "He was very, very impressed," she said as if consoling a child over the loss of a toy.

My neck and back muscles tightened. I got up and moved toward the sink. Blarna leaped down from her comfortable perch and jumped up onto my right leg, wagging her tail and barking. So I had to reach down and pet her.

She continued to bark until I unbent and said, "All right, all right. I give in." She hopped back to the ground and looked up at me. I was under strict observation from the hostess police.

"I'm sorry, Isabelle. I still find it hard to accept. You may be correct. I never understood what happened that afternoon. It was all very strange." I shook my head, walked back to my chair and sat down again.

"Barbara, please, rest assured. My brother never told me any details. All he said was that it was a miracle to him."

It had been a miracle to me, too.

Then, it seemed easy enough to explain to this virtual stranger what had happened.   One long-forgotten detail after another flew through my mind, out my tongue and into the air between us. The words hung there, as we puzzled over the events together.

Isabelle clapped her hands with delight and exclaimed, "But it is marvelous, that!"   Her eyes flashed golden blue and her face sparkled.

"I still don't understand what happened.   I have never talked it over with anyone, not even with your brother. It seems, well, sort of weird." That last word came out in a derisive whisper.

Isabelle's eyes glinted with amusement. "Well, perhaps you should."

By the following morning, all of us gathered on the street to wish Megan a safe journey. It was an odd farewell, a bit of an anti-climax with no private moments.   All had been decided, and we were just going through the final motions.

We did get a few hugs in, but that was about it. Megan clung to me when she said good-bye. My ribs would recover later.

Tears gathered in Megan's eyes, but she controlled them as she hugged Colleen, Horatio Caesar and Isabelle. Michael kissed her on both checks. She blushed and smiled, but there was no time for more. And off she went.

Blarna ran after the vehicle.   I wanted to run, too, but I called Blarna back.

XIX.   Dancing in the Spring

Within the hour, the shops and streets were filled with visitors and we had no time to think, no time to eat, no time to pause for a deep breath. *Charmed Necessities* filled with chatter as one clump of visitors after another burst in the front door.

My relatives dragged with them their latest acquaintances staying in the twenty-first room at *Delights in Earthly Haven*. They wore the colored spandex material of an officer living on a ship in outer space.

Underneath all my busywork simmered the desire to investigate the full meaning of Megan's words. I also wanted to follow up on Isabelle's suggestion. But the timing was unfortunate. I would have to wait until after the conclusion of all the festivities. As our village began to burst at its seams, everyone was pressed into helping out for our Spring Equinox Celebration, the second most popular of all our events.

Horatio Caesar, knowing his limitations around delicate objects, didn't volunteer to help out in any of the shops. He was much better at directing traffic and people to appropriate locations. So, I couldn't ask him whether he had heard about Anne's offer to Michael. He would know if anyone else did, since he followed Anne around like a moon dog.

Patrick remained in his kitchens, creating the most delicious edibles, while planning ice sculptures for the culminating Spring Feast.   Even Colleen understood his absence.

Melissa popped by after school to help us out with restocking the shelves. She could reach most of the shelves without standing in her favorite ballet points.   Her long black hair was braided up on her head, and with her elegant, slender neck and beautiful posture she could easily pass muster as a very poised seventeen-year old.   I spoiled the dignity of her fictitious age by winking at her.   She was forced to wink back and grin.

Every   spare   moment   was   filled   with preparations for the Equinox Celebration.   In addition to her own tasks, Colleen took on Megan's allotted duties for our big event.   Isabelle was too recent an addition to our village to help out in Megan's place. Yet, Isabelle informed us that she had promised to help her brother at the inn after *Chalice Lore* closed.   Samek and his bride were still on their honeymoon.   Colleen and I nodded in empathy.

My three evenings before the Main Event were dedicated to the expertise of Bossy Barbs.   With my hammer once again in hand, I helped re-build the stage and sets.   Tom Bates was late as usual, and, as always, we argued over the proper design and the proper tools. We argued over anything we could think of.   It was fun.

It felt like old times to wear my pants again. They hung loose around my legs and even a bit bulky. But Barbie had not forgotten her skill with the nails, and Barbara was grateful.

Our Equinox Celebration began mid-morning on as lovely a Saturday in late March as could be imagined.   I buzzed around our village green early, making certain that the stage was ready and the backdrops were in place.   I spied Anne, with Horatio Caesar in tow, helping to place large vases of fresh flowers and village-made decorations on tables and in the trees.   Made of stiff paper and wood rather than glass, they were Owly-proof.

I waved, but there was no time for more.   We were   all   working   together   in   a   common   cause–

welcoming in the Spring. Only a few moments remained to return home and change.

The weather was soft and clear. Wild spring flowers burst forth among the tender grasses. In honor of the strengthening sunlight of Spring, yellow was the main color of the backdrop on the stage and all the village-made decorations.

Each villager wore a touch of yellow. For some, it might be a spray of yellow flowers in the hair or on a lapel. For others, it was a yellow tie, or a yellow shirt, a skirt or even socks. Others had created costumes with yellow accents just for this event.

The old Barbie had worn a white shirt with the word "SPRING" painted on it in bright yellow. The Free Barbara was more decorative and a bit more imaginative.

All sorts of puns had run through my mind. I could be a SPRING-board, or a seat-coil (SPRING). But others might choose similar puns.

Instead, I made a long dress out of brown material that could stretch to embrace my more enthusiastic movements. Then I painted the dress in vertical stripes to resemble rows of tilled earth. At the top and bottom of each row, I sewed on small signs with the names of spring flowers, painted in yellow, of course. My neck, wrists, and feet were framed by the names of flowers. With my hair pinned up so that all the names were legible, I transformed into a walking, talking–and later on dancing–Spring Flowerbed.

As I headed toward the stage, my costume was awarded a few appreciative claps from visitors. Maybe it is not so bad after all to be The Free Barbara, rather than good old Barbie or Bossy Barbs.

Horatio Caesar was looking very fine, I had to admit, nice friend that I am. His grandfather's yellow jacket had been altered to fit him. In fact, I had never seen Owly look so strong. Closer observation revealed a much trimmer body and unprecedented neatness. Yes, he looked very manly indeed.

Anne's yellow cape inherited from her grandmother flowed to the ground in billows of bright silk. This was her first Spring Equinox in the village. What would she make of it all?

Watching Horatio Caesar hover near her, I began to wonder if he felt a connection to her deeper than infatuation. Both of them grew up with formative ties to grandparents, which might have created the most fertile conditions to generate a special bond between them.

Melissa skipped her way toward me with all the grace that I lack. Her black hair was threaded with tiny yellow flowers, dried from last summer's crop, and long yellow ribbons. And she was beaming. And I knew why. There would be dancing later, and any form of dance would do for her. Her anticipation was infectious; we beamed at each other.

Patrick boomed out orders in his paisley vest sporting various shades of yellow. He guarded his creations with all the eagerness of an overstuffed terrier, but lost little time in locating Isabelle, crowned by a delicate wreath of yellow flowers in hues ranging from pale to bold. Yellow-skirted Colleen, who organized the children's performances, was too busy to notice Patrick's distraction.

Samek strolled around with Jeanne on his arm looking quite pleased with himself. Both wore matching yellow poet shirts; his was huge, and hers tiny. Michael's bright yellow sport shoes and yellow cap matched the yellow scarf tied around his neck lending him a spontaneous air, so unlike him.

My relatives had outdone themselves. They had decided that they belonged to us, so they wore their allegiance with blatant enthusiasm. From head to toe, every bit of their clothing was yellow.

I giggled, as my eyes wandered over my businessman uncle, with his yellow sweater, no doubt cashmere, matching yellow shirt, yellow pants, yellow belt, and yellow shoes. Even his socks were yellow. I snickered again.

Uncle Christopher caught me at it. But he chose to be amused. "If my fellow board members could see me now." He chortled with an impish gleam.

Our festivities began by forming a long line of villagers and of a few brave visitors. Our oldest female inhabitant Grandmother Knowles, a spry 99 year-old great-great grandmother, knew the pattern by heart and headed the line.   She led us all in the song in praise of Spring, while skipping and weaving in and around the trees on the green. We bowed to them and to the flowers as we pranced by singing.

Melissa was close behind Grandmother Knowles, proud and happy. Soon more brave souls joined in.

Ahead of me, Anne kept pace with both song and dance. When I peered behind me as we looped around an ancient oak, Michael and Isabelle came into view. They were trying their best to follow, as were an increasing number of visitors.

Our leader, Grandmother Knowles, ended up at the stage, and without any help, danced up the steps to the platform and in clear tones, welcomed us all to the Celebration in Honor of Spring.

This year's Maid of Spring continued with the festivities, a vision of loveliness in a long ivory gown with yellow flowers at her waist and woven in her dark brown hair streaming down in her back.   She carried a basket filled with small yellow sacs, which are prized by visitors and villagers alike. Since I knew the routine, I made a run for it.

With one grand gesture, the Maid of Spring tossed the basket's contents into the crowd. Just as I leaped for a flying yellow sac, someone hit me with full force in the back and I collapsed, just missing my prize.

With my face full of grass, it was hard to see what or who hit me. I heard a gasp and a stammered apology and felt hands, any number of them, helping me up.   At least two sets of male hands lifted me upright. One of them was Mr. Mostly Green Eyes. But he was not the culprit.

I turned around to see a very apologetic Jeanne. I assured her that I was fine. Jeanne had been just as eager to get one of those yellow pouches.

Michael offered to get me something to drink, but I waved him off. I wanted to regain some dignity.

Mary Lisa Maguire, that expert at laughing in a horizontal position, launched herself again, not for a pouch, but over my predicament.   I sighed as her squeals of mirth carried far and wide. My dress now looked much more like a very real spring flowerbed.

As I picked clumps of dirt off of my face, hands and dress, the children's performances began. The youngest children acted out buds peeping out from the ground and spring flowers opening their first petals. Then, the Medieval Melody Merger, our classical ensemble burst forth with springtime melodies.

Michael brought me a glass of fruit punch–it was yellow, of course. Isabelle joined us, and so did Jeanne and Samek. Apologies flowed, as did music, food and good cheer.

The sumptuous luncheon feast would culminate with dancing on the green. While some sat at tables, others spread out blankets.

Patrick's little cakes garnished with yellow icing evoked groans of pleasure. Spying Isabelle, Patrick joined us, offering her a plate of marzipan and meringue flowers with a grand flourish. She laughed and her wreath tilted sideways, a sure sign of pleasure. Colleen stalked toward us looking like a thundercloud, but Patrick sprang up and offered her the plate of sweets as well.

And then the dancing began. In place of Chicken Charlie and his Gang, several local groups played promenades, polkas and line dances. Sitting still was not an option. Even my relatives formed a yellow ball as they danced together. All cares and concerns were shaken out of our bodies. I twirled away, swinging my arms and hopping in step with the beat. Remaining patches of earth on my costume went flying. To my delight, Melissa joined me; I skipped around with gusto, she with lightness, as the yellow ribbons streaming through her long black tresses swirled around her.

I wove in and out and panted my way around the village green, at times encircled by male arms. Samek actually lifted me in the air. Horatio Caesar did not stumble or bumble, a Miracle of Spring. My businessman Uncle was a lot stronger than I guessed; I began spinning like a robust top in his arms.

Patrick grabbed me, while his eyes strayed over my head. The object of his gaze? It was Isabelle dancing away with a nice looking gentleman, a visitor.

What a pattern we were weaving! Horatio Caesar danced with me again, and then Michael pulled me into his arms. I felt like a ping-pong ball, adjusting to one person, then to another. It would have been nice to continue dancing with one partner, instead of switching so often.

Michael asked about Blarna. I pulled us to a stop. How could I have forgotten! My canine friend, confined to the safety of my house, was overdue for some companionship. He offered to come with me, but I waved him away. He was needed at the festivities.

Blarna was so eager to see me that my guilt about leaving her alone quadrupled. So I brushed her, and petted her, and gave her a special treat. She licked my hands and then my face, and I loved her for it.

By the time I returned, the dancing had stopped. All the villagers who had caught a yellow sac formed a tight group. The rest of us gathered behind them. Singing away, they led the way through the village streets, out to a just ploughed field. The rest of us stood at the edge and watched as the villagers fanned out across the upturned earth. Facing the afternoon sun, they lifted their yellow pouches aloft in a final blessing of the spring sun. Then opening each sac, they poured the contents along each row of earth and covered them. The new seeds were now sown.

We clapped, hooted and hugged each other, and then drifted back to the green to begin cleaning up.

Aunt Phoebe bore down on me. "Barbara, what happens to the yellow pouches that the visitors catch?"

"Oh, they take them home."

"Are they that special?"

"They contain seeds from heirloom plants, Aunt Phoebe. They're impossible to find outside our village."

"Anyone can catch them?"

"Why, yes," I replied.   Aunt Phoebe's eyes glinted with a seed of resolve germinating in her heart, no doubt.   Next year, she would be right up near the stage, and who knows, perhaps she, too, would sail through the air to catch her yellow sac.

By dusk, most of the cleanup was completed. The festivities were over.   And Megan was not there. And I missed her.   And Megan said that Michael said. And then Isabelle said that Michael said.   And I knew I had to find out what Michael said meant.

XX. If My Wishful Thinking were like Steam

What is a Spring Equinox Celebration for but to welcome in the Spring, the returning sunlight (hence the yellow theme) and a fresh start! And I was determined, with somewhat mule-like tenacity, to focus on the new beginning.

I was tired of my yearnings for Sean, an old, engrained habit, which I caught myself slipping back into all too often. I was tired of my longing for my parents to be alive again. I was tired of my wishful thinking.

I was even tired of running away from my heritage, and from the knowledge that we had cultivated for generations, about that Energy, that M…Magic.

Where was I to begin, except with the questions? From that "why," or the "what," the truth would emerge, I was sure of it. Blarna barked up at me in agreement. It was time to act. But what to do first?

Blarna sniffed in the air and ran to the door with an excited bark. For the Sunday afternoon after our Spring Equinox Celebration, any knock on my door would be unusual. This was an afternoon for naps. This particular visitor was most unexpected. On my doorstep stood a bashful Horatio Caesar.

His clothes were even finer than those worn to the Equinox Celebration. His shirt was ironed, his jacket looked pristine. His hair was neat. Was this achieved with glue?

Catching my stare, Horatio Caesar flushed a little and explained that he had purchased some new clothes. Horatio Caesar? Buy clothes?

Before he sat down at the kitchen table, he took off his new jacket and hung it over the back of his seat.

"I don't want to wrinkle it," he mumbled.

"Good idea," was all I could think to say.

He drummed his fingers on the table, a sure sign that his thoughts were elsewhere. I made a pot of tea and wondered about getting down the porcelain cups.

But this was Horatio Caesar, and we never drank out of the porcelain cups together. I reached back in the cupboard for the mugs with the fewest chips, my contribution to the occasion.

When I asked him how he had enjoyed yesterday's celebration, he pushed his glasses back up his nose in a familiar gesture. Those thick lenses made his hazel eyes look very large and a bit unnerving. Owly he was, and Owly he would always be.

"It was..." he paused to search for the right word, "special."

"Special? In what way?"

"I, ah, liked the dancing."

"You did?" my eyebrows formed twin peaks. An endearing, life-long klutz enjoys dancing. Revelations never cease.

"What made you like dancing all of a sudden?"

Owly blinked and turned his head away. "Oh, BB, do I have to explain?"

His old nickname was heartwarming, true, but that didn't stop me. I was after the Truth, my springtime vow.

"Did you enjoy dancing, or did you just enjoy dancing with someone in particular?"

His face flushed, but he looked back at me and blinked. "I don't know where to begin."

Never known for my tact, I plunged right in. "Does this have something to do with Anne?"

His hands jerked, but I saved his mug in time. "Yes," he croaked, running his hand through his hair, ruining the glue job.

"She *is* very special," I agreed. Apart from my niggling feelings of being left out of the loop, when she didn't inform me of her job offer to Michael, Anne was quite amazing. "I'm *so* glad she moved here."

Horatio Caesar's face broke out into a smile, not just any smile, but a radiant one. It started with his curved lips that were a lovely shape, I realized all of a sudden. The smile continued with light pouring out of his eyes. So, he wasn't just an infatuated former schoolmate, Horatio Caesar was in love.

"So what do you want me to do?" What had I to offer to an Owly in love?

"Oh, BB, can you teach me to dance better?"

I burst out laughing; I couldn't help it. I'm known for my generous enthusiasm, not my flowing movements. My rather broad shoulders and sturdy feet are not those of a nimble dancer. But how could I refuse my beloved friend and schoolmate? Blarna barked her consent.

So, we pushed furniture aside, started some music and began. Blarna followed us around, yipping at our heels, until I told her to sit and stay. She obeyed me, and watched as we tried to avoid the furniture.

An hour flew by, and we were breathless, but Horatio Caesar no longer bumped into me. We agreed to practice in the evenings after *Charmed Necessities* closed.

Horatio Caesar kept looking at his watch, then exclaimed. He rushed for his jacket and ran out the front door. I forbore to ask him where he was going. Wasn't that nice of me?

This was yet another Sunday that I wouldn't hear from Sean. Megan was with him, and I didn't expect to hear from her either. To break my maudlin mood, I reminded myself of the pattern woven by the birds outside my kitchen window.

The week that followed passed by in a blur; it seemed almost as hectic as the week prior to the Equinox Celebration. I managed to converse with the remaining visitors and finish putting things in order. I even gave my relatives presents to thank them for all their unstinting help.

Isabelle continued to ask Colleen many questions, while I took care of Blarna and *Charmed Necessities*. Colleen loved to inform, so she grew to enjoy Isabelle's frequent visits.

Horatio Caesar got more practice dancing. "Lesson" would be too grand a term to describe our antics. He had a definite sense of rhythm, one that matched the music, much to my surprise. He only bumbled when he got nervous. So gaining confidence was the key to preserving my toes.

By Sunday afternoon, I was more than anxious to talk to Anne in my Pursuit of Truth. I headed over to her house, taking Blarna for her first official walk through the village. Most of the time, she kept up with my pace. When magnificent odors lured her, I reminded her of our destination.

Anne welcomed us both with warmth, and an extra special pat and treat for the smallest one among us. Blarna began another sniffing campaign, and then ended up in heap at my feet under Anne's kitchen table.

Anne looked tired and explained that she had some things on her mind. My cue to begin my Quest for the Truth.

"Before Megan left, she told me that you offered Michael a job." Try as I might, I couldn't keep the edge of hurt out of my voice.

Anne smiled. "She overheard a conversation that was not meant for her."

"Can you tell me, Anne?" The plaintive tone in my voice hovered between us.

"I'm happy to relay my part in this, Barbara," Anne replied. "For the rest you must ask Michael."

I sat up straighter. This lesson in ethics was making me uneasy. "I don't intend to pry, it's just that," I paused to find the right words, "I didn't know how to help Megan, or even if she needs any help." I let out a big sigh. "Everything seems so complicated."

Anne's cheek muscles twitched. "Do you really need to know?"

"But, of course!" Bossy Barbs overcame any inhibitions that the Free Barbara had developed.

So Anne began, and I stayed quiet. "As I got to know Michael, I had a feeling that, if you wish, a gut feeling, that together, we could accomplish many helpful things for others. But this possibility was only validated a short while ago. When Michael took such quick and efficient care of Blarna, I knew for certain that we could make a good team."

Her words made good sense, but something was missing. "Was Michael looking for a job in order to stay on here?"

"That's a question you should ask him."

I persisted. "Do you think he's in love with Megan, and wants to live with her in the village?"

Anne laughed. "Only Michael can answer those questions, Barbara."

A wall, yes, and I deserved it, too, unethical Bossy Barbs that I was. Some more habits of Barbara Blue to let go of.

An unrelated question popped into my head. I blurted it out regardless of the consequences. "Have you ever been in love, Anne?"

Surprise stilled her amusement. "Oh, many times when I was growing up."

"What happened?"

"Grandmother would visit and talk with me. She was wonderful," Anne exclaimed. "She taught me the difference between infatuation, and being in love. I thought that I was in love, oh, so many times, when in fact I was in love with what I thought I saw."

Her words made me squirm a bit. Did I know the difference? I wasn't so sure any more. Sean was, well, he was Sean.

"Have you ever been truly in love?" I just had to ask.

"Once," she murmured.

"What happened?"

"He wanted to explore the world. His purpose, his goals didn't include moving to this village and living here with me."

This was an all too familiar scenario. "Was his name Sean?"

Anne looked up from her reverie and smiled. "It could have been."

"So what's his name? What does he do? This must be recent. What did your grandmother say?" I discarded tact in a heap along with dignity and any form of sensitivity. Bossy Barbs was at it again.

Anne hesitated a moment. "He's a teacher, a very gifted one. Grandmother liked him very much, but she knew and I knew that my future lay in the village. She even hoped that he would change his mind."

"Do you think that he will?" Bossy Barbs puts two big feet in her mouth.

Anne looked beyond me as if she were seeing him, this man she loved. "No, I do not." Her face was composed, calm, the face of acceptance.

What could I say to that? She was certain. If she held even a grain of hope in her heart, she wouldn't be open to another man. Doubt is as far way away from certainty as red is from blue. Horatio Caesar had a steep mountain to climb.

Before I walked out the door, Anne revealed a bit more. "He's devoted to Yoga. He spends many months of the year studying advanced spiritual practices in India."

Blarna and I staggered home under the weight of these revelations. Anne had been, perhaps still was, in love with a man dedicated to studying and learning, a gifted teacher, whose heart lay in another continent, in another way of life. He must be devoted to helping others. Our village would seem tame and insignificant to him. True, there is teaching to be done in our midst, but many places in the world needed expert assistance. We would never qualify.

Knowledge is a powerful thing; it can put things in perspective. Sadness for Anne welled up inside of me. And in the grand scheme of things, Sean's and my broken dreams paled a bit in comparison.

XXI. Falling Armor

For days, I walked around *Charmed Necessities* in a light daze. Sympathy for Anne welled up, unbidden. Colleen thought that I was mourning the loss of Sean and the absence of Megan, and gave me a scold. She ordered me to let go of the past, and seize the present.

Colleen was right. Anne had accepted her situation and had established her new life, spreading cheer. It was my turn to do the same.

Michael continued to work at *Delights in Earthly Haven*. Samek and Jeanne strolled around arm in arm in honeymoon-mode. Michael managed to pop by to check up on Blarna. Colleen hovered, so there was no opportunity to question him about his plans.

Michael invited us both, the humans that is, to Haven's Ale on Saturday night. He looked like he really wanted to invite Blarna, too. And before he left, he thanked me again for recommending Isabelle for managing *Chalice Lore*. When he smiled, I couldn't help but smile back.

When Anne popped by, I asked her whether Michael had accepted her offer of a shared practice. Her response was scribbled on her face.

"All right, all right, I'll ask him." I said, forestalling any remarks about ethics.

Horatio Caesar was part of the equation as well. True, I was giving him practice dancing, but he might need more assistance in his own unspoken quest.

"Have you ever thought of doing some yoga?" I asked him in an off-handed manner during a dance break.

Owly looked blank. "Me? Yoga?"

"Have you read anything about it?"

"Oh, No," his reply was quick and reassuring.

As I continued to gaze at him, he shifted his feet and asked, "Should I?"

"Why not? And why not keep it a surprise!"

At our following dance session, Horatio Caesar informed me that Ronald had dug up all sorts of old books on yoga for him at the library. It had ancient roots, he explained to me with an earnest mien.

Horatio liked the ancient part, and also, that it wasn't Roman. His grandfather's obsession always aroused mixed emotions. If I had been dubbed a name like his, I would have rather fierce anti-Ancient-Rome sentiments, too.

Early Saturday evening, a small but merry group gathered for Haven's Ale. Isabelle, Colleen and Michael awaited us. A sunny Horatio Caesar arrived with Anne, like an Irish Wolfhound dragging his prize toy. His movements were a bit stiff; he mouthed one word in explanation over Anne's head–'Yoga.'

Anne caught my eye and smiled. It was a full smile, with no hidden meanings, no rancor, no bitterness or yearning, only friendship.

Patrick strode in carrying a large platter in one huge hand. Nestled in fresh fruit lay a succulent array of fresh cheeses and homemade pâtés. Patricia and Ronald brought with them a large basket of warm breads from *Butter Fingers*. We embarked with gusto on an unexpected feast with our ale.

I sidled up to Michael and asked in an undertone, "You planned all this, didn't you?" He gave a quick disclaimer and moved away to get dishes for us all.

When Patrick began paying Isabelle a multitude of compliments, she brushed them off like an expert. Even Colleen could tell that Isabelle was not taking any of Patrick's easy phrases to heart. Patrick looked frustrated, as well he should.

Halfway through our eager consumption of the paté and rosemary garlic bread, Samek boomed out a hearty greeting to us all from the pub's entrance.

Jeanne twinkled up at him, and then dropping Samek's arm, began to twirl.   In her spinning, she knocked against the suit of armor. I launched myself to rescue it and arrived one second after Michael. My hand landed on his arm. A jolt of fire ran down my arm. Michael saved the French knight's gear inches from the floor.

No one else seemed to notice. They were busy making certain that Jeanne was all right. The suit of armor was secondary.

"Michael!"   He looked up at me, pale and withdrawn. "Can we talk? Would you have some time tomorrow?"

"Of course," he heaved a sigh and shook himself. This encounter with the suit of armor had *not* been a pleasant experience, either for me, and from his pained demeanor, or for Michael.

The rest of the evening passed without further incident. Colleen took me aside and informed me that she was going to talk to Patrick tomorrow.

What would the morrow be like? I planned to discuss this strange armor experience with Michael, and Colleen wanted to have it out with Patrick. What else would fall down before I learned the Truth?

XXII.   The Marriage of Knowledge and Happiness

My sleep was disturbed by vivid dreams. I wanted to speak to my parents and I felt that they wanted to communicate with me, but there was a soundproof transparent wall between us. I woke up in the darkness of pre-dawn trying to decipher their lip movements.

Blarna stirred in her sleep, and groaned. Was she re-living her accident? When I patted her, she stopped moaning and settled down. I gave up the notion of further sleep and crawled downstairs. I sat at the kitchen table watching the dawn light creep toward me with steaming mug of tea for comfort.

Blarna joined me as soon as the sun was up. She was frisky and ready for food, play, and her toiletries. She led me through the morning's activities making certain that I fulfilled her agenda, while allowing me a few moments for my own grooming.

Even before I heard the knock, Blarna was ecstatic. She barked and jumped at the front door so hard, I was afraid she would hurt herself again. When I opened the door, Michael was laughing. He patted and played with her until she settled down under his touch.

When we sat down at the kitchen table, Blarna insisted on being on his lap. The same treatment that Isabelle received, only Blarna went one step further.

She curled up in his lap and closed her eyes. 'It's safe here,' her little body said.

Michael sat sideways away from the table giving Blarna plenty of room, but facing me, so that we could talk. And he began.

"What did you do last night, Barbara? It felt like a jolt of electricity went down my arm!"

"I didn't *do* anything!" I was quite incensed. "All I wanted was to save that suit of armor from crashing to the floor." I moved a bit in my chair. "My father loved it."

Michael looked at me, hesitated and then grew serious. "Isabelle's and my parents died within weeks of each other two years ago."

"Oh my. I'm *so* sorry. I didn't know." I paused to think of something appropriate to say. "It must have been a tremendous shock for you both," I blurted.

Michael looked down at Blarna, his expression hidden, and began to stroke her. It was a comforting gesture.

I continued, blundering from one inane comment to another. "As you may have heard, my parents died over six years ago." Well, perhaps it wouldn't hurt to explain what had happened.

"It was an accident. They were killed instantly. A beam in the barn fell on them. I was at the library with Ronald. Tom Bates came to get me. He was supposed to meet them later that morning to discuss repairs to the barn. He arrived early for once, and found them."

Michael's hands stilled. Blarna snored away on his lap. "I am glad they were together, Barbara, however, hard it was for you. Our father couldn't accept our mother's death after her short illness. He never recovered."

After a moment's hesitation, I conceded, "You have a point." It would be really hard to watch anyone close suffer like that, and feel so helpless.

Michael broke our silence, with a surprising question.

"Do you ever feel your parents around you?"

"Why yes, sometimes I do." Caught off-guard by his question, I said more than I intended. "I dream about them, as well. Last night we were trying to talk to each other, but I couldn't read their lips."

Michael's mouth twisted in a rueful grimace. "I've had dreams like that, as well. Only we try to communicate with each other by exchanging thoughts."

My face became blank. What did he mean by that?

"I find it easy to communicate with dogs, cats, and other creatures."

"You understand their barks and meows and such?"

Michael shook his head. "No, no it's not that simple. It sounds quite odd, but somehow I can hear their thoughts. "

As my eyebrows rose, he looked rueful.

"I discovered this as a boy. I don't know how it works. I've never understood it, and usually don't discuss it."

"But what a wonderful gift! It must help you to help them." I blurted out, and then blustered, "I mean, that is to say… Ehem. I did *not* mean to imply that you are not a good veterinarian."

Michael laughed. "Praise is always welcome."

It was time to shift topics; Ms. Manners would want me to, even if the hostess policewoman was snoring away on our guest's lap. I was just about to ask him about his plans for staying on in the village and working with Anne, when he brought me back on track, his track.

"Did you send that jolt into my arm?"

I shook my head hard. "Send you a jolt? Never! Wasn't it the other way around? You sent that jolt into *my* arm!"

Michael shook his head with grim vehemence.

I wasn't convinced. "The first time I endured that stabbing fire was when we worked on that bed-frame."

Michael looked skeptical. "Not once prior to that occasion?"

"Not once. Not ever. It was all so very odd. I thought that you must have had your other hand in an electrical outlet. I often puzzled over what happened at the inn and meant to talk to you about it, but there have been so many distractions. And last night, was doubly odd. There is no outlet near that suit of armor!"

"Distractions. Yes. While you were making up your mind whether or not to join Megan's brother in Argentina?"

"How did you know?" That was a stupid question. Disguising emotions has never been a Barbie-trait. Anyway, Megan must have told him all about my encounters with her brother.

I shrugged. "Well, yes, I guess you're right. That was a preoccupation, but now that all that is settled, I want to figure this out."

Michael grinned. "I like that idea." I smiled back. A moment of accord. Not bad.

"So, where do we begin?" I was clueless and didn't mind admitting it.

Michael proceeded to relive the whole experience at *Delights in Earthly Haven* from the beginning to that first jolt. He asked me how I knew what to do. He asked me if I had any idea why the pieces were falling down or flew apart when he left those three rooms. It was like piecing together bits of a puzzle, without having any idea what the final picture looked like.

Michael made a number of interesting observations. One of them was that the staff of the inn *knew* that I could help. Another point was that my knowledge of what to do must have been coming from somewhere.

Michael then proceeded to quiz me about my family and my ancestors. He was searching, he explained, for any special "gifts."

I squirmed, and with tremendous reluctance, talked a little bit about those "gifts." He was due some explanations. I revealed the history of my disbelief, and how that dreaded "M" word had haunted me growing up. And how I used some form of Energy for the first time on Blarna under Anne's supervision.

"So that explains it! Blarna recovered much faster than I thought she would."

My smile was weak. It was hard admitting that I was wrong, and they, my ancestors and my village, were right.

Michael followed his sister's train of thought. "Could it be that you were using some sort of Energy or Special Power or Magic at the inn?

It would make some sort of logical, if irrational, sense (all right, so I *am* a slow learner). At least, it made more sense than anything else we had come up with.

"In that case," Michael continued, "maybe that's why the staff knew you could help. They knew about the Energy you could call upon, if you wanted to."

I groaned. If this were indeed "true," then I felt very, very silly. All those years resisting something that could be useful. For Bossy Barbs, a humbling assessment. For The Keeper of Practical Order, it was shameful. Blarna sniffed in her sleep. She had every reason to. I felt quite idiotic.

"But I still don't understand that jolt when the suit of armor fell over," Michael pursued.

"Perhaps you have access to some sort of Energy, too?" My suggestion was as logical as one plus one equals two. When two people with access to Energy work together, a jolt occurs due to the added power.

It was Michael's turn to squirm. It's rather funny how much we don't like to admit Special Powers into our lives.

However, he had the strength of mind to acquiesce. So far, he showed superior strength of mind to Bossy Barbs.

"You think the jolt is the result of both of us using a similar kind of power at the same time?" He phrased that quite well.

"It sounds plausible."

"But if I were able to use this power myself, why did all those objects fall down or break apart?" Michael pondered.

"Perhaps so that you would become aware of your own ability?"

"And you, too." he countered.

"And me, too." I agreed in all fairness.

As he was leaving, Michael asked me whether I would join him later in the week for a walk after work, in order to conclude our analysis of these strange events.

I agreed, a great idea indeed. I would then be able to pin him down about his future plans. But for now, I was content to figure out if any bits of this puzzle were missing.

XXIII. If Life were Simple

Since her talk with Patrick, Colleen's behavior was edgy. Her red locks shone, but her face was pale. I asked leading questions hoping to draw her out. For three lengthy days, her silence remained heavy and determined.

My patience wore thin.   Using Blarna as enticement, I sat Colleen down at my office desk. Looking down at her from my full height, I scattered my intentions of discretion like the flyers on my office wall and plunged in.

"What *is* the matter, Colleen? You have not been your cheery self. Is there anything I can do?"

She put her face in her hands and muttered something.

"What did you say?"

She dropped her hands, revealing eyes filled with tears.   "Patrick's not certain whether he ever wants to settle down."

"Well, I must say, I am not surprised." Blunt Barbara was at it again.

Deep down, I was quite surprised at Patrick's behavior, having been witness to the most promising beginning of new love. I could think of only one reason why he had a change of heart-Isabelle. But I wasn't going to mention this possibility or her name to Colleen.

"Why not?" she fired back.

Another possibility came to me out of the blue. Whew, a way out of an impasse. "His devotion seems centered on his culinary feats. Look at his cakes and ice sculptures, and everything that he creates that could possibly come with any sizable feast!"

"But he behaved with such devotion to me!" Colleen wailed.

"Oh, yes, he did. In fact, it looked to me like he fell in love with you."

That was not the right answer. Colleen wailed with greater fierceness. I was hopeless at this, I sighed. I tried again.

"But he may not know how to love any woman, Colleen."

She looked up, affronted.

"I mean, that is to say, he may only know how to love food, or the creation of great food."

This was more promising, and Colleen, though skeptical, listened. I scurried further into my argument. It was a good one.

"Patrick is an artist, a true artist. He's more than a chef. Look at the number of former apprentices, who continue to be devoted to him. They come from all over just to be around him. I've always wondered why he didn't leave our village and acquire the fame and fortune his culinary creativity deserves." I was getting off track.

"Some artists have one muse, like Salvador Dali. But others have many, like Pablo Picasso. Patrick may be more like Picasso and require many muses, not just one." I paused, rather pleased with myself for having remembered that particular lesson from school.

"Only time will tell whether Patrick changes his mind. If *he* does not know whether he will ever commit to one person, then how can *we*?" I concluded, using my considerable skill with ice-cold logic.

Colleen's tears dried on her cheeks. "Then I shouldn't give up hope?" Eagerness crept into her voice.

"It may be more realistic to let go of Patrick." I retorted. Blunt Barbara had no shame.

Colleen didn't like my words. But what choice had she? I was only repeating Patrick's terms.

Much later, she surprised me with a hug. "Barbie dear, how right you are! Thank you for being so candid with me. I won't indulge in wishful thinking. At least I'll *try* not to. Your months of misery going back and forth with Sean will serve as my lesson. I will *not* torment myself, like you did."

While glad to see her restored to a state of cheer, I wasn't pleased to serve as a lesson for her. Foolish Bossy Barbs.

But Colleen was not finished with me. So I sucked in my breath and it was my turn to listen. Where, oh where, was Colleen's charm then? She swung a verbal battleaxe aimed straight for me.

"Now, I'll be blunt with you, Barbie. Even if Sean had agreed to live here, there's someone else here in the village. He suits you far better than Sean ever did. And I'll not say his name because you have to find out yourself, with your own heart!"

I froze and could think only one thought: 'He's already taken.' Horatio Caesar was the only person, who fit Colleen's description, and Anne was the object of his devotion. In the last months, he had lost much of his extra girth, and even changed his appearance with new clothing and new glasses. And with his secret practice of yoga postures, even in such a short time, he had become even more fit and much more attractive, and much less like my would-be brother.

Tom Bates had cleaned up his act as well. And the last time we met, he was friendly and even, gasp, nice to me. He also looked trim and very fit, or maybe I just hadn't paid attention before. Did Colleen mean Tom? We certainly shared interests, or rather The Keeper of Practical Order had.

Tom had a twinkle about him, not like Sean's easy charm, but he could spin a good yarn, and was quite entertaining when he wanted to be. In fact, he could be quite fun. Hmm. Something to consider.

By the time Michael came by for our walk, I had thawed a bit. My romantic future was as elusive as the scent of fresh rain on a sunny day. Colleen was wrong;

she had to be. Horatio Caesar showed no indication of shifting his affections from Anne to me. Tom hadn't popped by to say hi. All I cared about was solving a mystery or two. This was the only logical thing to do.

Blarna led the way as eager as any hound. Michael and I walked up the street and into the woods. She nipped at our heels whenever we paused to think. No delays for her, she wanted new sniffing grounds.

Michael cleared his throat and began. "We are missing part of the puzzle."

I stopped dead in my tracks. This was what I had concluded as well, but I had no idea what that missing part could be, and told him so.

Michael resumed. "First of all, how did the staff at the inn know you had this special power?"

"Perhaps knowing my family and my heritage, they assumed that I could access it, if I tried." This was a bit lame, but the best I could do.

"But is that power genetic?" Michael was persistent. I could just imagine him taking care of a hurt animal with the same dogmatic tenacity. I was getting off track again.

"I'm not certain. But I remember hearing tales about how some kind of ability is passed down through the female line. You must ask Anne. She would know. Speaking of which, what are your…?"

He interrupted me without apology. "That may explain why that strange jolt, that power, ran through my arm. Although I never knew her, Samek and I had the same grandmother. Her family came from the village. "

Michael was right. An inherited ability of some kind would explain why we both felt that power surging through our arms. We could stop our analysis here. Lurking in the fringes of my mind was a vague impression that the puzzle, in some mysterious way, was still incomplete.

He picked up on my thought, or had I picked up on his? "I am still not convinced we have the full answer." He stopped us both. And for once, Blarna stopped nipping at us.

"Nor am I."

The eyes that looked down into mine were pure green in the forest light. Mr. Green Eyes, now. "The jolt that ran through us both only occurred twice." He looked at me for corroboration. I nodded.

"When I touch your arm," he put his hand on my arm, "it doesn't occur." Strictly speaking, this was true. There was no jolt. I nodded.

"When we dance," he put his arm around me as if to dance, "it does not happen." No jolt, that was true. I nodded, a little breathless.

"Then why did it happen at *Delights in Earthly Haven*?" He dropped his arms and turned away.

"You're right," I replied, recovering from a twinge of feeling bereft. "Both jolts occurred at the inn. I wonder why?"

When he started walking again, I followed pace. An odd fancy passed through my mind. Michael, it seemed, was as logical and down-to-earth as I was. What if we escaped logic altogether?

"Maybe it has to do with working together? Which reminds me, I heard..."

He interrupted again. "You are right! We were both working, were we not? How clever of you!" I preened, dolt that I am. "I wonder what all this means? I have to admit that talking about a phenomenon called 'whatever,' Energy for example, is not what I'm used to."

I nodded in sympathy; nor am I, nor am I.

Horatio Caesar was waiting at the house for his dance practice. Michael nodded and promised not to tell anyone. There was an alert—or was it an amused—look on his face.

Before leaving, Michael invited us both to join him and his sister for dinner on Saturday night. Horatio Caesar agreed with unusual eagerness.

My suspicions were aroused after Michael left.

"What's so special about this Saturday?" Bossy Barbs returned yet again.

"It's Anne's birthday." Horatio beamed.

"Oh! Will she be at the dinner?"

"Michael and Isabelle invited her to dinner to celebrate her birthday."   Horatio Caesar puffed up with pleasure.

"Anne told you that?"

Horatio Caesar reverted to Owly in an instant. "I asked her out for dinner and she explained that she had a prior commitment."

No wonder his eagerness.

When we tried a glide, glide, step, step together, Horatio didn't step on my toes, trip or stumble.   He held me with a firm arm, and danced with confidence, not the limp and tepid gestures I was used to.   He seemed less like my would-be brother at that moment than at any other time in over twenty-five years of friendship, assuming infants create instant bonds.

I sighed.   Life was getting complicated again, just when I thought it was getting simple.

XXIV. Curiosity to Forget

Isabelle was a boon. For all her chic and delicate airs, she took over Megan's duties with aplomb and discreet efficiency. When I checked up on the Sullivan house, I found it cleaner than it had looked in years. Even the garden was tended, and the vegetable plot showed abundant signs of fresh plantings.

We were to gather at the Sullivan home for dinner. I had been uneasy about being in this oh-so-familiar house for a party without a Sullivan present. But no memories lurked in the shadows to haunt me. The Sullivan spirit was in hiding.

The house was shining and tidy, the generous chaos of the Sullivan household had been put away. Isabelle used candles and cloth to create a new atmosphere. We felt welcomed and warmed by the golden glow and the crisp linens.

By the time Anne and her escort Patrick knocked on the front door, Horatio Caesar, Jeanne, Samek and I had concealed our tokens of birthday joy in the adjacent room, as well as ourselves. The curtain hiding me was a little dusty from years of use, but with considerable effort I suppressed a sneeze.

When Isabelle escorted Anne into the room, we jumped out yelling, "Happy Birthday!" Anne laughed and laughed, amazed by us all. It felt so very good to surprise her.

Dinner was delicious; no corners cut on any front. Isabelle disclaimed, but she earned every bit of the praise we showered on her. Patrick, who was already taken with her, was swooning as only a big hulk of a man in a bright red vest can. It was as if he had found a fellow artist, someone who spoke the same language, but with fresh vocabulary. The rest of us were a bit dazed as they bantered back forth about reductions and coulis and the precise timing of adding the tomato in order to form the perfect consommé.

With the ease of an experienced hostess, Isabelle brought the attention back to Anne. Samek began to talk of Anne's grandmother. Horatio Caesar sat as still as an Owl, whose entire persona was focused on Anne. At first annoyed, I shrugged and then laughed. Our individual and collective futures were just too mysterious to predict.

Michael continued to remove plates, bring dishes and serve wine with practiced ease. And I continued to vacillate between Barbara, the refined appreciator, and Barbie, who was a bit too gung-ho with her guffaw and her gestures. So here we were, a merry bunch, four of us born and bred in the village matched by four living in the village by circumstance, of whom three were women.

That evening left a glow that lingered through the night and into the next morning when Blarna woke me up with a warm and wet face lick. Her legs had healed so well that she had managed to get onto the bed without waking me, and was peering down at me with eyes that said, "Wake-up, dummy, it is so beautiful outside, let's go!"

When Michael arrived in the afternoon to unravel our puzzle further, he observed my hovering glow, but said nothing and took his tea mug and cookie and sat down with his back to the sinking sun that filtered through the kitchen window. I couldn't resist asking a personal question.

"Where did you learn to be such a consummate waiter? I mean host?" I tried to cover up my social blunder with a saucy smile.

Michael's face went blank; this was not a topic on his agenda. "Well, ehem, the parents of a classmate own a hotel in the Swiss Alps. They felt that I was a good influence on their son, so they invited me back for several summers. I got very bored just hanging around, so with great reluctance, they agreed to permit me to learn about hotel management including how to wait tables."

His smile was rueful. "The head waiter, who trained me, was quite a stickler for correct behavior."

"Ah, the taming influence of mentors," I murmured, gulping down hot tea, and then regretting it.

Michael got me back on track. "Have you had any further ideas about the jolts?"

"Have you?" I countered. If we were going to play the information game, then I would play tough. On two occasions, he had brushed aside my questions. I was not about to be generous.

"I doubt it."

His answer did not convince me. He had some sort of idea or additional information, but wanted me to say something first. So I did, giving it my best volley. "On another note Michael, are you planning to stay on in the village?"

I got him all right, but he was a good player, indeed, an excellent one. "Would you like me to?"

I stumbled and groped for my shot back. "You make a nice addition to our village life." I gulped too much tea, and regretted, again.

"Thank you." His answer was stiff, but he rallied. "Why do you ask?"

"Well, I heard that Anne offered you the opportunity to share a practice with her."

"That's confidential! How did you find out?" He sounded quite miffed.

I had to be honest. "Megan mentioned Anne's offer before she left."

"How did she know?" Michael looked puzzled and upset.

An honest volley back was all I could manage. "She, ah, overheard your conversation with Anne."

Michael's hands clenched. "So that's why Megan thought of offering Isabelle the partnership in her store."

I paled. After all, it was my suggestion to Megan that got Isabelle her current job.

"But Michael, Isabelle is so very capable." My open-handed gesture matched my placating words.

Michael's countenance was stiff and unconvinced. He thought for a moment and then asked me a most unwelcome question. "Is Isabelle's skill the *only* reason Megan offered her the partnership?"

I blushed a full, apple red, for the first time in the many months since viewing the video of The Full Summer Moon Party at the library. The sensation was unpleasant, a slow heat that burned up my neck and covered my cheeks.

It was impossible to meet his eyes. I cleared my throat and croaked out "mainly."

Michael shot up from his seat, spilling warm tea left and right. "She told you more?" He was close to shouting.

It was time for the most profound soothing.

I touched his sleeve. "Megan has been my neighbor and friend all my life. When I helped her pack, she mentioned some of her personal wishes."

Michael looked down at my hand on his sleeve and used his other hand to run fingers through his thick hair. Not satisfied with his gesture, he pulled away and ran both sets of fingers through his hair. He turned so I couldn't see his face. He was wordless, his shoulders tight. I could only wait, helpless.

Half turning, he muttered, "Sorry. I need to go for a long walk. Alone."

Blarna and I, each in our own way, were bereft. And Miss-Know-It-All-Barbs was mystified.

The door slammed in my face. Maybe, just maybe, being so curious was not always such a good thing.

My pained reflections included what was in all likelihood Michael's point of view. It dawned on me that my curiosity, though in keeping with one of my unofficial roles in the village, might be too invasive and prying, and therefore inappropriate for such a recent inhabitant, let alone for someone that Megan knew much better than I did.

Perhaps he felt a blow to his pride that he hadn't asked Megan to marry him before she left, and I knew about his deficiency. I replayed our conversation in my mind until I knew it by heart.

One thing was for certain. This Barbara was chastened. No more volleys for me. I was *not* going to ask him about his future plans. Ever. My curiosity could just go hide out in a dark closet for a few weeks until Megan returned.

Such was my lingering dismay that I was uncertain whether Michael would show up for our mid-week walk. But there he was, efficient and competent, patting Blarna and looking as if nothing unusual had occurred between us. I was relived, yet cautious. Blunt Barbara went into hiding.

We talked only about matters pertaining to those strange jolts. Not one word about the future, his, mine or anyone else's, left my mouth.

Michael had done his homework, however, and had queried Anne about these Unusual Powers, as Michael preferred to call them. According to Anne, these special abilities did indeed run in families. Inhabitants of the village had cultivated all forms of these Special Abilities with such heroic flair that anyone with even distant kinship to the village would have some sort of ability for unexpected manifestations of these Unusual Powers.

For Michael, a very relevant example was how such a small staff at *Delights in Earthly Haven* could accomplish so much when the need arose.

Another form of these Unusual Powers, he explained, was the ability to make accurate predictions.

"Yes," I chimed in eager to make amends. "Megan has always had some ability with that. She can see ahead, if she wants to."

Michael stiffened. More amends to make.

"But she can't see anything for herself or about any of her own concerns."

Michael unbent and I sighed.

Talking with him was like walking among nests of fresh eggs. The Chastened Barbara was going to have to be oh-so careful where she stepped.

Michael concluded. "A similar ability may have enabled the staff to identify you as the best person to make those unusual repairs."

I nodded. If they had the ability to keep the inn clean and tended when all the rooms were occupied, then they could pinpoint the person to make those repairs.

I began to think out loud, a habit usually reserved for former classmates like Horatio Caesar or members of non-human species.

"It was so odd. It was almost as if the broken pieces were telling me what they needed. Maybe that is it! The pieces *did* tell me what to do and I just followed their instructions." What did I just say? Bits of furniture and a painting talking to me? Crazy Barbara was more like it!

To my consternation, there was no reprimand or scornful repartee.

Instead, Michael stopped and turned toward me. "Yes, a bit like animals 'tell me,' what they need. And so the bed frame must have conveyed to you that it needed us both for such a major repair."

When he said it, it didn't sound quite so outlandish.

He thought a bit as I began to relax. "And the suit of armor, as well. One of us alone might not have saved it from crashing."

"Oh, Michael, it all makes sense now! Those jolts helped to reinforce the fact that we were both needed to help repair or save those precious objects."

We had completed the puzzle. All the pieces fit well together. Michael was pleased, I was pleased, and Blarna was pleased by the scents around the old maple tree.

XXV.   Puzzle-Solver

I looked down at my hands, palms open to my gaze. Their square shape and blunt fingertips were the same. But they looked gentler than in the prime of Bossy Barbs. Furthermore, I had to admit, they looked a tad more feminine. Some familiar calluses had softened.

This realization sent goose bumps down my arms. I was overcome with a sense of considerable foreboding; just around the corner was something that I didn't want to see.

I closed my eyes and repeated out loud: "I'm an adult. I'm strong, even though I don't wield my hammer as often as I used to. I have adopted a dog." My brave words acted liked a talisman and the foreboding evaporated.

In spite of becoming a chastened information-gatherer, I was more flexible and generous in my manner of living, as proven by Blarna's ongoing presence in my daily life.

In return, Blarna couldn't have been more expressive of her gratitude, or more insistent that I remain somewhere in her vicinity. With persistence, she trained me to suit her needs. In fact, it would be more appropriate to state that Blarna had adopted me, and not vice versa.

After solving The Puzzle of the Jolts, my sense of self-worth inflated like a giant red balloon. True, I was chastened. But I now managed to hold my curiosity in abeyance, and pause for a few seconds before rushing in with a question.

Michael's information about those Unusual Powers, which I had heard about and ignored in my childhood, seeped through my mind in waves of increasing acceptance. In my own manifestation, some sort of something, an Energy, had poured out of my hands. Afterwards, Blarna's recovery was faster than expected.

I also used my hands to make those repairs. True, I hadn't come up with the right method of repair, but some place inside of me had "heard" the correct methods that my hands then fulfilled. If I had any sort of natural ability for some kind of Unusual Power, it manifested through my hands. I still had no clear idea what it was, or how to produce it on demand.

The now thirteen-going-on-seventeen year-old Melissa interrupted my reverie. I was sitting in my garden surrounded by untouched tools, when she called to me from the garden gate. I waved for her to come join me, and moved implements aside to make space for her.

Her dress was devoid of a single wrinkle and her shoes were immaculate. So, she looked with some misgiving at the grass, which was alive with small bugs. However, she didn't want to disappoint me, so she folded her legs and sank down on to the turf in one fluid movement. I was in awe. Even the Free Barbara couldn't match that ease of motion.

After chatting about her class and homework, Melissa looked at me with a curious expression. It made me rather nervous, but I was clueless.

"Sean really liked you." Melissa began.

I was dumfounded. I had witnessed Melissa's first steps, her first day at school, and the first time she won the Hapless Hatless Potato Race. And here she was, speaking to me like a fellow adult about a man I had yearned for. My state of shock was palpable. Another first?

"How did you know?" I could only utter the same boring question that is used, no doubt, in conversations of this nature in every language around the world.

"He told me."

"Oh, he did?" Brilliant Barbara, just brilliant.

"And Horatio Caesar liked you, too."

"What?!" Who was the adult around here? And who prided herself on being informed?

Melissa's cheeks acquired a rather becoming shade of pink. "He never said anything to me, like Sean did. But I watched him, and he liked you a lot."

My eyebrows formed two inverted v-shapes with a deep frown line separating them.

"He looked at you when you were busy, you know, in that special way."

Since I didn't have eyes in the back of my head, I could be excused, perhaps, for not even noticing. But I felt foolish and forlorn. What had I missed out on? Regrets filled every awkward corner of my mind.

"But he likes Anne, now." I blurted, all discretion scattered to one side like my gardening tools.

Melissa put her hand on my arm, and said in the manner of an adult consoling a child over a lost toy, " I know."

Well, since we were having such an adult conversation, albeit with our roles reversed, it was the time to lay down all my cards for her to see.

"Melissa, none of this is working out like I thought it would. Sean didn't like me enough to move back here. Or rather, it would have been so unfair of me to insist that he give up something he loved so much."

Melissa's eyes widened, like she hadn't considered the unfairness issue.

"Horatio was always like a brother to me." I paused, and then honesty overruled discretion. "He's much more appealing now, but he's not available."

Melissa nodded with a glum expression that matched my own.

"And Tom Bates, he looks more appealing too, but he prefers to argue with me."

I brushed the grass with my fingers and thought about what remained unspoken: no hope for Barbara. I sniffed and shifted my weight. Time to be positive about something, anything.

Then it came to me what to say, something I had never told her. A touch of sweetness lay hidden underneath my dismay. A heart-to-heart talk with Melissa held the promise of much more to share with her.

Looking into her eyes, the shade of rich, hot cocoa, the kind that warmed the body and the heart on a winter's day, I went straight toward that sweetness. "If I could have a sister, Melissa, it would be you."

There, I said it, and received a bundle of undignified Melissa energy around my neck. It was a nice kind of acquiescence. Very nice, indeed.

When Melissa left, I decided that the garden could wait. I wanted to start something unusual. I went upstairs to the New Projects Room and sat down with some fresh paper to create something novel, or different. My source of inspiration followed me with gentle clicks of nails on wood floors–Blarna. I began to draw something I had never even considered before.

When I began to build the doghouse that I had designed for Blarna replete with a turret, she watched with one ear cocked. She gave up trying to distract me into a game of fetch, curling up instead on a pile of wood shavings. Horatio Caesar helped to hold parts together while I hammered and screwed.

During the ensuing dance practice, he gathered up courage for more audacious moves such as twirling. In earlier dance sessions, my words about making smaller steps sank in. After all, large steps are much harder to follow than small ones. Owly had had a definite tendency to lunge.

Now he twirled with precision, even grace. I was having a hard time adjusting to the New Horatio Caesar, who was resembling less and less my would-be brother. The doghouse was a good distraction from attraction.

Isabelle made repeated visits, although I didn't have a clue why. She had the shop and house under better control than any Sullivan ever had as far as I could remember. She would pop by with a homemade creation and ask me how I liked it. What could I do but be honest and drool? Blarna joined me in that endeavor.

I showed her the doghouse in its various stages. Her suggestion to show Blarna different paint colors was an inspiration. Why not let Blarna choose her own colors? Even if a dog can't see colors as humans do, maybe she could feel an energy or vibration, preferring one shade over another. Let Blarna paw at the color samples she liked best!

Michael no longer came by for walks; his absence troubled me. The reason was obvious. I was still very much aware that I had overstepped his boundaries and wanted to make certain that no further amends were necessary.

Isabelle warned me that Michael was hard at work at *Delights in Earthly Haven*. Jeanne enlightened us further when she popped by just as Isabelle was handing me some custard tarts topped with fresh fruit. I insisted that they both stay. We could all have some tea and enjoy the fruits of Isabelle's labor.

She smiled at my pun. Some people are so kind.

So there we were, the Chic Isabelle, the Petite and Country-Bred Jeanne, and the Transformed Barbara, to whom Magic was inching ever closer to becoming a tolerable word. We devoured Isabelle's creations together.

"Michael seems to be very preoccupied," Isabelle observed.

Jeanne threw up her hands and laughed. "Mais, oui! He is making a special effort. You must know, Michael agreed to redesign our system for reservations. Samek desires to make it easier for me to make the bookings."

"So you will be taking over soon?" My manner was as casual as I could manage.

"It will take some time for Michael to make the changes," Jeanne demurred. "He's working very hard. He's devoting all his free time on this project." She hesitated, and then added, "He knows that the system needs to be finished very fast."

Our mystified expressions spurred Jeanne on. "I must learn how to make the bookings with the new system as soon as possible because," she paused. Isabelle's eyes were speculative, and mine were blank. "Because," she continued in a rush, "I am, we are..." she blushed "Our baby will be born soon."

With quickness of mind, Isabelle congratulated her, and I followed with much more awkward phrases.

While Isabelle gushed, I considered the implications. The explanation for Michael's absence alleviated my concern. He had an urgent reason for not popping by to see us. Underneath my relief was a rather strange feeling, one that was very hard to put in to words. Perhaps the closest description was that life, with all its complexities, was passing me by.

XXVI. One Haven Too Many

Blarna cheered me up with her antics. She was relentless in her pursuit of any game, tempting me to play with her from the moment I opened a bleary eye until I collapsed in bed in the evening. She pranced around me, tail wagging, dark eyes glowing.

Resist her? The Free Barbara could not. Besides, with Spring all sorts of wonderful new fragrances and colors were emerging, and all the deciduous trees were clothed in shades of green again. And Megan, my best friend, would return soon. It was all very reassuring.

After a busy day at *Charmed Necessities*, I planted seedlings in the vegetable plot. Blarna learned to participate; she pawed at the ground creating holes for the baby plants. We had a slight disagreement about where she was to dig, but I won out. A few dog treats still warm from the oven helped convince her that I was right. She pawed where I pointed.

Blarna kept me from brooding about the inequities of life. And Colleen kept her vow as best she could, only flinching a little when Patrick stopped by next door one afternoon and not by us. She hovered about me, making mysterious phrases about "opportunities."

I was at a standstill. Horatio Caesar's devotion to Anne showed no sign of abeyance. While practicing his dancing skills, he continued to mention odd facts about yoga. His arms and shoulders were now firm and strong under my touch, a result, he explained, of "Down Dog."

Blarna tilted her head at his words, and then with some reluctance, sank down to the ground. Horatio Caesar grinned when I pointed out Blarna's response; in terms of the yoga posture, she had it wrong. As her caregiver, I was quite pleased with her performance.

Isabelle kept popping by with fresh morsels of food that were so irresistible that my self-pity was forced to lift. She also dropped into my half-listening ears morsels of information, such as Michael leaving our village for a few days.

"He needed some assistance with the new booking system?" I was still thinking about those firm muscles under my grip.

"Michael didn't say," Isabelle complained, pouting. "He doesn't tell me much these days."

How does one respond to such a plaintive comment? I chose silence, after reviewing all the responses I could have made such as, 'Maybe he is too preoccupied by Megan's absence and is just counting the days until she gets back,' or 'He must be spending all of his spare time devising the very best way to propose to her.' They were all too risky, so I just bit my lips in frustration and swallowed hard.

I couldn't resist one question, however. "Isabelle, have you seen much of Patrick since your magnificent dinner for Anne?"

She looked up with narrowed eyes. Then she smiled just a tiny bit, like Mona Lisa. "He came by the store one afternoon."

Right, Colleen tried to hide her dismay about that from me. But only one visit? I would have guessed many.

"I think that," she paused for dramatic effect, leaning forward a bit, "he was a tiny bit impressed by my cooking for that dinner."

"We all were, Isabelle," I exclaimed. "You could open your own restaurant if you wished. Your cooking is first-rate."

Isabelle's face reflected the very essence of disbelief. "But I never studied at a cooking school."

"Then you have a tremendous natural talent. You must know that." She shrugged and shifted the topic to inquire about Anne.

That conversation proved to have an effect. I popped by to see Anne on the next non-dancing evening. She gave me a spontaneous and very warm hug, and thanked me again for being part of her birthday party. She then reverted to her usual calm, which was rather comforting to one whose inner spirit was in inexplicable turmoil.

"I'm sorry that I haven't been in touch since then," I blurted out, "but I have been a bit, ah, confused."

Anne led me to her kitchen table and we began an unforgettable conversation, one that I will remember even when I am an old woman. When she asked me for particulars, it was hard not to sniffle.

"I feel as if life is passing me by!" I moaned.

"Why is that?" Anne looked quite puzzled.

I relayed much of what had been on my mind, leaving out, of course, all mention of Horatio Caesar, yoga and burgeoning muscles, let alone dancing lessons.

Anne smiled at Colleen's mysterious statements and at Jeanne's news. And then, looking into my eyes with kindness and concern, she grew serious and spoke with hesitancy, as if feeling her way between of the shoals of the Overly Sensitive Barbara.

"From what you told me, you made some major changes in the recent months. In some ways, one might say that you started a new pattern in your life."

That was acceptable, but it got me nowhere.

Anne persevered. "So, you are in the beginning stages, with many discoveries lying ahead of you."

I remained skeptical while she went over all the changes I had made in my life, to the store, to the house, to putting down my hammer, to adopting Blarna.

Overall, she had a point. I made more changes in my life in the last six months than in the previous six years.

"Also," Anne hesitated. "You underwent a big shock."

I looked up, startled.

"Forgive me, but you never had the opportunity to say good-bye to your parents. So it was only natural to go through a substantial period of adjustment."

Anne spoke with such gentleness; I was touched by her concern for my prolonged bereavement.

"It sounds as if you've finished with that process and are now ready to continue with the next phase of your life."

Not bad, something to look forward to.

"Do you have any idea what will happen next?" I couldn't resist asking.

"After Megan returns, many things will become clear, I hope." Anne replied in a reflective tone.

Colleen's repeated admonition to let go of the past acquired an urgency that I could no longer deny. Talking with Anne helped clarify what I already knew, that I was ready to get on with My New Life.

So, I had better be prepared. Bossy Barbs and Barbara were determined to unite with Barbie, Barbara Blue, and BB and address the situation with a familiar tool–a pair of blunt-tipped and square hands.

The mix of emotions about my past was like a mushy ball. Feelings were all jumbled up: my grief over the death of my parents, my yearning that my mother would have been less regal, less remote, and my father more practical, not delegating quite so much to me, my regret about my stubborn resistance to that long dreaded M word, and my shame that to Bossy Barbs, The Most Practical of her Lineage, her childhood dreams of Sean could have ever seemed realistic. What was I to do with this heavy, watery sphere that weighed my heart down?

My hands knew the answer even though my mind did not. Somehow, I wasn't sure how, I would offer this tangled ball to my favorite tree. Not the wishing tree on the village green, where for decades, people from all over would come and tie a ribbon on a branch when they made a wish. No, I would go to the old, wizened oak tree on the edge of our forest. No one knew its exact age; its roots ran down into our mythic past.

I knelt by its trunk and felt for this mushy ball around my heart, hoping that no one would see me. I scanned the field behind me. I was alone with the tree and this thing inside of me.

I cupped my hands over my heart and blew out that ball of old emotions as I exhaled, feeling the weight of all those feelings transfer from my heart to my palms. My hands guided me to I lay the heavy ball, invisible to all but me and the oak tree, down between two thick roots. I thanked the ball for what all those conflicting emotions had taught me, about myself, about my life, about others. I was no doubt a nicer person because of them. Then I asked the tree, in its wisdom, to transform these old emotions into energies that could benefit the tree and all that lived.

My hands then touched the trunk; it was done. I thanked the tree for its wisdom and left with a lighter step. This Barbara was truly Free.

More than ever, I was eager for Megan's return. I had little more than a week to wait. My spirits soared, clarity was in sight.

The morning of her return was bright with sunrays filtered by soft thin clouds, so like the layered and wispy clothing that she liked to wear.

To our communal joy, Megan arrived on schedule. My first thought was how different she looked. Her soft, white skin had acquired a light tan. Instead of draping wispy clothes around her body, she wore a tailored skirt and jacket. She looked, well, successful.

We all clamored around her, and some of her new sophistication melted away when she hugged us with her familiar warmth.

We were not about to let Megan out of our sight. The many weeks had been long, much too long.

When Isabelle took Megan on a tour of *Chalice Lore*, we followed them both around like the ardent fan club we were. Megan gave her whole-hearted approval to Isabelle's management. We all beamed.

When we followed them both to the Sullivan home, Megan exclaimed in amazement. The garden boasted a multitude of neat rows of seedlings, and displayed the results of much attention and hard work. The house was immaculate, even the windows gleamed in the morning sun. Megan was just delighted and said so. We all beamed again.

Isabelle's luggage sat on the floor by the front door. She apologized that her brother had not yet been able to come over to pick the bags up. In front of us all, Megan hugged Isabelle and asked her to stay on. After all, there was plenty of room for them both in the large house. Isabelle hesitated.

"You must stay on, Isabelle," Megan insisted. "I'm counting on you to become my partner in *Chalice Lore.*"

Isabelle demurred, while Megan tried to persuade her. We looked on, hopeful that Isabelle would agree.

The impasse seemed insurmountable when, to our relief, Michael arrived. His welcome to Megan was the same as his farewell, efficient and effective. When Megan opened the door to his knocking, Michael smiled and kissed her on both cheeks. Megan's face shone.

When the situation was explained to him, his whole demeanor changed. Instead of clarifying the situation, his presence made our little gathering choppy and uncertain. Megan glowed while Michael's back went rigid. Isabelle became even more hesitant about what to do.

Michael took the situation in hand and asked to speak to Megan alone. Megan flushed under her tan and led the way into the farthest room of the house, while the rest of us gathered around Isabelle and pretended not to be interested in what was going on behind closed doors.

We did not have to wait more than fifteen minutes. Michael pushed past an ashen Megan, picked up the luggage and asked Isabelle in a curt voice to follow him.

Startled by these unexpected events, we remained frozen in place, like dolls in a toy house.

Megan was so distraught that we thawed enough to gather around her. She sobbed onto Colleen's shoulder, while the rest of us petted and stroked her as best we could.

If only my hands would emit that power, that special energy, and I could somehow help soothe Megan. They remained square and powerless.

When her sobs quieted, she told us between short breaths what had happened. Michael had insisted that Megan's offer to Isabelle be without any strings attached. When Megan asked what he meant by strings, he replied–it appeared with reluctance–that the offer to Isabelle must be made independent of him. Whether he chose to stay on in the village or not, should have no bearing on Megan's offer to Isabelle.

When Megan asked what his plans were, he said that he didn't know. When she suggested a shared future in the village together, he grew silent.

Then he made it clear: even if he did decide to stay on in the village, he would not be involved with Megan, let alone consider a future together. When she begged him to tell her why not, he replied that he liked her very much as a friend, but that was all.

We were shocked. Better yet, I was stunned. Wordless. Airless. Bamboozled. This just could *not* be true. All the evidence over the past months pointed to the contrary. Michael had always seemed so pleased to be in Megan's company. They were always doing things together. I recalled Michael's special smile when he looked at Megan, the way he gravitated toward her at every public event.

Megan tore off her jacket, mumbling that she was going to get some sleep since Isabelle was still in charge of *Chalice Lore*. I promised to bring her some dinner later and we all left worried. The happy outcome that we had planned to witness hadn't occurred. Instead, distress and unease reigned.

None of us could act or think with any clarity. I closed *Charmed Necessities*, hanging a sign of apology on the front door. Colleen went to *Butter Fingers*, her favorite place of solace, and I went back to my house and, with Blarna's assistance, continued the springtime planting.

At any other time, Blarna's antics would have amused me. But when I didn't throw the sticks that she brought to me, or scratch her ears when she begged me to, she plopped down on the ground and just looked at me. The earth warmed by the sun was inviting, so I plopped down as well and tried to clear my head.

After going over all the evidence of the past months and the events of this distressing morning, I decided that there could only be three options to explain Michael's behavior toward Megan.

The first possibility was that Michael felt that Megan should only make an offer to Isabelle, that his sister deserved nothing less. And any other offer with "strings" would be demeaning of his sister's abilities. Isabelle's skills deserved the highest praise.

The second option made particular sense in light of the Michael I had gotten to know during the past six weeks. His nature was independent. He disliked any hint that Megan could see his future, or their future. He may have felt that he was being 'forced' into a choice; even if that very choice matched his desires, his nature would rebel against it.

I had to consider the third option. Michael could have special feelings for someone who was not in the village. Although he never mentioned anyone, he seemed quite private. He left the village for some days in the middle of revamping the inn's booking system. He may have discussed with "her" the possibility of moving with him to live to the village, should he accept Anne's offer.

While taking dinner over to Megan's house, I decided to tell her about these three alternatives. She would have caught up on sleep. She would hear me out and feel better, I hoped.

I found the Sullivan household in familiar turmoil. Stuff was strewn everywhere and dismay gripped my stomach like a heavy lead pipe. This amount of chaos created in eight hours did not bode well for a Megan in a stronger frame of mind. I shoved my tray of warm food onto an overloaded table and went in search of my childhood friend.

Restless and feverish, she moved about her room, darting from her closet to the battered chest of drawers. Ashen before, she was now a mottled red. Her sleeves were rolled up.

When I told her about the food, she didn't hear me. I shook her shoulders and asked her what was going on; her dinner was waiting and she needed to eat.

"But I have so much to do," she wailed, allowing me nevertheless, to drag her downstairs to her food.

Once she settled down and had taken a few bites, I began to relay my insights about Michael. Before I finished expounding on my three theories, she shoved aside her tray, leaving most of the food scattered on her plate. Megan cut me off.

"Mother and Father called this afternoon."

A rare event and very bad timing, in my opinion. Now, they would be worried about Megan.

"They heard me out, they listened." Tears formed in Megan's eyes. I reached out to touch her, I couldn't help it. Her distress was so hard to see.

She grabbed my hand and spoke in a thick voice. "We came to a decision, a big decision. I know you won't like it, but it's the best choice."

She paused and watched my expression change to alarm.

"Barbie, I am leaving." Megan said, as if that explained it all.

"Leaving? But you just returned!"

"I'm moving, moving away to share house with Sean."

"What?!!" I was more than aghast.

"Everything you said about Michael sounds right. I thought about those possibilities, too. But there's still only one outcome. He said that he won't even date me." Megan caught her breath, her face bleak.

"There is no going around that. He won't change his mind, not in the near future, for sure. I know that much about him," she concluded with some bitterness.

"But move away? Megan, this is your home!" I wailed this time. Did I say I was strong?

"Not any more." It was Megan's turn to shake me. "Look, Mother and Father were quite right. We considered all the options. They don't want to live here again; they prefer to wander around, they like that freedom. They also know that Sean will never come back here to live. When they heard that I don't want to live alone any more, they made a suggestion. It made sense to me. Why not sell *Chalice Lore* and the house and move away to share a home with Sean? When I was with him, I found out that I enjoyed being in the real world."

Those last words cut like a knife. "But this is just as real, Megan. You know it! Think about how we all accept and practice some form of Special Power. It's real, in fact it's more real than anything else."

"Coming from you, Barbara Mahoney, that's quite a statement."

I bit my lip. "You're right, Megan. All these years, you've been right, and I've been wrong. Very wrong. I was just scared and didn't want to face something that I couldn't put a nail into."

Megan took a deep breath and looked at me, then past me as if she were seeing something. She smiled a little and then said, "Your parents are very pleased, Barbie, they are saying 'Welcome, Home.'"

My eyes got damp. Megan had never given me 'a message' from them before. This was a momentous first, but the timing was lousy. Megan was my oldest and best friend. The Sullivans were family.

Megan took my hand. "Barbie, you know what it feels like to be alone. In some ways, you are luckier than most. As an only child, you grew up being used to spending a lot of time by yourself." I nodded, trying to calm my groaning innards.

"I grew up with a beloved brother, who will never come back here to live, and parents who feel the same way. It's always hard to compare, but I've felt lonely, maybe lonelier than you. This house is too big, it's meant for a large family."

But the Sullivans are family, *my* family, my mind screamed.

"What a selfish friend I have been to you, Megan!" I had never even considered that she might be that lonely. Blind Barbara, indeed.

"Barbie, listen. You've always been so close to me. But you had your own responsibilities to take care of. I've yearned for a partner to share my life with and share this old house. And the only man I want," her voice caught, "doesn't want me."

How could I not empathize? I wanted her brother to share my life for some of the same reasons.

"And Barbie, when I saw Sean in his new home, I realized just how happy he is with his new life. You were right, by the way; he would never be as happy in the village, even with you. You're both too different. You want dissimilar things in life."

This was such a change of heart that I couldn't think of a single argument to counter it with.

She hugged me, and stood up. "It's all settled. I'm leaving in the morning. You must visit me, Barbie. And don't think otherwise, I'll be visiting you too."

I stared at her. "But what about this house? And *Chalice Lore*?"

Megan smiled down at me as if to a toddler. "We're selling the house and store to Isabelle. We agreed on all the details this afternoon. My parents will have a nice retirement fund to draw on wherever they want to travel, and I will have enough funds for a new life with Sean nearby."

And with that the changes to my life were irrevocable.

XXVII.   The Hammer in My Head

Megan managed to leave the next morning after signing papers about the house and *Chalice Lore*. Isabelle was going to pack and ship all Megan's belongings to her.

In anyone else's hands, I would have said, "Impossible!" But recent weeks had convinced me that Isabelle could accomplish huge tasks and make them appear effortless. Move over Bossy Barbs; make way for Isabelle In Charge.

Megan, bless her, gave me the clock that I had always admired. A Sullivan ancestor in love with all things Swiss had carved it by hand. In addition to the cuckoo that jumped out on the hour, the clock was embellished with a leaping cow set in front of a backdrop of carved and painted mountain ranges dotted with tiny villages and even tinier people.

In return, I promised to stay in touch on a regular basis, and keep her informed about village affairs.

Michael did not show up to say good-bye. Instead, Isabelle handed Megan a letter from her brother for her to read after her departure. Megan paled and stuffed it into her bag.

In her farewells, Megan clung to each of us, and we to her. I still could not grasp that this was her final gesture, that Megan, my lifelong friend, was leaving the village for good, her good. Her last words whispered into my ear as she clung to me were, "I think your third option is the correct one."

Grief hung in the air like a silver cloud, shiny and wet. My head was pounding. Colleen took over *Charmed Necessities* and Blarna's care, and shoved me out the door, telling me in no uncertain terms that I was to take the rest of the day off. I was too scattered to be of much use anyway. She gave me an impulsive hug, and the cloud lifted for a moment.

I walked around for a while, uncertain what to do with myself. Go to the library and sit in those warmed seats and pretend to read a book on Gaelic?

I started walking up the street, passing by *Butter Fingers*. Hot chocolate sounded very comforting, but I did not want to speak to just anyone, not even Patricia. Bereft of my lifelong friend and neighbor, I couldn't think of any chatter that mattered. It was better to keep on walking.

As I stood in front of the library, that odd conglomeration of structures each from a different part of two centuries, I glanced down the street. Tom Bates was striding toward me in his patchy work clothes. It was too late to run up the front stairs and pretend that I hadn't seen him.

"Heard about all the goings on," Tom muttered as he drew up beside me. "It's not right. It's just not right. We need some peace and quiet around here!" This, from the man who always argues with me about construction.

"Well, there are bound to be changes in the village from time to time," was all I could think of in reply.

Tom looked at me with derision, and I deserved it. "Thought you had more spunk in you, Barbie!"

I shuddered. Other people had much more spunk. But this was not something I wanted to discuss with anyone.

In a tart voice, I replied, "Well, I left my hammer at home today, Tom."

"Why then, Barbie, what's gotten into you?" His eyes narrowed. "I heard about Megan leaving and selling out." With more kindness than I ever credited him for, he said, putting a huge and oddly comforting arm across my broad shoulders, "I know you'll miss her, and am sorry for it, and for her choices."

I leaned against him; his large chest was comforting. "Maybe she didn't have a choice, maybe she's just following her destiny." I had to defend Megan, even though I agreed with Tom.

He snorted, "Destiny? My foot! Destiny isn't set in stone." He paused and added for my benefit, "Destiny is like a metal tape measure, you can bend it!"

He gave me a final, comforting hug, and I was left to ponder his words as my feet walked me toward the garden gate of Anne's house.

Wearing a thick apron, Anne welcomed me in, and seeing my expression, hugged me with special warmth. Her kitchen was in disarray; she was in the middle of preparing batches of herbal remedies. I offered to help out. She handed me a knife and bundles of herbs, some of which came from greenhouses in the village. She showed me how to cut the leaves off the stems. A mortar and pestle stood waiting for the dried herbs to be ground up.

Anne had several pots simmering on the stove, and as we talked, added measured quantities of specific herbs to each pot. Heady scents of lavender, rosemary and sage filled the kitchen, as well as comfort and a sense of timelessness. With modern equipment, we were doing what our female ancestors had done for hundreds of years–brewing healing substances. This was a new activity for me, but in some undefined manner, it felt reassuring.

Anne only knew about Megan's return. While we worked, I described the events of the last twenty-four hours. I expounded on my theories concerning Michael's inexplicable attitude toward Megan. I concluded with Megan's opinion that the third option, concerning Michael's involvement with someone outside the village, was the correct one. Anne nodded, stirred, and asked a question or two when I lost my thread.

"I just can't fathom that Megan has left us," I muttered.   "Our village without Megan, without a Sullivan. It's unthinkable!"

Anne's smile hovered in her round face and her blue eyes twinkled just a bit.   I was not amused. "Barbara, you explained to me once that people leave the village when they need to, just as they move here for the same reason.   I am just one example: I only moved here about nine months ago."

She had a way of throwing my words back out and into my face that was quite disconcerting. And her memory was too good for my liking.

Anne grew more serious, as befitted the occasion. "From what you say, it seems as if Megan had lost her will to stay on in the village. Her parents and Sean had left her with a huge responsibility.   It must not have been easy for her to maintain the house and *Chalice Lore* in their absence."

"Isabelle seems to manage quite well."   My voice was bitter with disappointment. I didn't mention that I had managed quite well myself with the house and store that I inherited.   The comparison was not fair. The Sullivan house was much larger and I grew up with more practical, every-day skills than Megan, and besides, Colleen shared the burden of *Charmed Necessities* with me.

"Isabelle seems quite capable of asking for help when she needs it." Anne sounded amused.

Well, Isabelle had not requested my assistance. She only asked me about those Special Powers, and I had had very little to say.

Anne continued.   "With her cooking skills, many will want to help her out."

Isabelle had brought me many samples of her culinary skills and asked for nothing in return. Curious. Maybe I had nothing to offer her.

I shook myself, my lamentable habit of getting sidetracked. I like pursuing my own line of inquiry too much.

"But Michael might have changed his mind about Megan after Isabelle worked for a while as Megan's partner."

"I agree," Anne said all too quickly for my peace of mind.   "But it sounds as if Megan was convinced that he would never change his mind."

"But she's running away!   She should have stayed and convinced him otherwise."

"That's what you would do, I'm sure," Anne chuckled.

I was incensed. This was not a laughing matter.

"Yes, but Megan loves Michael!" I insisted.

Anne continued as if I had not uttered a word. "Since I arrived here, Barbara, you welcomed me and explained about village life and people's stories. From what you told me, Megan didn't choose to ally herself with our village heritage in one fundamental way: Megan didn't develop the talent, the second sight that she was born with. She used it, but only when it suited her."

I nodded, but without a glimmer of dawning comprehension.   Barbara-in-the-Dark-Once-Again.

Anne's blue eyes grew darker and sharper. "You resisted the existence of Special Powers and your own abilities, Barbara, but, and please correct me if I'm wrong, this seemed to be more out of a need to test them on your own, and to discover whether or not they contained any validity, without being told by others what to think, or do."

What a nice way of putting it.   Much better than saying I was a stubborn dunce.

"However, one might say that Megan was almost lazy in her approach to her own gift.   In fact, she didn't seem that interested in it.   She took it for granted, and thereby ignored its potential."

Counterarguments rose to my lips and evaporated as Anne's words sunk in. They made more sense the longer they rattled around in my head. Megan always argued for the existence of Special Powers, but she never developed her enviable natural talent for them.   When I looked beneath the surface of both of our lives, the true state of affairs was quite at odds with outer appearances.

Megan dressed and acted as if Energy or Magic filled her life and being, from the ethereal clothing, to her manner, to her occupation. But she didn't believe in it with her whole being, or she would have developed her own ability and put it to use for the benefit of all. Even the so-called Unusual Power of her Kissing Bough, the object that she crafted while growing up, was fine for others, but she didn't use it herself.   She fell in love with Michael and was persuaded that he was her life-partner, without a single encounter with him beneath it.

We were an odd pair of friends, Megan and I. Perhaps she argued for Magic for all those years, just because I was so against it.

"Since I met you, Barbara, you've never doubted that you belong here, even when you refused to acknowledge your own Special Power or the legacy of our ancestors, and even when the temptation to move away to join Sean was so enticing."

Again, I could only nod. Sean was the ultimate carrot for the Mule-Headed-Barbie.

"You said that this village felt like home to you, even when the unusual abilities that all villagers are born with, didn't appear real to you."

Home, yes, my ancestors' home was my home.

"Furthermore, the situation that you described about the Sullivan Family appeared to be fraught with difficulties. Megan's heart never seemed to be engaged in her work."

"She was always daydreaming rather than helping out visitors, or cleaning *Chalice Lore*," I added.

"Perhaps she preferred to daydream about her brother living here again, and if not, then about finding a substitute for Sean, a partner. What a dilemma! Megan yearned to be with her brother. In turn, Sean didn't feel that he belonged here with us, even though he tried to reconsider his position with you in mind."

Anne added one final point. "It seemed like he cared for you, but another part of him is by nature restless. He may never need a home like you want, you crave." I agreed one hundred and one percent (the one was for good luck).

It was my turn to add, "And you helped me realize that being part of the village makes me feel free,

free to express who I am." And that freedom felt so good.

For my entire life, I've been accepted in the village as a non-believer. I could be myself, even when my father's interest in history bordered on obsession. While I respected his interest, he respected my disinterest. I ignored our history and the myths that surround the origins of our village. I yawned through those classes in school. I still would. But in light of that strange power that runs through my hands in recent times of need, I give those myths a bit more credence than I did before.

Only one topic remained to be discussed. "Is Michael going to stay on now that Isabelle will be living and working here?" I tried to sound casual, but couldn't quite manage it.

Anne laughed. My ruse was unsuccessful. All she said was to ask him.

I left her house in a much more cheerful frame of mind. The wet cloud had lifted, and peace embraced me with a warm, fuzzy sensation. Anne's own Special Power. The herbal remedies and common sense were only a small part of her contribution. If Horatio Caesar won her, he would be a lucky man indeed.

I had no idea what the future held for Horatio Caesar, Anne, Tom Bates or me. Colleen and Patrick might end up together after all, as might Horatio Caesar and Anne, or I and Tom Bates. Maybe a fondness for arguing over tools was as good a basis as any for a shared future, or a big and comforting chest and underlying kindness. I may just choose not to share my future with anyone in particular, and surround myself instead with my friends and the events in the village. Anything is possible.

XXVIII.   When My Destiny was Bent

Jeanne waved to me from across the street. I crossed in quick strides to greet her. Her look of concern cleared up after she greeted me. She explained that she'd been worried about me and had sent Michael to check up on me.

How fortuitous! I would never ask Michael about his future point-blank, of course; I was the Discreet Barbara now, where he was concerned. But Michael might mention something about his plans in passing. That was enough. I would not ask for more.

"You should listen to him, Barbara. You should. Michael is a fine man, with a good heart."

My face betrayed my bemusement.

"Ah, Barbara, you have been through so much. I will not say more. Just please; take a moment to listen to him. I, but yes, Samek and I both, we wish you so much happiness."

Her enigmatic phrases were perplexing. Here was Jeanne, a relative newcomer in our midst, who was growing a new life in her body, and had much to preoccupy her. Yet, she showed concern for a Barbara whom she met for the first time only about seven weeks ago. I was touched.

My next encounter was just as unexpected. School was still in session, but there was Melissa, looking downcast and, by her standards, bedraggled. Was she feeling unwell?

Stomping her feet on the stone sidewalk, Melissa informed me with mottled checks that she was never going back to school, ever. Not even if they added a dance class.

Memories surged up of a much younger Barbie, with similar emotions, just as dire, just as intense, but without the guts to tell either parent. All I did was to hide out in the barn for much of the day. I was lured back home by hunger and the faint fragrance of my favorite meal, which somehow made its way to the barn through an open kitchen window.

Using my new status as an older sister, I picked humor as a strategic response. Soon Melissa was laughing at the young Barbie's antics to avoid school–all of them unsuccessful.

Then I distracted her with a very adult conversation, by giving her the details of Megan's departure. Melissa's eyes grew round and even darker than their habitual hue, turning from hot cocoa with steamed milk into pure dark chocolate, as she forgot her woes with school. She plied me with so many questions that she soon knew just as much as I did.

Megan's desertion of our village did the trick. Melissa shot me a speculative glance, and then promised me that she would turn around and go back to school. My good deed for the day was complete. I could be on my way.

So where was Michael? Isabelle had hung a sign on the front door of *Chalice Lore*, her shop now–I must remember that–stating that it would re-open tomorrow. I assumed that she had begun packing up Megan's belongings. And Michael must be helping her.

When I arrived at the no-longer-Sullivan house, Isabelle was organizing objects by size and degree of fragility. She stopped what she was doing and welcomed me. Then she motioned to her helpers how to pack the larger objects. One of the helpers turned out to be Patrick. Her whispered reason explained his presence. She had promised to give him her family's much-coveted recipe for mousse au chocolat.

Clever Isabelle!   Patrick brought all his assistants in anticipation. She had an abundance of helping hands. Megan would receive her belongings much sooner than anticipated. And Anne was right; Isabelle could get any help she needed. No one could resist her cooking.

Isabelle explained that Michael was looking for me, just as Jeanne had requested him to. First, he had stopped by *Charmed Necessities*, but Colleen was uncertain of my whereabouts. His next stop was to look in with his sister in her new home. He left a message with Isabelle that if I did turn up, he would be at my house checking on Blarna. I rushed off, leaving Isabelle with a smile lurking on her lovely face.

The front door was ajar, and as I hurried inside toward the scuffling noises, I found Michael and Blarna playing with each other in the very room that Horatio Caesar practiced his dance steps with me. With a nod and wag, they acknowledged my presence, and continued their game. So I went to the kitchen to make tea.

Michael interrupted me with Blarna yapping at his heels. He informed Blarna in a stern voice that she was to guard the house, and dragged me outside and up toward the path we had wandered before.

He walked with such speed that I had a hard time keeping his pace. He was determined and distant. I was bemused and breathless.

As we neared the trees, Jimmy Delane stood at the edge of the field with arms outstretched and began to warble. All sorts of birds flew over our heads straight toward him. Jimmy didn't even glance at us; we were not birds.

Michael grinned and nudged me in the ribs. He had a point; it was a pretty funny sight.

Once in the woods and a safe distance from Jimmy and his flock, Michael whirled me around to look at him. I couldn't tell whether he was angry or defiant.   His intense green-eyed gaze killed any lingering questions churning in my mind. He spoke.

"There was another reason for those jolts we both felt." His eyes bored into me. "Can you guess what it was?"

I was mesmerized and could only utter, "Well, uh, no. I thought we had solved the Puzzle of the Jolts. Did I miss something?"

Michael's hands flew up in despair. "Yes, you did! This was the reason."

He pulled me to him, pressed me against his chest and then kissed me hard. The kiss softened as his lips stayed on mine. The wild jolt, springing up from nowhere, went through my entire being and the current began to flow as I felt it reverberate in him. We became one closed circuit.

When we parted for air, he was looking as dazed as I felt. We held each other for support, catching our breath as our hearts pounded in our ears. We both saw it in each other's eyes–awe for the power that we had just felt. Without exchanging a word, I knew that we had both felt it with equal intensity. There was no going back.

In that moment, everything became clear; the rightness, the irrevocable nature of shared feelings.

"I'm planning to stay on here, in the village, Barbara, if you'll have me." Michael looked into my eyes, and elaborated. "Have me, that is, for life."

As he paused, I let his delicious words sink in.

"Will you marry me, Barbara? Will you marry me and create a life here together?"

My reply was to the point, "Finally, you asked!"

He grinned as he slid a ring on my finger, the one he had gone to the city to search for over a week ago, he explained. It took him several days to find what he wanted.

His absence from the village was clarified, but I had been wrong about his mission. Isabelle had helped him by observing my hands close-up and guessing the ring-size. There had been a secret purpose to her frequent visits to the house, after all.

The ring glistened, but I only glanced at it. Michael, and only Michael, Mr. Mostly Green Eyes, who became Mr. Green Eyes in the forest light, had my complete attention.

We belonged to each other. This was a truth that shivered through my body and his with such intensity that we could only embrace each other.

We staggered from the enormity of it all, and then laughing, walked arm-in-arm the longest way back toward the house. Words came, insights about past events filtered through our togetherness, and true understanding was born.

Michael's words of love were as fervent as the jolts we had just experienced.

And when did all this happen?

I acknowledged that the signs were all there from the very beginning when I first looked into his mostly green eyes. My revolt against every Special Power forced me to deny any attraction that I felt toward him.

He smiled, his expression rueful. My subsequent actions and words convinced him that the attraction we had both felt was a figment of his imagination. After all, I made it very clear to one and all that I was in love with Sean.

I hung my head; I'd been in love with a dream. The reality behind the dream didn't involve Sean at all, but rather the man I was holding snug against me. This Mr. Mostly Green Eyes.

Did his sister know? Isabelle guessed shortly after Michael's and my first encounter at the Full Summer Moon Party. But even before she took over the management of *Chalice Lore* in Megan's absence, she had heard all about Sean, so had thought that her brother's situation was hopeless.

And Megan? Michael squirmed a bit. He still felt awkward about her assumptions. He assured me, that he felt only friendship for Megan. In a strange way, spending time with her was a means to get to know me better. She spoke a great deal about me.

He was careful never to give Megan any real cause to think that he cared for her. No, he had never tried to kiss her, except on her cheek. Megan wanted a reason to stay on in the village; he was just convenient, that was all.

He had asked for my help at *Delights in Earthly Haven* against his better judgment. He was trying to stay away from me. But those events shook him, even more than they shook me. After witnessing those repairs, he felt that in some way that we were kindred spirits.

How right he was! I had denied it all, while clinging to the illusion that Sean and I could share a life together. My final dismissal of Sean gave Michael renewed hopes, and even more so, my adoption of Blarna.

Blarna? Yes, Blarna played a very real role in bringing us together.

Michael was impressed by my healing ability; he hugged me harder as he spoke of it. He was also impressed by all my transformations, from my house, my dress–he eyed me–to my adoption of a dog. It took courage, and he admired that. Even more so, he admired the opening of my heart, when I invited Blarna to share my life.

But even with all those changes, he still hadn't understood those jolts. Our talks helped to clarify them, and just as I had concluded, he thought that we had found their cause and full meaning.

Anne's offer to share a healing practice with him was a marvelous opportunity, and he could imagine, if I were willing, that I could help with the healing of some of the injured animals. Working together made sense, on a very literal level. He found it hard to resist giving Anne an immediate and resounding "Yes!"

Had Anne known about his feelings toward me? He was quite certain that she did, but she never spoke about them, or about me. She had been discreet, a true friend in every sense of the word.

Colleen guessed, but reassured him that she would not interfere. She was convinced that I had to make the discovery of our rightness together with my own heart.

Horatio Caesar and Patrick, as well as Tom Bates, were absorbed in their own worlds and never noticed, as far as Michael could tell.

Jeanne, newcomer though she was, guessed his feelings and wanted to help his cause. He was a bit daunted by her offer of support. With considerable reluctance, she promised discretion. She succeeded in keeping her promise. Her phrases to me earlier that day (or was it a lifetime ago?) were perfect enigmas.

Michael was upset about having to tell Megan what he did, but he saw no other solution. The letter he wrote for her to read after her departure explained all of his feelings for me from the very beginning, including his fateful encounter with me under Megan's Kissing Bough. He hoped that over time, she would understand.

The final explanation for those jolts came to him when we were talking after Isabelle's birthday party for Anne. It just dawned on him.

He would have acted then and there, but felt that Megan had to return so that he could clarify Isabelle's position, since Isabelle loved her work and wanted to stay on in the village. He had to make it all clear, for his sake, for Megan's sake, for Isabelle's and mine. That was the main reason he stayed away from me those final weeks.

He groaned: "Dislike" was too kind a word for his feelings about database management, but he volunteered to redo the booking system in order to keep his mind off of me. He had to stay away since the urge to tell me the whole truth was overwhelming.

As we walked back to my house, his hug developed into a lingering kiss, right in the middle of the street.

My overwhelming curiosity was understood now. I had a very personal, if unacknowledged, reason for wanting Michael to stay on in the village. I had always noticed him. I had done so from the very beginning. I had cared too much about what he thought and whom he looked at, or paid attention to.

But I was afraid that I had no choice in the matter, that the event of the Kissing Bough was fated.

And I wanted to choose my own destiny. My first, somewhat childish choice of wanting to be with Sean had to do with old dreams and old habits, but also with running away from Michael, just as I had run away from my own gift all my life, or indeed the presence of Energy or Special Powers.

My parents played a crucial role. I can see that now. For all my mother's aloofness and my father's abstraction, they never forced their opinions on me. If they had, I would have run away from home. The recent visions I had of them helped me accept Special Powers into my life.

On some elemental level, I forgave them for their untimely death, and for leaving me with such heavy responsibilities. I have to admit that I have a knack for running things. Even without Colleen's help, I would have managed. Since their death, I discovered more abilities than I ever thought I had.

I liked the respectable mantle that our village presented to visitors. I had no need to know about, or practice, what lay underneath it. But I'm no longer rebellious of that heritage; it serves a useful purpose, and we can either recognize it and use it in some way, or let it dwindle.

I was born with my feet on the ground; I like the practical, the down to earth. No theory for me! But thanks to these extraordinary months of changes that I chose to make, I can appreciate the unseen, the intuitive, and the mysteries a bit better. My hammer is still my close friend, and my hands will always be my carrier of any special talents.

For this year's Full Summer Moon Party, I allowed Tom Bates full reign with the platform for the festivities. Tom was delighted. And I was fully occupied helping Michael convert two rooms in Anne's house for his practice. My hammer found abundant usage in that project.

What transformations one year can bring! Along with my lingering sadness at the loss of Megan's company, indeed of all the Sullivans, new friendships have opened up new ways of living.

In the year since I first met her, Anne seems much more relaxed. She laughs a lot more. Horatio Caesar looks taller, much fitter, more focused. He's quite good-looking now. But underneath his new appearance and manner, he's still the ever-endearing Owly. Perhaps Patrick has changed the least. He still pursues Colleen and flirts with Isabelle, or is it the other way around?

This year's Full Summer Moon Party shared a few similarities with the previous one, but with some twists. Michael gathered me up at *Charmed Necessities* and we raced together over to the green. Horatio Caesar saved two seats next to his in the fourth row, so we could slip onto them, just as the opening speeches began. We listened to Bessy Macintosh's poem of welcome, having been too busy to hear her rehearse. When she spoke of the beauty of changes, I glinted at Michael, who answered with a grin.

After the Hapless Hatless Potato Race, in which Melissa was now too old to participate, we sauntered over to Uncle Christopher and Aunt Phoebe.

"Are you ready?" Uncle Christopher barked.

"Ah, yes. I guess I am." I answered in my most demure manner.

He led me to an area under a large oak limb. Aunt Phoebe led Michael. Horatio Caesar and Anne followed, as well as Melissa, Isabelle, Patrick and Colleen. Jeanne, who was quite large now, was already there with Samek. When I saw the crowd of friends, I nearly balked. This was more than I had bargained for.

In a high-handed manner, Michael pulled me to him before I could protest and kissed me in front of all those pairs of eyes. Our friends applauded, a few hooted, and I blushed as deep a shade of crimson as my mother's dress.

Michael pointed upwards, and sure enough, there was the Kissing Bough dangling over our heads. Megan left it behind for it to be used in village events, the very same one under which Michael and I had had our fateful encounter last summer.

Michael grinned broadly. "You see? It worked!"

I glowered. He was just too proud of himself. But he was right. Whatever Unusual Power it possessed from Megan's lineage, it *had* worked.

Michael and I are to be married in October, on a special date, the anniversary of our first jolt at the *Delights in Earthly Haven*. That Unusual Power feels like Magic, whatever it is.

In a few quiet moments as our wedding approaches, I ponder the choices that I've made in this last year. Would I have remained happy in our village, denying my own abilities and our heritage? I'm convinced that I would have, but I would have missed out on so many dimensions to our life, to our community.

With some help from the Kissing Bough, Michael and I were brought together by the power that runs through my hands. I will always be grateful for it and for all who helped me; Megan, Anne, Colleen, Horatio Caesar, Jeanne, Samek, Isabelle, Tom Bates, Melissa, Aunt Phoebe and Uncle Christopher and beloved Blarna, who is looking up at me, as I write these final words, with glorious brown eyes encircling small dabs of gold. She approves. She jumps up and gives one yelp and puts her front paws on my left knee, wagging her tail. Or maybe she knows the finish is near and I will attend to her.

So this is how I found my freedom. With the man I love from the depth of my soul, and who loves me with keen awareness. The man I will share my life with. In our house, in our village.

Interview with Anne Barclay Morgan, author of *Bending Destiny*

Interviewer: What inspired you to write this book?

A: I began writing a funny short story to entertain myself that lengthened into a novel as the characters introduced themselves to me as I was writing, and told me what they wanted to hear and say and do. The writing process was very spontaneous. When I started writing, I didn't know the outcome. I didn't even know whether the story would take place only in a single village.

Interviewer: Where did the idea for the village originate?

A: I became intrigued with the Isle of Avalon of Arthurian legends, and wondered how such a mythic place could present itself in today's world. So I imagined an unusual community that chose a way to co-exist with our contemporary society. Visiting places such as Sedona, Arizona, made the concept of a village with curious energies even more plausible.

Interviewer: Where in particular is this village located?

A: The village was purposely not named because it could be anywhere. It's for all of us to imagine that we could find that village, or that we could create it anywhere we want, at the very least in our own imagination. Due to the climate, the seasons and weather patterns, and the fact that the novel was written in a North American style of English, it is probably a village somewhere there. It's really up to the reader's imagination to locate this village.

Interviewer: What is this concept of 'energy' that is called by different names in the book?
A: Energy work, as it is now known, is not magic. However, to those who aren't familiar with it, it may appear magical. A prime example in use today for both humans and animals is acupuncture, which is finding increasing popularity in Western cultures. Barbara's energy work on Blarna could be defined as 'extraction,' a technique used by shamanic healers in many parts of the world today.

Interviewer: The psychic abilities, the Special Powers, seem to be passed along in families. Can you comment on this?
A: Often people with various forms of psychic ability will mention that their parent or grandparent had a similar, but not the same, ability. An intuitive knowing that many people have, like a hunch about what to say or do, a gut feeling, is a version of that ability.

Interviewer: Do you identify with the main character Barbara since she is the one telling the story, or with one of the other characters?
A: They're all people that I've never met. They have their own likes and dislikes, their own personalities, quirks and traits, their own life paths. In writing the story, I was getting to know them, just as the reader is, when reading the story.

Interviewer: But one character shares the same name as you, even spells it with an "e," why is that?
A: Someone pointed out to me that people with the name Ann or Anne are often healers. In the community of shamanic healers, of which I am a member, it is the most common name. Otherwise, I'm dark-haired and dark-eyed and slender, while Anne Beauchamps is blond, blue-eyed and has a broad

frame. She loves the color beige, the minimalist style, has few possessions and is also gifted in herbal healing. I admire minimalism, but do not live that way, and have not studied how to heal with herbs.

Interviewer: Tell us about Barbara since you're writing in her voice.
A: I have wonderful friends named Barbara. However, Barbara Mahoney is a person I've never met. Yet, I discovered to my delight through writing in her voice that I could empathize with some of the dilemmas that she was going through, and how profoundly difficult it was for her to make the choices that she did in *Bending Destiny*. Ultimately though, the choices she made, led to a much deeper and greater happiness than she would have experienced with different choices, otherwise.

Interviewer: Tell us more about Barbara's personality, and why she's so interesting.
A: Like many of us, Barbara's personality is full of contradictions. She's bossy and a busybody and overly inquisitive, but with the very best intentions. She's convinced that she can organize better than others: she wants the very best for her village. She also wants to find out 'information,' not so much for her own gain, but rather for the benefit of her beloved village. During the unfolding of the story she realizes that her inquisitiveness is not always appropriate, and she tries to rein it in.
She resists change, and yet change was forced upon her when her parents died.   What makes her more interesting to me is that she is not stubborn. When the opportunity arose for her to grow in new and unexpected ways, such as discover an innate ability for energy work, she was willing to try it out.
She's very observant, such as noticing the details of eye color, and yet, she is clueless about herself, her own emotional depths, and also clueless about the feelings of those around her toward her. Being oblivious to her own possibilities and her own future makes Barbara a bit more human, since this is something many of us

can identify with. Aren't we all to some degree blind about our own lives, and what's right in front of us?

In addition, Barbara has a very profound desire to determine her own way of thinking, to make her own choices and not blindly accept the teachings and the histories that she grew up with. Yet as her story unfolds, she grows in quite extraordinary ways within the span of one year. One could argue that she grew up.

Interviewer: How are you the same and how are you different from Barbara?

A: Apart from being female...Let me put it this way: I have an intense admiration for people, who are really good at practical problem solving because I'm not. I've had to learn little bits here and there. I much prefer to live in my mind and my creative imagination rather than deal with the nitty-gritty of everyday life. I admire Barbara's ability to do that. I also admire her ability to take on a store that she's inherited from her mother, realize that it needs to be improved, and then renovate. On another note, I'm an avid traveler in contrast to Barbara.

Interviewer: In many ways, the story focuses on personal growth. Can you comment on this?

A: Many of the characters choose to grow in unexpected ways. Ironically, the family with the easiest circumstances, the Sullivans, grows the least. Professional success and paths in life all seem quite effortless to Sean and Megan, and indeed their parents. Sean sails through life on his charm and talents for dealing with people and skill with languages. Megan never embraces her innate psychic abilities. She wafts. Overall, no effort is put into things. And perhaps because they didn't grow in profound ways, they couldn't stay in the village, they had to leave.

In contrast to Sean, Michael really works at his life: he's paid attention. He learns how to wait tables, instead of just having a good time on vacation. He studies to become a veterinarian, and understands the responsibility of that profession on a deeper level.

Interviewer: You describe different forms of romantic partnership. What creates a true partnership?

A: Barbara tries to figure out an answer that is right for her. Is it in her long-held dreams of a life with Sean? What they share is the past having been next-door neighbors until Sean leaves for studies when Barbara turns 14. The familiarity of a language and the way of life with mutual friends and references seem to be the perfect basis for a partnership. But is it? Barbara has to figure this out. Only at the end of the story does she realize that true partnership is about the present, and about how two people with different histories can have so much more in common than would first appear to be the case. For Barbara, wood speaks to her. For Michael, animals speak to him, and together these 'gifts' or innate talents are enhanced. Together their gifts are stronger, and isn't that the very definition of a true partnership?

Interviewer: You wrote the novel, set it aside and then after a number of years came back to it. What caused you to set it aside?

A: I allowed the story told in *Bending Destiny* to evolve over time. When I completed the manuscript, it sat for eight years as I thought about it, and life took me other directions.

One of the things that happened is that my husband and I had the great fortune to have a puppy enter our lives. She was not even a glimmer in her mother's eye when I completed the novel, and all the dog scenes had already been written. We had no idea that we would even be getting a dog. After eight years, I re-read the passages containing Blarna and realized, "Oh my goodness, that's just like our beloved dog!" I created a reality by envisioning it to begin with, and that is quite amazing to me. It was as if I was writing about a personal future that then manifested. Contrary to Blarna, however, our own dog is a white, very tall, stubborn, and much loved standard poodle named Amma.

Interviewer: And why are there no ninjas in the book?

A: (Laughing) My husband Brent jokingly told me that I needed to add a ninja in the book to make it more interesting and marketable. Yet this novel had its own trajectory and ninjas just didn't seem to pop up anywhere.

Interviewer: Tell us a little more about the title of the book and where it came from, what it implies, what it means.

A: *Bending Destiny* is based on the idea that we may have a certain life pattern that is pre-determined for us by our parents, our genes, our environment, such as where we grew up and what kind of education we have, our physical attributes, and our likes and dislikes, but at the same time we are not bound by them. The character Tom Bates, an important member of Barbara's community, explains at the end of the novel that there are ways we can "bend" our destiny.

Interviewer: Is there a message in your novel that you want readers to grasp?

A: The messages in the story are ones for the reader to discover. One question to ponder, though, is how much free will do we have?

Similarly, what is important in considering the choices that we make, and how fundamental are those choices to our lives?

Another underlying question is to consider what creates community. And what creates a sense of belonging and why is that so important? And how do you create it in your own life?

Interviewer: Tell us more about what you mean about this emphasis on community.

A: One of the reasons Barbara is so happy in the village, and is unhappy when she leaves it for any length of time, is the sense of community that exists in the village. This community is unusual, because the characters are all quite different with diverse professions, although many of them are directly or indirectly working in hospitality.

Another point to emphasize is that the community is continually being reinvented with newcomers, who plan either to stay in the village for a while, or marry someone from the village. It's not just a group of people who have known each other since childhood. It's a community that is changing, shifting, evolving.

Interviewer: Colors seem to be mentioned often. Why the emphasis on this, is that the way you tend to think?
A: Barbara has an unusual trait: she picks up on people's eye colors with extreme precision. This is one of the quirks of her personality; she tends to notice details, in particular color. Since she is telling the story, color is emphasized in the book. As for myself, I *love* color and change the colors inside our home for every season using a variety of fabrics and linens.

Interviewer: One of my favorite elements of the book was the inn called *Delights in Earthly Haven*. Where did that come from? Have you stayed at a place similar to that?
A: Never. It just came to me in the writing process and it was amusing to imagine what such an inn would be like, and to mix up the sources for the interiors. They weren't all going to be from the same culture historically. For example, the thirteenth century room was not a medieval English farmhouse the way some visitors were expecting, but was inspired by the thirteenth century Sufi poet Rumi. So *Delights in Earthly Haven* was completely a work of my imagination, and I hope someday it will manifest in physical reality. I would like to stay there and try out each and every room.

Interviewer: Do you have a specific writing style?
A: I'd like to think that my writing style is entertaining, fun and quirky with some less common vocabulary sprinkled here and there, while dealing with serious topics relevant to all of us.

Interviewer: How much of the book do you think is realistic?

A: It's quite realistic in the sense that the events that happen to the characters could happen in our reality. The only paranormal event is the apparition of ghosts. I have never seen a ghost, but I know very well educated and rational people who have.

Interviewer: Who did you imagine would be your target audience, your typical reader?
A: The story deals with the choices we are presented with, and focuses on one of the pivotal choices we make, namely, who we decide to spend our life with. The story evolved into a novel with romantic elements, as well as mystical or spiritual elements and a touch of the paranormal.

Interviewer: You've written non-fiction for many years as an art writer. Is this your first work of fiction?
A: I've written a number of short stories, but this is my first full-length novel. It began as a funny short story, but then evolved into a novel as I realized that the characters had stories to tell. I'm still discovering the deeper meanings of the story.

Interviewer: Do you see writing fiction now as part of your career?
A: The characters showed me that they wanted to tell their own stories. We will see whether there are opportunities for other characters to share their trajectories.

Interviewer: Tell us more about your own background.
A: How about growing up on four continents (including Africa), learning four languages? I ended up in the French educational system, specializing in Mathematics, Physics and Chemistry at the lycée and later receiving a doctorate in Psychology from the University of Vienna in Austria. Because I specialized in research methods, working at the Children's Hospital in Vienna with epileptic children and those with learning disabilities was a revelation. I went from authoring and co-authoring scientific research papers

in journals to helping scientists in other fields with publications. Later on, due to my profound love of art (with intermittent studies in ceramics and sculpture and architecture), I ended up writing about it. I earned a Masters in Art History from the University of Florida and began a career writing about contemporary art for magazines and catalogues, and making art documentaries. Meanwhile, I started attending classes taught by Rev. Eloise Page, a spiritual teacher and psychic medium in Cassadaga, Florida. I also studied shamanism through the Foundation for Shamanic Studies and with Sandra Ingerman, as well as Native American teachers Beautiful Painted Arrow (Joseph Rael) and Oh Shinnáh, becoming a shamanic practitioner and teacher, and more recently a Reiki Master. So my professional trajectory went from scientific research and writing in professional journals to art writing, to developing intuitive and spiritual skills.

Interviewer: Give us three 'good to know' facts about you.
A: I'm not a trained gardener, yet nature is always teaching me something. A bloom that appears way out of season, or tomatoes growing way beyond the normal life span of the plant. Nature is always teaching me to pay attention, to notice. Also, I thrive in a creative environment, so in addition to writing, I've always made works of art whether sculpture, prints, drawings or photographs. I feel it's all part of the same continuum, the same thing. And I truly enjoy creating community.

Interviewer: Is there anything specific that you would want to say to your readers?
A: Just enjoy. Just enjoy!

Biography of Author

Anne Barclay Morgan writes about contemporary art in magazines and books and has made art documentaries. *Bending Destiny* is her first novel. She lives in Florida with her husband Brent Mashburn and their irresistible standard poodle Amma. Her website is www.annebmorgan.com.